romancing the workplace series

Hot Off the Press

alia smith

BAL KON media

ROMANCING THE WORKPLACE SERIES

The Plus-One Clause (Novella)

Bookish with Benefits

The Maine Event

The Midnight Meet-Up

Hot Off the Press

Mind the App

HOT OFF THE PRESS
Published by Balkon Media

Paperback edition ISBN: 978-1-916970-16-8
Also available as an E-book

A CIP catalogue record for this title is available from the British Library.

Edited by Hanna Elizabeth

Cover Design: graphichouse123

www.balkon.media

*To finding the person who makes all the sentences make
sense.*

ONE

♥

GRACE

I thread my way through what used to be the respectable half of *The Chronicle* newsroom, counting the number of new espresso machines and 'breakout areas' since the merger with *The Express*. Today, the open-plan is even more open than usual—whole banks of desks have been razed overnight, leaving tumbleweed clumps of Ethernet cable in their wake. Every face I pass is glued to a screen or a phone, but the air is thick with anticipation: something big is coming, and for once it isn't a police tip-off or a celebrity snorting coke in a pub toilet.

I clutch my coffee cup like it's a holy relic, thumb hooked through the handle, my last vestige of order in the chaos. The mug itself is a limited-edition *Chronicle Christmas* 2022, long since faded to a diseased grey. Some bastard has drawn a penis in Sharpie over the commemorative masthead. I don't even mind; it feels honest.

I skirt around a cluster of interns in slogan T-shirts, all of them speaking in that Gen Z rising inflection that makes every statement sound like a question. Over the low privacy wall, the Crime desk is already breaking out the gin. Typical. There's *The Express* Features team, who moved into the office last week, glowering in their glass box like a pack of hungover wolves. You can tell my fellow Broadsheet lot by their scarves and the way they look at everything with faint, cultivated disappointment.

My 'hot desk' for the day is in no-man's-land: the buffer zone between the dying world of print and the bloggy, viral, click-chasing disaster that is our digital future. I can see the wreckage of both from here.

I lower myself into a chair and do a quick visual sweep for hazards—spilled energy drink, errant Post-its, last week's newsprint ground into the carpet like ash. Satisfied, I open my laptop and spend two full minutes pretending to read my inbox while actually observing the movement patterns of my colleagues. From here, you can tell who's been called into a morning meeting with their editor already—everyone else walks like condemned prisoners, resigned but hoping for a last-minute stay.

A chirrupy ping from my phone: Dad, reminding me to "make the family proud." Because nothing screams pride like cross-checking the PM's decade-old expenses claim against a spreadsheet of sugar-baby subscription receipts. I text back a thumbs-up, then tuck my phone away with a sigh.

It's 09:29. The meeting is at 09:30. I glance at my reflection in the black screen of a powered-off monitor. Hair scraped back in an overworked ponytail, suit jacket aggressively navy, lipstick still (miraculously) present. I tug at my jacket, flatten the lapels, and pinch some colour into my cheeks. Mum would call it "polishing the armour." I call it survival.

The Editor makes her entrance at exactly 09:30: a middle-aged tornado in a trench coat, shoes sensible but eyes pure murder. She wields a novelty megaphone—another of her motivational gifts from management, I assume—and smacks it on the edge of a desk to get everyone's attention. A hush falls, broken only by the faint whirr of the Features team's coffee grinder.

"Right, listen up!" Her voice booms through the megaphone, setting off a minor panic in the sports corner. "As you all know, we're in the exciting, challenging, and frankly bloody terrifying first week of the new-improved *Chronicle* following our merger with *The Express*. Some of you have been here since we were using carbon paper and faxes. Some of you can barely spell your own names. Together, we're going to make this work, or die trying. Are we clear?"

A few mumbled affirmatives. The Features team, never ones to show weakness, merely arch their eyebrows and keep typing.

"Good!" The Editor grins, wolfish. "Now. One of the big changes is our cross-pollination of talent. That means all desks are hot desks, all stories are open for pitch, and you're all about to get very, very intimate with someone you may or may not like."

The room shifts, uncomfortable. I feel a low pulse in my throat, a kind of lizard-brain panic, but I keep my chin up and my gaze flat.

"Pairings will be announced now," the Editor continues, "and yes, it is random, and no, you can't swap unless there's an actual court-ordered restraining order." She rattles a sheet of paper. "First: Anna and Jacek. Second: Monty and Prisha. Third: Grace Hampton and—" She pauses, and I already know, even before she says it. "Paul Callaghan."

I freeze, coffee cup halfway to my lips. Somewhere nearby, a stapler drops to the floor with a muted clatter. I count one, two, three heartbeats before I set the mug down, careful not to spill. Every muscle in my face has been trained for composure; only a tiny twitch in my jaw gives me away.

My vision narrows, a pinhole camera trained on the far side of the room. There he is. Black jeans, white shirt, sleeves rolled to the elbow, stubble a few days past respectable. Paul Callaghan leans back in his chair as if the last seven years have been one long, slow grudge. He meets my gaze and gives the tiniest shrug, as if to say: *Well, this should be fun.*

I manage a tight smile. Professional. Polished. And one-hundred percent fake.

My brain does a quick rerun of the past: Sheffield University, the student paper, the kind of late-night magic that burns too hot to last. The debates, the deadlines, the inside jokes that turned to arguments. And then the internship—mine, not his. A single decision that blew everything else to hell.

I thought the sting had dulled over time. But apparently, bitterness has a hell of a memory.

The Editor ploughs on, oblivious. "You'll be given a desk together and a weekly brief. Output will be monitored. If you can't work together, you'll both be fired and replaced with AI." She scans the room for questions. "No? Get on with it, then."

The meeting dissolves into murmurs. I stand, legs rubbery but serviceable, and feel the eyes of at least three people burning holes in my back. I manage to collect my laptop and the relic mug without looking at anyone, but as I pass the Features team, I hear them: "Is that *the* Grace Hampton?" "Didn't she used to be—?" "Yeah, with him. Drama."

I clamp my mouth shut, bite the inside of my cheek until I taste copper.

At the new desk—one of those ghastly modern things with a glass surface and no privacy—I arrange my things with surgical precision. Laptop exactly centre. Coffee to the right. Notepad to the left, pen uncapped and at attention. I focus on my breathing, force it to slow, force my hands not to shake.

Paul slides in opposite me with a nonchalance that is almost definitely rehearsed. He doesn't speak, just opens his laptop and begins typing as if the past seven years have been a mere prologue. He's as tall as ever, legs sprawled out under the desk, taking up more space than strictly necessary.

I sense, rather than see, a ripple of interest from the rest of the newsroom. Some people are here for the stories; others just want blood. Bloody journalists.

Paul looks up finally, and gives me that infuriating crooked smile. "Well," he says, "fancy seeing you here."

I smile back, tight and professional. "Small world, isn't it?"

He inclines his head. "Some would say inbred."

It's a test. I refuse to rise to it. Instead, I check my lipstick in the reflection of my screen and start drafting the day's column.

By noon, the first email arrives from HR: "Welcome to the new *Chronicle Express* Team!" There's a cartoon of a bee on it, in case we didn't get the cross-pollination metaphor.

I delete it unread.

By one p.m., I have typed and re-typed my opening paragraph twelve times, but can't get Paul's presence out of my peripheral vision. He hums while he works; a habit I'd forgotten and immediately resent. He writes fast, then stops, drums his fingers, and stares at the ceiling like a man searching for God in the air conditioning.

I get up to refill my coffee, and as I pass his side of the desk, I catch a glimpse of his screen: it's a spreadsheet of old *Chronicle* exposés, names highlighted in lurid yellow. There's a column headed "Untapped Stories." My own name sits at the top of one cell, right above the word "Skeletons?"

I don't break stride. I don't give him the satisfaction of looking back.

At the coffee machine, I steady my hands against the counter. They're shaking, just a little, but enough to make me hate myself for it.

It's not like we ever dated. Not really. What we had was

too quick, too bright, and burned out before either of us could claim it. But the anger—that's eternal. The memory of his hand on the small of my back as we ran to a student paper deadline; the way his eyes would go flat and cold when he was about to wound me, just for the sport of it.

I top up my mug, take a scalding gulp, and steel myself for the walk back.

At the desk, Paul is watching me. Not openly, but enough. I sit, log back in, and fire off a pitch to the Editor: "The death of print journalism—report from the trenches." She replies in three seconds: "Love it. Pair up with Callaghan, see what you come up with."

Of course.

I paste the pitch into a shared Google Doc, email him the link, and wait.

Paul types: "Nice opener. You've softened up since uni."

I reply: "You're just used to working with children."

He responds: "They're easier to train."

Me: "Less likely to stab you in the back, at any rate."

He doesn't answer, but I can see the twitch of his mouth, the way he's enjoying this. I refuse to give him more.

By five, we've drafted the column, edited each other's work, and managed not to murder one another. Barely. We've also hardly spoken, with communication limited to in-document comments. Bizarre. I gather my things, stand, and look him in the eye.

"See you tomorrow," I say, voice like ice chips.

He leans back, stretches, and says, "Looking forward to it."

I believe him.

As I leave, I can feel the newsroom watching, waiting for the first sign of blood. I give them nothing. My hands are steady, my mouth unsmiling, and my armour is back in place.

Tomorrow, I think, they'll have to try harder.

The next morning, Paul Callaghan makes his entrance as only he can: swagger dialled down to plausible deniability, sleeves rolled to broadcast a willingness for hard labour, but with that signature crooked smile to remind you that all of this is a game, and he's the reigning champion.

He pauses on the bullpen threshold, taking in the territory as if it's a wildlife documentary and he's sizing up the new alpha. The effect is immediate—conversations slow, screen-saver glows multiply, and a heat-seeking wave of attention finds him, then rebounds to me, then back to him. Across the divider screen, the Sports desk starts a betting pool on how many days we'll last before HR gets involved.

He knows the room is watching. He plays to it, hands in pockets, chin up, eyes scanning the horizon before finally locking on me. Our gazes collide. My body betrays me with a full systems check: pulse up, shoulders back, jaw locked so tight I'll be massaging it for days.

He grins wider, lifts an eyebrow. Raises his hand in a lazy, ironic salute. The simple bastardry of it almost makes me laugh, but I force my expression into the granite calm I spent the whole bus ride perfecting.

He cuts through the desks with slow, measured steps, an assassin who wants everyone to see the knife. At three metres out, he stops to lean over the desk of a junior reporter—probably feeding them an obscene pun for the next day's headline. Two metres. One.

He stops in front of me, lingering just long enough to register the collective inhalation from the entire Features section. "Morning, Grace," he says, all politeness and mischief.

"Morning, Paul."

We stand there, old enemies, new partners, facing off with the polite grins of politicians before a televised debate.

The Features Editor, Sarah, summoned by some sixth sense for drama, swoops in with her arms already outstretched. "Here we are!" she crows. "The Dream Team!" She says it with the same tone most people reserve for calling pest control.

She plants herself between us, radiating synthetic warmth. "Now, I know the last-minute desk arrangements are a shock, but think of it as an opportunity to, you know, build trust. Collaborate." She pauses for dramatic effect, her gaze bouncing between us. "Two of our best, together on one hot desk. The office is buzzing!"

Behind her, it is. Literally. At least five people are holding their phones in such a way that I'm ninety percent sure this is already being live-tweeted.

Sarah gestures to the pristine glass-topped desk directly under the big window—prime real estate, but with zero privacy and the least ergonomic chairs known to man. "This is you. Make it work. Keep filing your own pieces, but send your first joint column by Friday. Remember, the key theme: partnership." She claps her hands together, and the sharp sound lingers, a slap to the face.

She leans in, lowering her voice to what she probably thinks is a confidential volume. "I mean it, you two. The higher-ups want to see chemistry. Even if you have to fake it." Then she's gone, off to break up a minor insurrection at the News desk.

We're left staring at the glass slab, our own little island in a sea of anticipation.

Paul slides his messenger bag off his shoulder and drops it on the floor with a heavy thunk. "I hope you don't mind," he says, "but I took the liberty of booking us in for a brainstorm at the pub after work. Neutral ground."

Of course he did. I force a smile. "Not a chance. I wouldn't want to give the office pool an early payout."

He laughs, quick and sharp. "God forbid. I've got money on us holding on 'til Thursday."

I sit myself at the desk and begin the ritual of marking my territory: notepad, pens, mug. Paul sets up directly opposite, mirroring every move with infuriating precision. We're so close that our knees nearly brush beneath the table.

He opens his laptop, the lid plastered with a sticker that reads: "Ask Me About My Data Breach." He makes a show of firing it up, drumming his fingers while the login screen loads. It's the same rhythm he used to tap on my thigh under the table at the Red Lion, the night we broke the story that made us both legends and, indirectly, mortal enemies.

"Do you want to write directly in the Google doc, or just shout over each other until something sticks?" he asks, voice pitched low so only I can hear.

"Whatever works for you. I'm flexible." I can hear the challenge in my own words and hate myself for it.

He tips his head, conceding the point. "I'll start with some research, then?"

"Perfect." I start typing, but every keystroke is haunted by the possibility that he's watching, judging, waiting for a mistake.

From the corner of my eye, I can see the newsroom's attention still locked on us. The Features team has a sweepstake grid going, red marker dotting our names in various cells labelled "fatalities," "romantic relapse," and "mutual destruction."

I decide not to dignify it with a reaction. Instead, I dig into the brief, determined to outpace him, out-write him, outlast him. I know how this will go: he'll try to charm, to provoke, to needle me into dropping my guard. But I'm older now, harder. I won't give him the satisfaction.

An hour passes like trench warfare—periods of tense

silence, then sudden bursts of volleyed questions and passive-aggressive document edits.

At one point, he clears his throat and says, "You know, I've always admired your work ethic. Ruthless. I mean that as a compliment."

I keep my eyes on the screen. "And I've always admired your creativity. Even if it's mostly in service of self-preservation."

He leans in, folding his hands. "That's the only kind of creativity that matters, isn't it?"

I look up, let my gaze linger just a second too long. "Depends what you're trying to preserve."

He doesn't reply right away. He looks at me, really looks, and I feel my stomach lurch in a way I thought I'd trained out of myself.

A silence stretches between us, until the Editor's voice blares from across the room: "Hampton! Callaghan! How's the new arrangement suiting you?"

Paul lifts his mug in a mock toast. "Seamless integration," he calls back.

I raise my own cup, chin up. "Like we were made for it."

Sarah beams. "That's the spirit!"

When she turns away, Paul drops his voice again, just for me. "You're really going to make me work for this, aren't you?"

"You expect anything less?" I say.

Our knees bump under the desk, and neither of us moves away.

For the rest of the day, we play at truce. But everyone in the office knows it's only a matter of time before the first shot is fired.

And that, I realise, is what I've missed most of all.

TWO

❤

PAUL

The new office looks like an Apple store had a one-night stand with a WeWork, and now no one knows whose kid the bastard is. There's not a single soft edge in sight—everything is glass, chrome, and LED strip lighting set to a shade of "clinical optimism." I pause at the edge of the bullpen, two carrier bags weighing down my left hand, and take in the carnage. Even the air smells hostile, off-gassing from cheap furniture and management desperation.

My new desk for the day is front and centre, directly in the blast radius of the open-plan, and so transparent I can practically see my own shame reflecting back at me. There's Grace, already in place and radiating a weirdly tranquil aggression. Her jacket today is navy, sharp enough to be considered an offensive weapon, and she's arranged her notebook and phone in perfect parallel to the edge of the desk. There's not a single coffee ring or dog-eared Post-it in sight. Just like her to stake out territory before the ink is even dry on the seating plan.

I dump my carrier bags at my feet, making sure at least

three people hear the thud. Someone in Features looks up, recognises me, and then ducks down again with a speed that suggests we're back in secondary school and I've just been let out of isolation. The rest of the room does a decent impression of working, but I can feel the low-frequency hum of rubber-necking. I know how this looks. The prodigal shit returns. The exiled son of tabloid hell, home to roost in the big leagues—if the big leagues now meant writing three listicles a week and dying a little more inside with every clickbait headline.

Grace doesn't look up, but she clocks me. Her eyes flick once, lightning-fast, then back to her laptop. I see the slight tension at her jaw—the tell she thinks nobody knows about, but is as obvious to me as a fire alarm. I almost smile. Instead, I press my palms flat against the glass and let the cold work up into my bones.

The ergonomic chair is set at a height appropriate for a toddler. I lower myself in, limbs unfolding like a deck chair that's lost the will to live. The upholstery squeaks. I make a mental note to sabotage it for maximum comic effect during a future staff meeting. For now, I just slide forward until my knees threaten to knock into Grace's. She doesn't shift. She wants me to know that this is her desk, her turf, her rules. She's *Chronicle* and I'm *Express*, and sharing a desk and even an office will never change that.

I oblige by making it a crime scene.

First, I open my battered laptop—the stickers on the lid have faded into a grey smear—and set it at an angle guaranteed to reflect sunlight directly into Grace's retinas. Then I extract my notebook, spine cracked, margins full of doodled gallows and anatomically improbable genitals. I place it on the desk with a soft slap, flipping open to a random page. For good measure, I flick at the surface, as if searching for invisible dust, and drag my fingers along the edge until the glass squeals in protest. Then I unpack my pencils, and line them up to mirror

Grace's neat selection. Grace still doesn't react, but I see her hand tighten on her pen.

We sit like this for two full minutes, the world reduced to a two-square-metre theatre of war. My entire body itches. The shirt I picked up off my bedroom floor this morning is at least half polyester and refuses to behave—static clings it to my chest, rides up at the shoulders, snags at my elbows. I pull at it roughly, then look at Grace, who is (of course) dressed in a perfectly ironed blouse so starched it could stand up on its own.

She's changed, but not really. There's a new coat of polish —lipstick darker, hair more disciplined, makeup hiding the bags under her eyes—but beneath it, she's still the same. Hyper-competent. Incapable of half-arsing anything, except maybe her own happiness. The kind of person who'd get a gold star for dying if it were on the syllabus. Seven years and she still smells like ambition and posh perfume, with a hint of ink if you get close enough. I wonder if she still corrects grammar on street signs.

I don't get close. I know better.

Instead, I log in and start to work, or pretend to. My first action: Google "How to fake your own death and get away with it." My second: type up a list of all the stories I'll never get to write now that my days are numbered. I'm halfway through "25 Most Corrupt Council Leaders: Ranked!" when I feel her looking at me again. I meet her gaze dead-on, and give her the smallest nod. I can see the question in her eyes, clear as print: *Why are you really here?*

I'd ask myself the same thing, if I didn't already know the answer. It's simple. I lost a bet, a job, and my self-respect, in that order. Now I'm here so I can pay my rent, avoid Mum's phone calls, and pretend like I'm not one bad day away from joining the gig economy. I tell myself it's temporary. One week. One column. Then I can slip out the fire exit and never come back, telling everyone—including myself—that I gave the merger a go, but it just wasn't a good fit.

Grace breaks eye contact first, scribbles something in her notebook. Her handwriting hasn't changed—impossibly neat, borderline erotic in its regularity. I wonder if she ever writes angry. Probably not. Probably compartmentalises, bottles, files away under "To Be Processed When Convenient." I try to picture her screaming at someone in traffic, and can't.

My phone buzzes in my pocket. I check it under the desk, out of sight. Three missed calls from an *Express* colleague who was offered, and accepted, a settlement agreement the day after the merger was announced. A voicemail from my mum. A text from my bookie, who still thinks I'm on the inside at the *Express* and therefore have a hot tip for Premier League leaks. I delete them all, then flick the phone onto the glass so it skids to a halt, centimetres from Grace's perfectly aligned phone.

The office is louder now, with people moving purposefully and actually doing some work. Sarah, my new editor, is in her glass box, typing with two fingers and frowning at her screen like it's personally insulted her. I catch her glance in our direction, then away, then back. She's waiting for us to combust. Maybe she's rooting for it.

I allow myself a brief, ugly satisfaction in knowing that if anyone's going to break, it won't be me. I'm an old hand at public self-immolation. Grace, for all her control, still cares. That's her problem.

My hands are restless. I drum them on the desk, then run my thumbnail along the seam where the glass meets the metal frame. I flex my fingers. The office feels colder now, and I almost want to shiver, but don't. Instead, I glance at Grace, who is rereading her notes with a look of mild disgust.

I wait for her to say something, but she doesn't. So, I do.

"Thought you'd have switched careers by now," I say, voice pitched low enough that only she can hear.

She lifts her chin, eyes flat. "Why? The pay here is so competitive."

I snort, half a laugh, half a warning shot. "Could have gone into management. Or teaching. They love a control freak."

Her mouth twitches, just for a second. "And you could have gone into advertising. Or prison."

"Not too late," I say, and actually mean it.

There's a brief *détente*. We stare at each other, then away, then back again. The newsroom feels smaller, the glass walls closing in. Somewhere in the background, an intern is giggling into her sleeve. The Sports desk starts a slow clap, then stop when they realise we're not actually about to throw hands.

Grace picks up her mug and takes a long, deliberate sip. She never did like confrontation, but she's good at it when forced. I respect that, even as I make it my life's mission to force her into it as often as possible.

I watch her over the rim of my own mug, and for a moment, I remember what it was like to be on the same side of something. There was a time we could finish each other's sentences, and not always with a punchline. Now, we can barely stand to finish the same conversation.

"So." I clear my throat. "We going to pretend this is going to work, or are we just here to provide morale for the masses?"

She sets her mug down carefully, and smiles. "Why limit ourselves?"

I nod, conceding the point. "Always the overachiever."

There's a beat of silence, then Sarah's voice cuts through the noise: "Callaghan! Hampton! My office, now."

We stand at the same time, neither giving way, and collect our things with matching efficiency. As we pass through the bullpen, I feel the eyes on our backs, the betting pool updating live. I hope someone's smart enough to put money on the dark horse. If I have to go down, I'm taking at least three careers with me.

In the glass box, the Editor is waiting. She gestures us in, then closes the door behind us with a soft hiss. The walls are thin enough that if we shout, the whole office will hear.

I catch Grace's reflection in the glass. For the first time, she looks almost nervous.

I decide to enjoy it.

Sarah's glass box is more of a meeting room than an office. The big table has been set up like a breakfast bar, so tall my knees threaten to tangle with Grace's every time we shift in our seats. There are three glasses of water on the table, each poured to a different level, like some kind of psychological test. I claim the fullest, out of principle.

The Editor herself—Sarah, but always The Editor, even when off duty—perches on a stool and glances between us with a look usually reserved for bomb disposal. Her phone is glued to her palm, thumb twitching over the screen as if at any moment she might be called away to something more important, like a mass redundancy or a dog stuck in a drainpipe.

She clears her throat and puts on her best "fun boss" face. "Right. First of all, I want to say how thrilled I am that you two have been paired up. Truly." She nods at Grace, then at me, as if expecting us to catch contagious enthusiasm by eye contact alone. "You're two of our respective papers' most decorated writers. Your work speaks for itself."

Grace sits up straighter, pen poised. I slouch just enough to show I'm not buying it.

The Editor checks her phone again, then powers ahead. "I know this is a bit of a shock—merging the desks, the joint column. Management's really pushing for… integration." She grimaces, the word leaving a bad taste. "They want this to be smart but accessible. Hard-hitting but light-hearted. A bit of healthy back-and-forth." She gestures between us, like we're two sides of a novelty salt and pepper set. "You know, 'charmingly combative.'"

I make a note in my pad: "*Charmingly combative = punchable.*" Then, for my own amusement, I doodle a hangman. The Editor watches my pen, jaw tensing.

Grace is all business, scribbling notes in handwriting so neat it could be a font. "Are we keeping the *Chronicle* style guide, or are we meant to dumb down for *Express* readers?"

The Editor blinks. "Oh, there's a brief. It's in the shared drive." She doesn't say whether she's read it. "But really, it's about chemistry. You two have history, right? I thought, why not use that to our advantage?"

I cough into my hand. "Not sure weaponising unresolved sexual tension is HR-compliant."

Grace's pen stops. She doesn't look at me, but her cheeks flush a shade darker.

The Editor ploughs on. "Right, well... think of it as an experiment. All the best columns have a bit of friction, don't they? The readers eat it up."

I say, "So you want us to bicker in print, and call it journalism."

She shrugs. "Worked for the *Telegraph* for years."

Grace jumps in before I can fire back. "Do you have a column title in mind?"

The Editor hesitates. "Well. Marketing has a few options, but I thought it might be better if it came from you. More authentic. Readers love authenticity."

She says "readers" the way politicians say "the people." I'm not convinced she's ever met one.

Grace nods, already listing options in her notebook. I can see her cogs turning—she's not above playing the game, as long as she gets to write the rules. I consider lighting a cigarette, just to see what would happen. Instead, I lean forward and drop my suggestion onto the table.

"He Said, She's Wrong."

The Editor blanches, eyes darting to Grace, who, to her credit, doesn't flinch.

Grace sets her pen down, aligns it with the edge of the notebook. "Or perhaps something less... inflammatory. 'Two Sides of the Story'?"

I grin at her. "Yours is more diplomatic. Mine will get the clicks."

"Mine won't get us sued."

The Editor exhales, a long slow leak of hope. "Why not brainstorm a few and send them over by end of day? I'll run them past legal, just in case." Her smile is now pure hostage video.

She slides two folders across the table, one for each of us. "Drop whatever you're working on. Your first topic is 'The Death of Truth.' Make it snappy. Maximum twelve hundred words, fifty-fifty split." She looks at Grace, then at me, then back to Grace, as if pleading for one of us to act like a grown-up. "You have seventy-two hours. There's a launch event Friday, so please try to have it in before then."

Grace opens the folder, already annotating. I glance at mine, then shove it into my bag unopened. I'll read it later, or never.

The Editor fiddles with her phone, then looks up. "Any questions?"

I ask, "Is this a test, or are we being punished for something?"

She laughs, but it sounds like a death rattle. "Bit of both, I suppose."

Grace smiles, professional to the end. "Thank you, Sarah. We won't let you down."

I nod, not quite agreeing. "Looking forward to it."

The Editor looks like she might vomit. "Right. Well. Off you go, then."

We stand, Grace gathering her things in perfect order, me knocking over my glass of water for effect. Grace doesn't comment, just hands me a tissue from her bag. I wipe the spill, but leave the glass right where it is, a half-moon of water spreading slowly toward the centre of the table.

Back in the bullpen, the tension has lifted. The Sports desk is arguing about something unrelated, the interns are playing games on their phones, and the Features lot has returned to their natural state of brooding. I follow Grace back to the desk, and for a moment, we walk in step, as if we've always done it.

She sits, then looks up at me. "We should meet after work. Actually brainstorm, if you're capable."

"I did offer a night in the pub."

She sighs. "Fine. But I pick the place."

"Deal. Nine?"

She hesitates, then nods. "Nine."

I watch her re-arrange her workspace, making small, invisible corrections until everything lines up. I wonder if she does the same with her life—endless, tiny adjustments, hoping that one day everything will just click.

It won't. Not with me here to fuck it up.

I flip open my notebook and start my draft, underlining the words: "*Death of Truth*." I resist the urge to draw a tombstone.

Instead, I imagine what it would be like if we actually won. If we write the column, become legends again, and prove everyone wrong. The thought is so alien I almost laugh.

I look across at Grace. She's typing already, face set, jaw tight, like she's bracing for an earthquake.

I could do worse for a sparring partner.

Probably will.

THREE

——— ♥ ———

GRACE

My flat looks like it's been raided by a very specific kind of burglar: one who is only interested in print journalism, caffeine, and the fleeting possibility of sleep. There's a half-drained wine bottle on the counter, a graveyard of mugs lined up on the window ledge, and a wild, spiralling diaspora of notebooks across every available horizontal surface. The only spot not colonised by paper is the laptop, which stares at me from the centre of the coffee table, work emails glowering from its unblinking screen.

I'm on my third glass of wine and my second hour of what Mum likes to call "catch-up." In reality, it's her attempt to crowdsource my happiness via Bluetooth. She's on speaker, voice as clear as if she's perched on my shoulder.

"I just think it's such a funny little twist of fate," she's saying now, for the fourth time. "You, him, back together at last, after all these years! It's like the universe is giving you a second chance."

"Mm," I say, tracing the rim of my glass. It leaves a wet,

perfect circle on a pad already soaked through with crossed-out ideas for our *joint* column.

She's undeterred. "And to think, I always said you two had unfinished business! Even when you insisted it was just a 'professional falling out.'" She puts so much emphasis on the phrase, I can hear the finger quotes.

There's a clatter from her end—probably the cat launching itself into a doomed vase—and then her voice again, closer to the mic, syrupy with nostalgia. "He was always so handsome, even with that ridiculous hair. Does he still have that hair?"

"Unfortunately," I say. "It's longer now. Looks like he's been living in a tent."

She laughs. "It suits him! He always did have a rebellious streak. I remember when he came to dinner, and your father nearly choked on his risotto because Paul was wearing a Sex Pistols T-shirt."

"Dad choked because Paul told a ten-minute story about the time he tried to unionise the catering staff at his old school."

She giggles, high and bright. "Well, it's not every day you meet a young man with principles."

"Or a juvenile criminal record," I mutter.

She hears, but ignores. "You know what I think? I think you're secretly thrilled. It's like Romeo and Juliet, only with more commas."

"More casualties, too," I say, pouring a top-up and immediately regretting it. I need to sleep at some point this week, but the odds are not in my favour.

She's on a roll now, powering through my sarcasm like an armoured car. "I know you say you're just colleagues, but I've read your writing, darling. Nobody can eviscerate a man so beautifully unless she's in love with him."

I close my eyes. "Mum, please."

She only gets louder. "Just promise me you'll give him a

chance, okay? You're both older, wiser, more... emotionally available." She delivers the last words like a prescription, knowing full well that I am neither wiser nor emotionally available in any sense that doesn't involve direct debit.

I take a long, purposeful gulp. "Mum. This is not a romcom. He's not even technically my ex."

"Technicalities," she says, as if waving away a minor parking ticket. "You always overthink these things."

My knuckles are white on the wine glass. I picture myself as a cartoon, teeth gritted, hair standing on end, little storm clouds above my head. I glance at the mirror above the radiator and see only a woman in pyjamas, mascara half-removed, surrounded by paperwork like a failed magician who couldn't make her problems disappear.

She's still talking: "Have you thought about what you're going to wear tonight? You should make an impression. I remember you had that lovely red dress—"

"It's a meeting, Mum. Not a wedding. And the dress doesn't fit."

She tsks, as if this is a moral failing on my part. "You're too hard on yourself. You always have been."

"Not hard enough, apparently," I say, thinking of the column I have to write, the meeting with the Editor, the fact that Paul Callaghan is now a recurring feature in the pitiful soap opera of my career.

She senses the downturn, and tries a new tactic. "What's really the matter, darling?"

I hesitate. I could tell her the truth—that the job is eating me alive, that I'm stuck in a loop of diminishing returns, that I'd bet my next payslip Paul will implode and take me down with him—but instead, I say, "Nothing. I'm just tired."

She doesn't buy it. She never does. "You've always had to work twice as hard, haven't you? Even when you were a little girl, you used to rewrite your homework if the handwriting wasn't perfect."

I want to say: *I only rewrote it because you made me.* But I don't. I just sip and stare out at the orange glow of the street-lights beyond my window. There's a fox rummaging in the bins across the road, eyes shining, tail a riot of smug defiance. I envy it.

Mum sighs. "You need to be kinder to yourself. And to Paul."

This is a new one. "Why does he need my kindness?"

"Because he's always been a little lost, hasn't he? You said it yourself. Maybe you're just what he needs to find himself again."

I laugh, but it's hollow. "Then he can use Google Maps like the rest of us, Mum."

She ignores me, on the final straight now. "Just try, Grace. For me. Give it a chance. You never know what might happen."

"I know exactly what will happen," I say. "We'll be forced to work together until one of us snaps and is found dead in a stairwell, probably me, and you'll still think it's a sign of repressed sexual tension."

She laughs as if I've told a joke, not a prophecy. "You're so dramatic! Anyway, I have to go. There's a new drama starting on BBC One, and the cat's already eaten most of the heads off the peonies."

She blows a kiss through the speaker, and I catch it out of habit. "Love you," she says.

"Love you, too," I say, even as I end the call and toss the phone onto the sofa.

For a moment, the silence is so dense I can hear the fridge buzzing. I stand there, glass in hand, trying to let the emptiness settle. Instead, my body vibrates with a restless, pointless energy. I turn in a slow, aimless circle, as if hoping the centrifugal force will flatten my feelings.

I catch sight of myself in the TV's black screen: a woman on the verge, hair exploding out of its grip, lipstick faded to a crime scene outline. I look like someone who's just been ghosted by a pizza delivery driver.

I set the wine glass down with more force than necessary. It chips against the rim of a mug, sending a spray of red onto the stack of half-written columns. I stare at it for a second, then grab a kitchen towel and blot the mess, movements frantic, as if scrubbing hard enough might erase the last ten minutes from existence.

When the counter is as clean as it's going to get, I plant my hands on it, lean forward, and let my forehead drop to the cool surface. For the first time all evening, I let myself actually feel tired.

After a minute, I sit back, haul the laptop onto my knees, and stare at the blinking cursor of my inbox. There's a fresh email from the Editor, subject line: "BRIEF FOR JOINT COLUMN (URGENT)." I click it open, and the body is just a single bullet point: "Make it punchy. Management will be watching."

I close the tab, open a new one, and type: "How not to commit professional homicide." The search results fill the screen instantly, a parade of clickbait and mental health hotlines.

For a moment, I actually laugh. It's not a nice sound, but it's better than nothing.

I drain what's left of my wine, close the laptop, and tell myself that tomorrow will be easier.

I know it won't. But I've always been a good liar, when it counts.

The Inkwell is pretty busy by the time I arrive, its windows sweating with condensation and its bar lined with people more interested in IPA than actual conversation. The place is exactly as I remember it from my intern days: wood panelling chipped at the edges, beer mats with passive-aggressive slogans, and an actual blackboard above the bar, still boasting the names of journalists who drank themselves into legend. I find the only free table—a corner two-top, squeezed between a fake plant and a wall of framed headlines—and stake my claim.

I unpack: notebook dead centre, agenda printed in triplicate, three different colours of pen (blue for notes, green for action items, red for emergencies only). I order a half-pint of Camden Hells and set it on a coaster that reads: "Alcohol: The Cause and Solution to All Newsroom Problems." The table is sticky; I reposition everything twice before it feels acceptable.

Paul is, naturally, twenty minutes late. By then, I've watched the barman close up a tab for a semi-retired war correspondent, clocked a former *Newsnight* anchor in the snug, and lost myself in a wormhole of tweets about our impending column. Most are sceptical, a few are vicious, one calls us "the Torvill and Dean of professional bitchery." That one I print-screen and send to Mum, who responds with a heart emoji and, for reasons best known to herself, a GIF of penguins falling over.

When Paul finally appears, he's managed to look even more disreputable than at work: shirt unbuttoned at the collar, sleeves rolled up, hair looking like it's survived a hostage situation. He carries nothing but a cracked phone and a look of absolute, unearned confidence.

He zeroes in on me with a lopsided grin, as if being late is a personality trait. "Didn't think you'd actually show."

"Didn't think you'd be sober enough to notice," I reply, standing just enough to make the handshake weird. He ignores it, collapses into the chair, and signals for a pint with a two-fingered salute.

"So," he says, "the famed Inkwell. Did you pick it for the symbolism, or just for the booze?"

I ignore the question and slide my agenda across the table. "I made a list of possible column topics. I thought we could go through them, pick the ones with legs."

He takes the page, scans it for half a second, and then places it face down under his elbow. "*Death of Truth in Modern Media.* Christ, Grace, why not just call it 'Please Like Me'?"

"Did you have a better idea?"

"I have several," he says, grinning wider. "We could do a live blog of pub quiz nights. I hear Millennials love participatory journalism."

I stare at him, deadpan. "You think we should anchor a joint column with pub reviews."

He shrugs, sips his pint, then leans forward conspiratorially. "Or we could do a running series where we review viral internet hoaxes and see who can get catfished first. The money's in humiliation these days."

"You're already ahead, then."

He laughs, full and unguarded, and the sound is infectious. I catch myself almost smiling, then check it, embarrassed.

He sees, of course, and softens his tone just enough to let me know he's not a complete bastard. "Look, Grace. If you want to do a column about the moral decline of society, fine. But you're going to have to let me take the piss at least once per paragraph, or nobody will read it."

"That's not true," I say, but I know it is. People read his stuff for the punchlines, the self-sabotage, the joy of watching someone set fire to his own career in slow motion. I write for the people who underline sentences and send polite corrections to the Features inbox.

He watches me as I process this, head tilted, eyes narrowed as if he's reading my thoughts and scoring them out with a red pen.

We trade ideas for twenty minutes, the table filling with notes and empty glasses. I pitch, he parries, I revise, he derails. It's exhausting and oddly exhilarating, like tennis with live grenades. The bar staff catch on quick; by the third round, our drinks appear without being ordered, and the regulars have started betting on who will land the first real insult.

Eventually, Paul leans back and stretches, arms behind his head, shirt riding up just enough to show a faded tattoo and the hint of a scar. "You know what your problem is?" he says, not unkindly. "You want to save the world, but you can't stand to get your hands dirty."

I snort. "And you want to set the world on fire, but only if someone else supplies the matches."

He looks at me then, really looks, and for a second I see something old and vulnerable and almost sweet. He says, "Maybe that's why we work."

The words hang in the air, so sudden and sincere, I nearly drop my pen. I reach for my beer instead, hoping the chill will smother the heat rising up my neck.

We sit in a rare silence, the pub noise swirling around us, and for a moment I let myself imagine it: us, not as adversaries, but as something closer to equals. Partners, maybe, if not quite friends.

Then Paul ruins it. "How's your mum, anyway?" he asks, feigning casual.

I stiffen, instantly wary. "She's fine."

He grins. "She used to like me, you know."

"She has poor taste."

He shrugs. "Runs in the family."

It's a good line, and I should let it pass, but I can't. Not tonight, not after the week I've had—and it's only Tuesday. "You think this is all a joke, don't you?"

He pretends to consider, but the answer is obvious. "Not a joke. Just—less tragic than you make it out to be."

I close my notebook with a snap, the sound loud enough to draw stares. "Some of us don't have the luxury of treating our lives like a failed sketch show, Paul."

"Ohh. Touchy."

"Try responsible."

The mood is ruined, the brief spell broken. I start stacking my notes, pretending not to care that he's won, again. He watches in silence, eyes following my every move, until I can't take it anymore.

"Don't you ever get tired of being such an arse?" I say, voice lower than I intend.

He leans in, elbows on the sticky table, all faux sincerity. "Not when it gets results."

"You think sabotaging everyone around you is a result?"

"It's better than sitting around waiting for someone else to give you permission."

I want to throw my beer in his face. Instead, I take a deep breath, count to five, and stand up. "You know what, Paul? I don't need this."

He watches me, expression unreadable, as I gather my things. "Where are you going?"

"Home," I say. "Unlike you, I have work to do."

He doesn't try to stop me. Doesn't even reach for my arm as I brush past him. I make it to the door in three quick strides, only pausing at the threshold to look back.

He's still sitting at the table, shoulders slumped, pint untouched. He looks smaller than I remember.

I step out into the night, air sharp with rain and possibility. I don't look back again.

FOUR

<hr>

PAUL

Nothing says career death spiral like a Thursday morning in a café where the linoleum floor sticks to your shoes and the beans are so institutional they come with their own trauma counsellor. I'm halfway through a sausage sandwich that tastes of pure sodium and regret, and I'm still not sure why I agreed to meet Jamie here. He's always been more of a Pret-a-Manger type, the kind of man who reads *Wired* on the toilet and believes in the curative power of electrolytes. But today, here he is, stretched out in a vinyl booth with both arms behind his head, legs open in an aggressively heterosexual way, watching me with the expression of a bored shark.

"Have you always chewed food like that, or is it just since the merger?" he asks, not looking up from his phone.

I swallow, wipe my mouth, and glare at him. "They say digestion starts in the mouth, Jamie. Wouldn't want to give myself a heart attack, not when the office is planning a sweepstake."

He smirks, still scrolling. "You realise it's not actually

mandatory to work yourself into an early grave? It's just a suggestion, like putting the bins out on time."

I ignore him, turning my attention to the mug in front of me. The tea is the colour of river water downstream of a tannery. I take a sip anyway. It burns my tongue and my will to live in equal measure.

The greasy spoon is quiet at this hour, the only other patrons a cluster of pensioners engaged in a pitched battle over who can complain the loudest about parking restrictions. The air vibrates with the combined force of burnt toast, deep-fried batter, and vintage disinfectant. I inhale, then cough. Jamie glances up at me, eyebrow raised, as if this proves some point only he understands.

I set my mug down, hands shaking slightly. "Honestly, the merger is a joke. They keep going on about innovation and disruption, but it's just an excuse to cost-cut by getting rid of all the staff journos and getting the interns to do all the actual work."

Jamie snorts. "You always did have a healthy respect for corporate bullshit. Now you're just inside the sausage factory."

"Yeah, well. At least at the *Express* you could tell who was trying to fuck you over." I stab at my food. "Now everyone's on LinkedIn pretending to be 'Thought Leaders,' but behind the scenes it's just passive-aggressive emails and sabotage by committee."

He puts his phone down, finally, and gives me the full force of his attention. "Is this about your new boss, or is it about Grace?"

I freeze, fork halfway to my mouth. For a moment, I think about denying it, but I'm too tired to lie convincingly. "She's impossible, mate."

He grins. "You mean she's better than you, and it bothers you."

"I mean, she's a sanctimonious, micro-managing, control-freak who spends more time colour-coding her inbox than doing any actual reporting." I scrape the last of the beans onto my toast, then regret it immediately. "She's obsessed with systems. Has a fucking spreadsheet for everything, including her coffee preferences. Who does that?"

Jamie leans forward, elbows on the sticky table. "So, what's the real problem?"

I take a deep breath, then let it out in a slow, controlled leak. "She's rubbish at sharing. Won't let me near the article, keeps giving me research tasks, and makes me copy-edit *her words* like I'm the office junior. And now we have to share a hot desk every day, so I get to listen to her 'efficiently' breathing all day."

He snorts, once. "Maybe she's just better at the job."

I consider flinging a hash brown at his head, but decide against it. "It's not that. She's always been like this. We studied the same course, worked on the student paper—she was News, I was Features—and every week she'd pick a fight over the front page. Didn't matter that I broke the story, or that she was technically on a different desk. She'd just—take it."

"Sounds familiar," says Jamie, looking entirely too pleased with himself.

I glare. "What?"

"Nothing. Just—you have a type, that's all."

I stare at him, then look away, tracing circles in the sauce on my plate. I don't want to admit he's right. Instead, I focus on the peeling posters above the counter. One promises "Free Wi-Fi" in Comic Sans, another advertises the café's sponsorship of a junior football team. Judging by the state of the menu, I doubt the Wi-Fi works, and the football team is probably on a watchlist.

Jamie goes back to his phone, but I can feel him watching me over the screen. He doesn't speak, which is almost worse than when he does.

I sigh, long and dramatic. "Look, it's not that I care. It's just —after the merger, things were supposed to get better. New management, new money, maybe a shot at something resembling a real career. Instead, it's just the same bollocks, different logo. Now I'm on a leash, and she's the one holding it."

Jamie puts his phone down again. "You know, some people would pay extra for that."

I flick a chip at him. He catches it, eats it, doesn't break eye contact. "Still not going to therapy, then?"

"Piss off. Anyway, I've got you."

He grins, and clicks his fingers. "You're not mad at her. You're mad at yourself, for letting it get to you."

"Are you writing a book? Save it for your Substack."

He makes a show of typing on his phone. "I'm just saying, maybe stop acting like you're the only one who ever got shafted by the system. If you hate it that much, leave."

"I need the money."

"So, go freelance again."

I laugh, short and bitter. "You know what freelance means these days? It means I get to fight over clickbait gigs with teenagers who think SEO is a sex position. And if I'm really lucky, I'll land a five-hundred-word listicle about 'The 10 Best Places to Cry in Public.'"

Jamie laughs, drawing the attention of the pensioners. "You'd ace that, actually."

"Cheers, mate." I crumple my napkin and toss it onto the plate, then lean back, the booth groaning in protest. "You know what the worst part is? She pretends like nothing ever happened. Like we didn't spend two years hating each other's guts, then another five years not speaking at all. Now she just —smiles, and asks if I've 'gotten over it yet.'"

Jamie drums his fingers on the Formica. "Have you?"

I think about it, really think, then shake my head. "Not even close."

He smiles, slow and knowing. "You know what I think?"

"No, but I'm sure you'll tell me."

He waits, drawing out the moment until it's unbearable. Then he says, "I think you're still pissed about the internship."

My whole body tenses. "That was years ago."

"Yeah, but you never let things go. Not really. It's like emotional plaque—you need a professional cleaning every six months."

"She said she didn't even want the job, then took it out from under me. And when I called her on it, she played the victim. Like I was the one being unreasonable."

Jamie shrugs. "Maybe she was just better at playing the game."

"I'm not mad that she won. I'm mad that she lied about it."

He watches me, silent again. Then, after a long pause, "Maybe she didn't lie. Maybe she just wanted to win, and couldn't admit it. You ever think of that?"

I don't answer. Instead, I stare at the contents of my mug, wishing I could will myself into a lower state of matter and just evaporate.

He changes tack. "You seeing anyone?"

I blink, thrown. "What's that got to do with anything?"

"Just curious. Last time you were *looking to mingle*, you were still using that photo from uni for your Tinder profile."

I feel my face heat. "It's a good photo."

"It's a photo of you in a toga, holding a can of Red Bull and trying not to throw up."

"Chicks dig confidence."

Jamie bursts out laughing, slaps the table, then picks up his phone again. "Just checking you're still alive, mate. Sometimes I worry you're going to dissolve into pure, uncut cynicism and drift out to sea."

I don't answer. Instead, I place my cutlery on my plate, then nudge it all away. The pensioners have moved on to comparing hospital parking rates, and the café is starting to fill with the mid-morning lot—builders, taxi drivers, women with NHS lanyards looking utterly spent.

Jamie stands, stretches, and tosses two tenners on the table. "We better get back to the office. You coming out to play on Friday?"

"Doubt it. Need to knuckle down for a week or two, show management I'm trustworthy."

He shrugs. "Suit yourself. Just don't let her win, yeah?"

I want to say something cutting, something that will put him in his place. Instead, I just nod, suddenly exhausted.

"See you later."

He leaves, the door clanging shut behind him. I sit there for a while, staring at the oily swirl on the surface of my tea, and wonder if it's possible to be nostalgic for something that never really worked in the first place.

Eventually, I gather my things and head for the door, hands jammed in my pockets. As I step out into the grey, a gust of wind nearly knocks me sideways, and for a second I feel weightless.

Then my phone buzzes, a new email from Grace, subject line: "RE: Tomorrow's Deadline."

I delete it without reading, and keep walking.

It's always the smell that gets me first—a hint of body odour, burnt ozone from dying computers, and the faint, tragic musk of energy drinks that have outlived both their prime and their legal sell-by. Seven years later, and it's the same chemical mix that hits me every time I step into a newsroom. Back then, in the basement of the Humanities building, it was stronger, almost intoxicating, but maybe that's just how nostalgia works:

it makes even the stink of failure seem like something worth bottling.

It's midnight. I'm in the office alone, or so I think. The strip lights flicker, casting epileptic shadows over the carpet and the carcass of a takeaway pizza that's somehow been both incinerated and left raw. I'm staring at the noticeboard, jaw locked, hand fisted around a highlighter like I might use it as a weapon.

They've just put the list up. "Internship Nominations: Final Round." Four names, two per department. I know before I even look that mine isn't on there. I also know, with the sick certainty of a condemned man watching his own funeral, whose name is.

Grace Hampton, in biro, with a little asterisk next to it. I want to set the board on fire, instead, I just rip the printout off the cork and start tearing it into strips.

The door creaks open behind me. I don't turn. I hear the careful step—heels clicking, then pausing, like she's deciding whether I'm a rabid dog or just a normal one.

She says, "You saw it?"

I keep my back to her, shoving the shredded paper into the bin and immediately regretting the melodrama of the gesture. "Congratulations," I say, but it comes out so flat it sounds like a diagnosis.

She waits, then crosses to the desk beside me, her hands folded, eyes fixed on the bin. She looks tired. Worse, she looks worried.

"I didn't apply," she says.

"Right," I say, and laugh. "Sure."

She shakes her head. "No, really. I wanted a gap year. I told them. My plan was to take a year out, travel, maybe freelance—"

"And *The Chronicle* just magically picked your name out of a hat?" I spin around, the words jagged. "Come off it, Grace.

You don't even want it? You've only been gunning for it since week one."

Her face goes red. "That's not fair."

I slam my hand on the desk. It hurts, which is good. At least something does. "You know what's not fair? I've been breaking my balls for three years. News Desk, Features, Sports, even the fucking crossword when they needed it. But the second you show up—oh, it's Grace, she's so mature, she's got 'leadership potential.' They love you. Always have."

She looks down. I realise I'm yelling, and that the only other sound in the room is the whirr of the ancient iMac by the window, trying to load the BBC homepage. I want to stop, but something in me won't.

She tries again, softly, "I'm sorry, Paul."

I want to believe it, but all I can see is her name, in pen, underlined, permanent.

"You're not," I say, and it's suddenly not about the internship, or the job, or anything except the fact that for once I needed her to be on my side and she wasn't.

I grab my bag, nearly wrench the zip off, and head for the door. She doesn't follow. She just stands there, statue-still, as I shoulder past.

In the corridor, I can feel my own heartbeat. I slam the door anyway, because it's the only victory left.

It's only when I'm halfway across campus, the cold chewing at my fingers, that I realise that I'm never, ever going to forgive her for it.

FIVE

♥

GRACE

If I'd known the day would end with me planning how to murder Paul Callaghan and make it look like an HR accident, I'd have worn something less dry-clean only.

The Features meeting is scheduled for 9:00 a.m. sharp, because Sarah—the Editor, and rumoured vampire—believes punctuality builds character. By 9:04, the glass-walled conference room is a sweat lodge of nervous energy, every journalist in attendance producing enough tension to turn a Geiger counter sentient. The long table is ringed by faces: some old, some new, all either pretending to check emails or white-knuckling takeaway cups like they're flotation devices. The lights are migraine-bright. The air smells of instant coffee, antiperspirant, and dread.

I take my usual seat, three from the left, and arrange my notepad, tablet, and Biro with the fastidiousness of a person who once spent a summer learning competitive calligraphy. My pulse is audible. I glance across at Paul, who is slumped in his chair as if it's a hammock, legs extended and arms folded.

His hair is, astonishingly, even worse than yesterday. He notices my attention, winks, and mouths the word "morning" like he's making a lewd suggestion. I look away before my expression can be cited as evidence in court.

Sarah waits until exactly 9:05, then claps her hands once. The sound is as sharp as a gunshot.

"Thank you all for coming, and thank you especially for bringing such positive energy," she says in a tone that dares anyone to challenge her sarcasm. She scans the room, eyes lingering on the more vulnerable freelancers like a house cat considering which mouse to torture first.

"We'll keep this brief. As you know, the *Chronicle* is in a state of"—she makes jazz hands—"evolution. Which means, yes, we're all slightly terrified, but also that there's opportunity for innovation. Good news! Features is leading in digital engagement for the first time since I joined the paper. Bad news: engagement isn't enough if we want to keep our jobs and avoid being replaced by AI."

There's a ripple of forced laughter. I don't join in. Instead, I steal another look at Paul, who is watching Sarah with the rapt interest of someone who has never once read an employee handbook.

Sarah continues. "The new approach is pulling clicks. That's good. But what management wants is a spike. Something viral. Controversial. Shareable. So, less 'think piece' and more 'think bomb.'" She smiles at her own wit, then gestures at me and Paul. "Which is where you two come in. You're both veterans of the outrage economy. So, next week's topic?"

A hush descends, punctuated only by the syncopated tapping of someone's thumb against their phone case. I wait one second, then two, then lean forward.

"Given the climate," I begin, "I thought we could do something on the ethics of reporting in the age of misinformation.

Maybe a joint investigation into the human cost of viral hoaxes. If we can get interviews, or even first-hand accounts—"

Paul interrupts, not with words but with a theatrical yawn, arms stretching above his head to fully expose a tattoo I'm reasonably sure is new and was definitely done in someone's kitchen.

"Or," he says, "we could do a stunt piece. Live journalism, real time. *Express* readers love a bit of blood sport."

Sarah's eyes light up. "Go on."

Paul sits up suddenly animated. "Send us out together, throw us into a situation, have us report back in alternate perspectives. Like Gonzo journalism, but with more emotional damage."

There's a smattering of interest around the table. I want to object, but I can feel my own idea slipping away, drowned in the tide of easy spectacle. Sarah is already nodding.

"I like it," she says. "What sort of situation?"

Paul glances at me, and for a second, I see the devil-child he must have been. "Speed dating. Or, failing that, anything that puts us in close proximity and high embarrassment. A blind date, a couple's yoga class, maybe even a relationship therapist—"

He pauses, lets the room laugh, then drops the real bomb. "Or we could do all three. See which one kills us first."

There's a real laugh this time, and even the *Chronicle's* old guard at the end of the table—the ones who still carry real notebooks and speak with full sentences—are smiling. I dig my nails into my thigh, careful not to leave a visible mark.

Sarah claps her hands again. "Perfect! That's the angle. We'll call it 'Modern Romance: A *Chronicle* Experiment.' Get it trending. Make the millennials weep."

My coffee cup trembles a little in my hand. I force it still. "We could do a parallel piece," I offer. "Compare experiential and data-driven perspectives. Add some actual statistics—"

Paul, already basking in the attention, waves a hand. "Or we could just document the humiliation in real time. No filter. Readers eat that up."

Sarah is writing this down, her pen a blur. She says, "I want the first draft on my desk by Monday. And Grace, can you do a sidebar on the cultural context? Paul, you handle the live thread. Get social to record the whole thing. We'll push it as a multi-platform event."

I nod. My jaw is tight enough to crack molars. Beside me, Paul leans back, satisfied, sleeves rolled up as if preparing for open-heart surgery. He catches my eye, and the smirk is back—full wattage, no mercy.

"Looking forward to it, Hampton," he says, low enough that only I can hear.

"Likewise," I reply, voice like dry ice.

Sarah dismisses the meeting with a "Let's make this one for the ages, team!" and everyone rises in a slow, resigned wave. Chairs scrape, people file out, the hum of pre-emptive gossip beginning before we've even cleared the door. I gather my things, hands steady now through sheer force of will.

Paul waits for me in the corridor, shoulder propped against the wall, as if he's just there by coincidence. He holds a can of something caffeinated, and the way he pops the tab is both juvenile and intimidatingly self-assured.

"Well played," I say, without looking at him.

He shrugs. "All's fair, et cetera. Besides, you'll get to write your treatise on romance and spreadsheets. I'm just here for the content."

I don't give him the satisfaction of a reply. Instead, I stride past, head held high, and make for the lift. I can feel his eyes on my back, a pressure that lingers long after the doors slide shut.

Back at my desk, I stare at the blinking cursor of a blank document and imagine, in slow motion, the various ways this assignment could go wrong. The mortification, the viral memes, the inevitable smugness of Paul Callaghan when it all goes pear-shaped, and the commentariat bays for blood.

But there's a kernel of curiosity, too. A part of me—buried under layers of caution and bitterness—wants to see how it ends.

Maybe, for once, I'll be the one who gets the last word.

The speed dating event is being held in a bar that looks like the set designer for Love Island ran out of money, then doubled down with a Groupon for LED strip lights. The official name is "Cupid's Table," but judging by the decor—streaky mirrors, sticky leather banquettes, a decorative neon arrow over the Gents—I suspect its main claim to fame is being within vomiting distance of the bus station.

I arrive five minutes early, because there is still a part of me, deep in the pit of my soul, that believes punctuality can stave off disaster. The rest of me is resigned to the fact that this night will be an exercise in self-sabotage, mitigated only by the number of receipts I can claim for the expense report. I scan the room, clocking a demographic spread from "optimistic postgraduate" to "divorced estate agent with novelty tie." The tables are set in neat rows, each decorated with a single candle, a pile of mini pencils, and a nervous-looking singleton. There's a bell on the organiser's podium, promising further indignities to come.

I'm wearing a suit jacket, paired with the only blouse I own that doesn't show wine stains under blue light. My notepad fits in my bag, but I opt to carry it, on display, a shield and a warning. I can't decide whether I look like an under-cover cop or someone about to conduct a hostile takeover of a vegan food co-op.

Paul isn't here yet. I stake out the bar, order a Campari spritz (to avoid suspicion), and watch as the room fills to its design capacity for loneliness. The organiser is a woman in a floral midi dress, clipboard in hand, smile as fixed and impenetrable as Sarah's at an all-staff meeting. She is marshalling the arrivals into gendered queues. I feel a momentary flicker of solidarity, then quash it.

Paul arrives at 6:58, looking like he's just sprinted here through three acts of a Greek tragedy. Hair wild, shirt untucked, five o'clock shadow morphing into what might be the world's laziest goatee. He clocks me at the bar, ambles over, and manages to lean on the counter with maximum nonchalance and minimum structural support.

"Fancy seeing you here," he says. His breath smells of chewing gum and, faintly, of something medicinal.

I raise my glass. "Didn't think you'd make it."

He grins. "Couldn't miss it. Been a while since I got to ruin your night in person."

The organiser catches sight of us, clocks the dynamic, and swoops over. "Welcome! Names on the list, please. We'll get you wristbanded and ready to mingle."

Paul shoots me a glance. "She's the competitive one," he says, nodding at me. "I'm just here for the research."

I roll my eyes, hand over my details, and allow myself to be tagged with a fluorescent pink band. Paul's is blue. "Traditional," he notes quietly, as if this is a coded message.

We're herded to opposite ends of the seating grid. "Gentlemen move, ladies stay put," the organiser announces. "Five minutes per table, then the bell rings and you're off to the next adventure!" There's a round of low laughter, and I see Paul slip a tenner to the barman before taking a seat. I'm half impressed, half disgusted.

My first "date" is a junior doctor named Olly, who looks at my notepad as if it's about to diagnose him with something terminal. He spends the entire five minutes reciting his CV, pausing only to check his phone. I make two notes: "NHS burnout is real" and "possible repressed mummy issues." I ask about his hobbies; he admits to war gaming, then goes red and tries to recover by claiming he's writing a novel. I suspect he's lying.

My next suitor is a solicitor, tight-lipped, all business, who spends half the round interrogating me about GDPR. I deflect by explaining the difference between slander and libel, which seems to arouse him. The bell rings before he can proposition me, but he slips a business card under my notepad as he rises.

Third is an accountant named Rohan, who tries to neg me with comments about journalists being "the real fake news." I respond by quoting his LinkedIn endorsements back at him until he sweats. The bell rings mercifully quickly.

Every other table, I catch a glimpse of Paul. He's doing the same—charming, sparring, occasionally staring straight at me, and pulling faces to make his dates laugh. He's a natural at this, which shouldn't annoy me but does.

After round five, a break is called and we cross paths at the bar. He's got lipstick smudged on his cheek, which he's either unaware of or is wearing as a badge of honour.

He looks at my notepad and says, "Taking notes? How very Grace Hampton of you."

"At least one of us is working," I shoot back.

He leans in. "Are you, though? Because it looks like you're just collecting blackmail material."

"That's what journalism is, Paul. Blackmail, but with footnotes."

He laughs, full-bodied, then orders us both a gin and tonic. "This place is hell," he says conversationally.

"Suits you, then."

Before he can respond, the bell rings again. We're back in circulation.

Midway through round seven, I encounter a man so beautiful I have to check he isn't a plant from the event's PR team. His name is Jan. He works in urban planning, and he has a Swedish accent that makes "infrastructure" sound like a come-on. For the first time all night, I actually listen.

He asks what brings me here. I debate lying, then admit the truth, or a version of it: "Work dare. I'm supposed to be chronicling the death of romance for my newspaper."

Jan nods, amused but not deterred. "And are you finding what you expected?"

"Mostly," I say. "A lot of men who think a personality is the same as a job title."

He laughs, then gestures discreetly towards Paul, who is at the next table over, hands animated as he regales a woman in a tartan jumpsuit. "Is that your colleague?"

"God, no," I say, with too much force.

Jan raises an eyebrow. "You look like a couple. The way you keep checking for each other."

I force a laugh, loud and unconvincing. "He's just a mate. We're... rivals. Professionally."

Jan smiles, like he's heard this before. "You know, when people protest too much—"

The bell rings. Saved by the metaphorical gong.

The rest of the night blurs together. There's a man who claims to be an "angel investor" but can't explain what he invests in; a stand-up comedian who tries out material on me and dies by degrees; and a game developer who spends four straight minutes explaining the difference between VR and AR. I'm running low on patience and gin.

In the final round, I'm paired with an architect named Daniel. He is gentle, thoughtful, and talks about buildings the way some people talk about pets. He asks if I've ever been to Barcelona and tells me about the Sagrada Familia, the beauty in unfinished work. It's almost disarming.

Midway through his description of flying buttresses, I feel a prickle on the back of my neck and glance across the room. Paul is watching me, not with mockery or a smirk, but with an unreadable softness. Our eyes meet, and for a moment, the noise of the bar fades out, the air thick with unasked questions.

I lose my train of thought. Daniel notices.

"Sorry," he says. "I ramble when I'm nervous."

"No, it's fine," I say. But my brain is stuck on the way Paul looked just then, like he wanted to say something but couldn't. Or wouldn't.

The bell rings one last time. Daniel stands, shakes my hand, and thanks me for a lovely chat. I watch as he drifts off, then gather my things and head for the bar, where Paul is nursing a pint and staring into the foam.

I drop onto the stool next to him, not sure what I want to say.

He speaks first. "How'd it go? Meet the love of your life?"

I shrug. "Maybe. If I develop a sudden fetish for spreadsheets."

He smiles, tired. "But you do have a fetish for spreadsheets."

I want to make a joke to undercut the moment, but I don't. Instead, we sit in a silence that is less awkward than I expect. After a while, Paul taps the rim of his glass.

"You know, I almost feel bad for some of them," he says. "Like they don't realise the game is rigged."

I nod. "We're all just here to be judged."

He looks at me then, really looks, and for a second I see the version of him from university—the one who cared too much and said it too loud. The one who broke things when he didn't know how to fix them.

"Did you ever think," he says, voice low, "that maybe we're the problem?"

I laugh, but it comes out a little cracked. "Only every day."

We finish our drinks. He pays. We walk out together, the neon arrow flickering above us like a cosmic punchline.

On the way to the bus stop, neither of us speaks. There's nothing left to say that isn't dangerous.

I'm home before midnight. I set my bag on the floor, peel off the jacket, and collapse onto the sofa. I stare at the ceiling, replaying the night in my head.

When I close my eyes, I don't see the architect, or the doctor, or the man with the novelty tie.

I see Paul, and the look on his face when he thought I wasn't watching.

I tell myself it doesn't mean anything. I lie so well, I almost believe it.

SIX

---♥------------------------

PAUL

It's not even noon, but the inside of The Blue Anchor is indistinguishable from midnight on the planet Neptune. All the bulbs are dead or dying, and the only concession to sunlight is a single window smeared so thickly with condensation and ancient fry-up grease that it's become a light-diffusing membrane. I'm installed at the usual table, a circular pit with one leg shorter than the others, so every time I put my elbows down, the whole thing shudders like it's got the DTs. Appropriate.

Jamie appears out of the gloom, bringing with him the static charge of someone who's already had three espressos and a Twitter spat this morning. He's in a crumpled check shirt and battered All Saints jacket that probably cost more than my rent, but his hair is the kind of neat that only occurs after deliberate, high-effort chaos. He stands for a moment, surveying the graveyard of pint glasses left by the early-morning shift—pensioners and off-duty nurses, mostly—then lowers himself into the seat opposite, wincing like he's about to undergo minor surgery.

"You look like shite," he says, not unkindly.

"Cheers. Good to see you too." My tongue feels like it's been sandblasted. I have the urge to click it against my teeth just to see if I've lost any overnight.

Jamie sets his phone on the table—face down, a rare act of respect—and leans forward, hands clasped, the way he used to when he was prepping an interview subject for a proper grilling.

"So, you're sticking with it for a second week. Still feels like a shift down a mine?"

"I'd rather be at an actual mine," I say, then instantly regret the self-pity. "It's fine. Journalism's a growth industry if you're measuring in unpaid overtime."

Jamie grins. "Saw your column last week. Wasn't sure if it was satire or just very postmodern self-harm."

"Suppose there's a market for both," I say, trying to smile and probably failing. The hangover is operating at a level that would breach the Geneva Convention. "Anyway, it's all click-bait. No one reads past the headline, so why bother writing the body?"

He studies me with the squint of a man who once tried microdosing for a feature and never fully came down. "You've got a fan in the comments. Someone called 'HampsterFan69' keeps writing treatises about your lack of moral fibre. I think it might be a Russian bot, but the syntax is too competent."

"HampsterFan's my mother," I say, deadpan.

Jamie gives me a look that says, *plausible.*

I flag down the bartender—same as always, heavy eyeliner, working the bar with an expression of imminent martyrdom—and order a black coffee and whatever breakfast they're still willing to serve after eleven. The bartender nods, her ponytail swinging like a judge's gavel, and vanishes.

Jamie watches the exchange with mild curiosity, then turns back to me. "So, the new double-act column. You and Grace. That was some high-level content generation. Truly viral."

I suppress a groan. "It was speed dating, not a prize fight."

He shrugs. "Tomato, *tomato*. Looked like a grudge match from where I was sitting."

"Where were you sitting?"

He grins, showing teeth. "Back left. Next to the stag-do in the 'Best Man' T-shirts. We were running a sweepstake on who'd get thrown out first, you or the guy in the Mr Bean brown suit."

"Mr Bean definitely had better odds," I say, closing my eyes. The memory of last Friday's "event" is a patchwork of humiliation and overproof gin. I can't decide if it's worse that Grace was actually quite good at it, or that I was so obviously out of my depth.

Jamie taps his fingers on the tabletop, five quick staccato bursts. "You've got a tell, you know. Every time her name comes up, you do this thing with your left eye. Like you're being interrogated with a desk lamp."

I fight the urge to touch my face. "Don't be weird."

He ignores me, picking up his phone but not unlocking it. "Do you like her, or just hate her enough to go full Sherlock on her sex life?"

"It's not—" I start, then abort the sentence before it can self-destruct. "I don't like her. It's just... history. We're both professionally obliged to pretend we don't remember uni, or the subsequent... fallout."

Jamie cocks an eyebrow, the universal sign for "explain yourself."

I scowl at the table, at the ingrained beer rings and the crude declaration of love carved into the wood ("FAYE 4 KELVIN 4EVAH," the 'FAYE' later obliterated with a cigarette burn). "She stitched me up for a job, years ago. Made it look like an accident, but it was textbook sabotage. Never admitted it, not even after."

He lets the silence marinate for a moment. "Are you still mad about the job, or about her?"

"Are you writing a profile or just trying to get me to cry in public?" My tone is too sharp, but I'm too tired to course-correct.

Jamie grins. "Just interested. You act like you're over it, but you can't shut up about her."

The bartender returns with my coffee—industrial strength, nuclear black—and a breakfast sandwich so dense it's actually sinking into the plate. She slaps the plate down with a flourish, then stalks off without waiting for thanks.

I take a bite of the sandwich, mostly to buy myself time, but also because I haven't eaten since yesterday's Pret wrap. The bread is solid, the bacon is real, and the whole thing is held together by a structural excess of ketchup. It nearly brings a tear to my eye.

Jamie stirs his own coffee, which he must have ordered on his way in, and fixes me with a look that's half amusement, half concern. "Look. I get it. She's *The One That Got Away*, except she didn't so much get away as beat you to the finish line, then tattoo her victory on your arse."

I snort. "Nice metaphor."

"You're welcome." He sits back, arms crossed. "It's just—maybe you'd feel better if you actually talked to her instead of lobbing grenades from your column every week."

"Maybe," I admit. "But then I'd have to hear her side of it. And what if her side's actually—"

"True?" Jamie supplies.

I shrug, staring into the void of my coffee. "That's what scares me."

We lapse into a silence that isn't quite companionable, but

isn't hostile, either. There's a comfort in the half-light and the safe anonymity of a pub in the off hours. Here, nobody expects you to be anything except alive.

Finally, Jamie says, "She's got a good laugh, you know. Not what you expect."

I blink. "How do you mean?"

"It's not posh, not fake. It's sort of... shattering. Cuts through all the shite. Like she's not afraid of being heard."

I think about that for a moment, about the way her laugh at the speed dating cut through the bar, the way it echoed after she'd already moved on to the next table. I can't remember the last time I laughed like that.

Jamie's watching me, waiting for a reaction. Instead, I pick at my sandwich, then say, "She still wears the same perfume. Some French thing. I kept getting flashes of it, even when she was across the room."

He raises an eyebrow, not even trying to hide his smile. "You're a real poet when you're hungover."

"Go to hell."

"You first, mate."

We sit like that for a while, me nursing my coffee, Jamie with his phone still face down, both of us pretending there's nothing lurking under the surface. I glance at my watch. Time has started to move again.

Finally, Jamie says, "You're going to write about her, aren't you? Not the job, not the rivalry, just her."

"I don't know how," I say honestly. "Every time I try, it comes out like a hit piece. Or a eulogy."

He shrugs. "So write a love letter and pretend it's a war report. No one will notice the difference."

I snort again, but this time the laugh catches in my throat and sits there, raw and embarrassing. I reach for my coffee, but it's empty.

Jamie stands, brushing imaginary lint from his sleeve.

"You're toast," he says, grinning. "If I were you, I'd get used to the idea."

He walks off, heading for the bar, and I'm left staring at the table, tracing the old knife grooves with my thumb.

He's wrong, I think. *I can still do this. I can still keep it together.*

But my fingers won't stop drumming on the wood, and the smell of her perfume is still in my head, sweet and sharp and impossible to forget.

After the pub, I walk the city for an hour, then another. In the end, I decide it's not worth even going back to the newsroom. The day is an indecisive bastard—half drizzle, half a bone-dry wind that cuts through my jacket and wakes up old, unhealed bruises. By the time I reach my flat, the taste of last night's cheap lager has finally stopped repeating on me.

There's a stale silence waiting behind the front door, thick as last year's dust. I toe off my boots, climb the stairs two at a time, and let myself into the tiny flat I've called home since I fled Sheffield and rocked up in London. The décor has not improved. Still a patchwork of second-hand furniture and condensation-mottled walls, still the same flickering bulb in the kitchen that threatens epilepsy but never delivers.

I dump my bag and flop onto the armchair, which is older than most European democracies and has the spinal support of a jellyfish. The room is half-light, half-gloom, all malaise. The only real change is the pile of unopened letters on the table— bills, bank statements, the unclaimed detritus of modern life. I shuffle through them out of habit, not hope.

I remember the only time I ever read something I received in the mail:

A battered postcard, blue air mail sticker, the exotic stamp a little blurred from rain. My name is written in slanting, spiky script. I know it before I read the return address: Vientiane. Laos. My hand tightens, thumb digging into the crease along the middle. The picture is of a monastery at sunset, all gold and orange, like a portal to another, less vindictive dimension.

The message is short. Grace's handwriting is neater than it was at uni, but still somehow urgent, as though the words are trying to outrun the ink.

> Paul—
>
> Didn't want to email. Thought a postcard would be more personal. Laos is beautiful. The light is different here. Have been thinking about you, about everything. Hope we can talk one day, properly.
>
> —G

The 'G' is looped, a signature but also a question mark.

I stare at it. The room vibrates a little, or maybe it's my pulse echoing up through the floorboards. My mouth tastes like copper and regret.

The postcard arrived a few weeks after I first saw her name in print, soon after she landed the *Chronicle* internship and I lost out to someone who used to write a heart instead of a dot over the 'i.' The week I started letting the bitterness grow teeth.

I remember the day it came, too. I'd seen her byline on the *Chronicle's* digital edition, a thinkpiece about post-truth and the illusion of objectivity. I'd read every word, dissected every clause, marked up the typos and the clumsy turns of phrase.

By the end of it I was vibrating with an anger so pure I could have bottled it and sold it as artisanal rage.

The postcard had been waiting in the letterbox, bright and innocent, like a bomb made of hope. I carried it upstairs, stared at it under the faulty kitchen light, then launched a pint glass at the wall so hard the glass spider webbed, then dropped in pieces all over the floor. The noise drew my flatmate, who looked at me, looked at the mess, and said, "Can you try not to do that before ten a.m. next time?"

I ignored him. Sat down at the table and read the card again, and again, and again, until I could recite it in my sleep. The last time, I tore it in half, then quarters, then sixteenths, as if by reducing it to atoms I could erase the fact that she'd written at all.

I still have the pieces, somewhere. I kept a few in my wallet for years, between my emergency fiver and an old student ID. I'd see them every time I paid for a kebab or topped up my Oyster card—tiny, sharp-edged reminders of the thing I destroyed rather than face.

Now, in the half-dark of my flat, I pull open the drawer where I keep old receipts and passport photos. The fragments are still there, faded at the edges, the 'G' just visible on one torn scrap. I line them up on the table, a jigsaw of what-could-have-been, and realise with a sick clarity that this is who I am: a person who tears up second chances before he's even read them through.

I'm supposed to be writing a column, some viral think-piece about modern romance, but all I can think about is this: the time I got a message from the only person who ever actually saw me, and I shredded it out of spite.

I reach for my laptop, open a new document, and stare at the blinking cursor until the screen feels as blank as my brain.

Outside, the rain has started again, gentle at first, then

harder, as if the city itself is auditioning for the role of world's saddest backdrop.

I write nothing. Instead, I imagine the postcard whole, the words unbroken, the message intact.

I imagine what I'd say if I could send one back.

I tell myself I'll reply next time. I lie so well, it almost feels like hope.

SEVEN

GRACE

You can always tell when you're the punchline of a joke because nobody wants to make eye contact, but everyone wants to see your reaction. The office is a living diorama of Schadenfreude as I walk in, ten minutes early and already regretting it: desks clustered in tight huddles, the hum of muffled laughter, the glow of a dozen phone screens angled just enough to hide content but not intent. My route to the Features bullpen is a gauntlet of "did you see—?" and "wait, wait, here she comes—" punctuated by the kind of smile you show a corpse in an open casket.

At my desk, someone has stuck a Post-it to my monitor: #GRALLAGHAN. I pluck it off, palm slick with sweat, and slide into my chair. The headline from our first joint piece is still up on my screen: "Love in the Age of Metrics: Two Writers, Twelve Dates, Zero Chemistry." Below it, the social counter spins like a gas meter in a leaking flat. Seventy-six thousand shares. The comments section is a radioactive wasteland.

Paul is already here. He's got his feet up on the rolling cabinet, chair tipped back so far the casters should sue for abuse. He's reading the article with a kind of lazy glee, scrolling at exactly the speed needed to make me think he's not reading at all. His hair is even worse than yesterday, and his T-shirt says, "Error 404: Motivation Not Found." He doesn't look up, but I know he's waiting for me to speak first.

Instead, I bury myself in the day's emails, hoping that maybe an actual crisis will erupt to eclipse the ongoing PR disaster of my own life. No such luck. The first six messages are from internal comms, subject line: "GOING VIRAL!" and "Keep the momentum!" The next four are from HR, reminding staff that the dress code still exists even if the newspaper is now "multi-platform."

A small, sharp pain lands on my arm. A rubber band, expertly fired. I don't have to look to know it's Paul.

"You seen this?" he says, voice pitched for maximum audibility.

"Unfortunately," I reply, flicking the band back at him. It bounces off his forehead. He grins.

He holds up his phone, screen turned my way. "We're trending. Even made it to TikTok."

He taps a link, and a video starts: a pair of teenagers in bad wigs, reenacting our speed-dating attempts in front of a kitchen sink, one of them screeching in a flat parody of my accent, the other smirking and monosyllabic in a way that actually flatters Paul. The comments are a masterclass in digital empathy, ranging from "OTP" to "these two need to shag or die trying."

I close my laptop with more force than necessary. "Remind me again why we're doing this?"

He shrugs, all feigned innocence. "I thought you cared about the mission. Raising the standard of public debate. Exposing the soul of modern romance."

"Funny. I thought the goal was journalism, not performance art for Gen Z."

He takes the hit, but only just. "It's a living."

"Barely," I say, but he's already gone back to the article, scrolling with his thumb while composing a tweet with his other hand. I want to ask how he can function with so little shame, but I know the answer: practice.

At 9:32 exactly, Sarah barrels in from the corridor, trailing the scent of bergamot and ambition. She's in her signature green suit—double-breasted—and she's carrying a stack of printed analytics, each page dog-eared and bruised by a highlighter. She slams the sheaf onto my desk, sending the Post-it skittering to the floor.

"People!" she crows, as if addressing the Roman Senate. "We are officially a phenomenon."

She fans out the graphs, each one an exponential curve, all steep ascents and annotated milestones. "Look at this. Look! Engagement up one-hundred percent. Page dwell times through the roof. You've single-handedly doubled our under-thirty reach."

I feel the warm rush of accomplishment, followed by the icy trickle of dread. "That's... good?"

"Good? It's viral, darling. It's the holy grail." She pivots to Paul, who has himself pivoted to a vertical stance in anticipation of the praise. "You two are the new face of the *Chronicle*. The banter. The chemistry. The violence. It's everything we ever wanted in a column and more."

"Great," says Paul, biting back a smile. "When do we start?"

Sarah claps her hands together, the sound sharp and final. "Next week. No—this week, if we can pull it off. We'll call it 'Modern Connection' or something more clicky. We want you two to co-author, real-time, maybe even livestream the process. The kids eat that up."

I feel my stomach drop, then keep dropping, as if the floor has suddenly disappeared. "I'm not sure—"

Sarah cuts me off. "You're journalists. You observe, you provoke, you connect. That's what we do. I mean, we could pivot to hard news, but who wants to read about the G7 when there's this?" She gestures at the analytics like a magician revealing a rabbit made of pure data.

Paul leans back, arms folded. "What's the brief?"

"Anything," says Sarah, eyes shining. "Dating, friendship, even hate-mail. God, especially hate-mail. Let's try to explore alternative venues for modern dating. I don't know—a cookery class, a climbing wall centre, something like that. Two lonely hearts, four hours, nowhere to run. Can you do it?"

He grins. "It's not like we haven't done worse."

I want to protest, to reclaim the last vestige of professional dignity, but the words stick. Instead, I watch Sarah tap her nails on the desk, the rhythm like a countdown to some inevitable disaster.

"Is there a pay rise involved?" I ask, knowing the answer.

Sarah's smile doesn't waver. "Not directly, but the exposure is invaluable."

The word "exposure" lands like a cold hand on the back of my neck. Paul's eyes flick to me, then away. I wonder if he's thinking the same thing: that we've been here before, chasing relevance down a dark tunnel, not sure if the light at the end is a sunrise or just another bloody train.

Sarah sweeps up her graphs, tosses a stress ball from her bag, and leaves as quickly as she arrived. The stress ball bounces off the edge of my desk, rolls under Paul's chair. He picks it up and squeezes hard.

We sit in silence for a long minute, the office returning to its normal hum. I check my phone, thumb hovering over the care home alert, then lock the screen and shove it in my pocket.

Paul breaks first. "You okay?"

I want to say yes, to pretend that the thing churning inside me is just professional anxiety, not existential horror. Instead, I say, "I thought I'd get to write something that mattered."

He tosses the stress ball from hand to hand. "Maybe you will. Eventually."

"Or maybe this is it. Maybe we're the joke now, not the punchline."

He looks at me, really looks, and for a moment I see something almost like sympathy. "At least we're getting paid for it this time."

I snort. It's not funny, but it helps. He passes me the stress ball. I take it, squeeze until my knuckles ache.

Across the office, someone starts playing the TikTok parody on loop. The laughter rises, then falls, then starts again. Paul grins, but it's softer now, less weaponised.

I watch the numbers on my screen, the counter ticking up in real time, and wonder how many of those are people rooting for us, and how many just want to see us burn.

I squeeze the stress ball until it almost splits, then open my hand and let it drop.

"Ready for the next round?" asks Paul.

I look at him, then at the article, then at another care home notification blinking on my phone.

"Not even close," I say.

But when Sarah's next email pings into my inbox—subject: "You Two Are Gold"—I open it, and start to read.

Seven years ago, I was not yet the kind of person who knew how to weaponise a smile.

I stand outside the glass fortress of the *Chronicle's* headquarters, arms pressed to my sides like I'm expecting to be frisked, and try not to stare at my reflection in the automatic doors. I look like a tourist in my own life—jacket too new, hair still refusing to settle after two months of tropical humidity, skin shockingly pale beneath the surface tan already leaching away. My bag, a knock-off Mulberry that smells of someone else's perfume, is so obviously not the real thing that I want to burn it. The city air tastes like cold metal and possibility, but the main thing I feel is a thin, pulsing sense of impending disaster.

I check my phone again. One new notification from my mum, three WhatsApps from uni friends (all variants on "you'll smash it"), and the pin on my Google Maps set to this exact spot. No voicemails. No last-minute calls telling me it was a clerical error and I should go home. I'm not sure if I'm disappointed.

Inside, the reception is all marble and silent judgement. The woman at the desk wears the kind of eyeliner that would get you expelled at my old school, and she scans my name badge with a laser that leaves no trace but shame. "You're early," she says, then gestures at a bench by the lifts. "Wait there, please. Someone will collect you."

I wait, knees pressed together, hands in my lap like an especially diligent nun. The bench is strategically placed for maximum exposure: every passing staffer, every visitor, every actual journalist sees me, evaluates, and passes on. A man in a Rolling Stones T-shirt gives me a once-over and makes a note in his phone. Two interns, still damp from the rain, whisper behind their hands, eyes flicking to the blond streaks in my fringe. I smile at no one and try to look like I belong.

After eleven minutes, a woman in a tan jumpsuit appears and beckons. "Grace? This way, please."

Her heels echo through the corridor, past open-plan pods

and glassed-in meeting rooms packed with people pretending not to stare. We take the stairs two at a time. I am breathless before we reach the top.

The editor's office is a greenhouse: triple-glazed, southerly aspect, every surface designed to blind. The man behind the desk is smaller than I expected, hair a thatch of silver wires, glasses perched on the end of a nose that looks manufactured for condescension. He does not stand up, just gestures for me to sit in a chair that squeaks and slides an inch backwards as I lower myself in.

He flips through my CV with a flicker of interest. "Hampton, right? Sheffield. A few articles for *The Independent*. That piece on Sri Lanka was very"—he waves a hand—"assured."

"Thank you," I say, aware that every word is being weighed.

He nods, tapping the CV with a fingernail. "You didn't apply for this internship, did you?"

It's not a question. My throat tightens. "No. I wasn't— I had planned to go travelling for twelve months and apply next year. Then I got the letter, and—"

He raises a finger. "We have a strong tradition here. If we see something we want, we ask for it. Not all candidates are so... proactive. Or honest, for that matter." He sets the paper aside. "Do you want it?"

I think about it: the rent I can't afford, the rows with my mother, the last argument with Paul, who said the system would always pick its favourite. I think about the spreadsheet I keep on my laptop, mapping out the next five years like a NASA mission.

"Yes," I say, and it's the most honest thing I've said all month.

The editor glances at the glass wall, then back. "You had quite the reference. Professor Harlow, I believe. He said you were"—He checks a note—"'disgustingly efficient. More driven than half the men I've ever taught.'"

A cold drop slides down my spine. Harlow. Paul's hero. The man who told him he had "the gift." I try to keep my face still, but the Editor is watching for it.

"Small world," I say, voice tinny in my own ears.

He doesn't smile. "Very. This world is even smaller, Ms Hampton. You understand the pressure?"

I nod. "I do."

He regards me for another moment, then stands. "You start Monday. Eight sharp. Bring a notebook, not a laptop." He extends a hand. His skin is cold and dry, like a pressed flower.

I shake, then stand. The chair makes the same undignified noise as before. I want to shrink, but instead I thank him—twice—and walk out.

The corridor is empty. I linger by the stairwell, hands shaking just enough to make my phone hard to grip. There's a message from Professor Harlow ("You'll be splendid, old thing—remember, nothing is ever as accidental as it seems"), and an email from the Chronicle's admin office confirming my start date. I scroll through, searching for something—some hint, some hidden clause—but it's all just perfectly ordinary, perfectly inescapable.

Outside, London is its usual off-white. The rain has stopped, but the streets are still slick, pooling in the gaps of the pavement like tiny unfinished lakes. I pull my jacket tight and start walking, unsure of where I'm going. The city sounds louder than I remember. I feel the weight of the building behind me, of all the invisible strings that dragged me back.

At the first red light, I unlock my phone again. Paul's contact is near the top, still starred. I hover over the call button, thumb poised for disaster. In another universe, I would press it—tell him the truth, ask if he knew, ask if he still hated me. In this one, I pocket the phone and keep walking.

The wind whips my hair, lifting the blond until it's almost white. I see myself reflected in a shop window, jacket and all, and I look like a child pretending at adulthood. Or maybe a ghost, already fading.

I keep walking, eyes fixed ahead. There's nowhere left to go but forward.

EIGHT

— ♥ —

PAUL

If coffee shops were people, this one would be the trust fund brat at an art-school house party: ostentatious, needy, and convinced it invented cynicism. The menu is in lowercase, the baristas all have tattooed knuckles, and the Wi-Fi password changes daily because "digital security is self-care."

I pause at the entrance, surveying the usual population of early-morning overachievers and failed screenwriters, and spot Grace in the back. She's always in the back—closest to a power outlet, farthest from the door, impossible to ambush. If I didn't know better, I'd think she's actually afraid of me.

Of course she's there already, even though I'm only seven minutes late, which in our mutual language is basically on time. Her laptop is open, a regimented garden of colour-coded Post-its sprouting from its edges. Next to it, her notebook— every page an act of calligraphic violence, the headings under- lined in three separate colours. I can see the agenda from here, even without my glasses: 1. Brainstorm. 2. Outline. 3. Deadlines. 4. Tone check. She's even drawn a little tick box next to each, ready for the dopamine hit of completion.

She doesn't look up when I approach, but she knows I'm there. She always does. It's like we're connected by an invisible tripwire, permanently set to "sarcasm imminent."

I make a show of reading the menu, ignoring the queue behind me, then order a double shot black coffee with oat milk and "whatever syrup is most expensive." The barista rolls her eyes, types it in with the kind of finger flourish that suggests a short course in interpretive dance, and slides me the point-of-sale device.

Grace's eyes flick up as I approach. She's in a black turtle-neck and a jacket so precise it could have been engineered in a wind tunnel. She looks tired, but the kind of tired that's been actively worked on; her lipstick is war paint, her eyeliner a dare.

"Morning," I say, dropping my bag and taking the chair opposite. I let it screech across the concrete floor, purely for effect.

"You're late," she says, ticking the first box on her agenda before even making eye contact.

I shrug. "Time is a social construct, Grace. So are deadlines."

She closes her notebook with a snap. "That's the spirit. This week's brief is in your inbox, by the way. I've already started a Google Doc. I notice that you haven't added anything. Let me know if you need help getting access."

I ignore the bait, instead scanning the contents of her table. Next to the laptop is a flat white, two sips gone, and a plastic tub of overnight oats with chia seeds and blueberries arranged in a pattern suspiciously close to the Fibonacci spiral. I lean forward and disturb it with the edge of my coffee cup.

She glares at me, but doesn't correct the pattern. Progress.

"So," I say, "what's the existential horror for today?"

She pulls up the brief, her fingers barely making a sound on the keys. "How to Fake a Relationship (and Why You Shouldn't). Twelve hundred words. Editorial wants it by Friday, but they'll settle for Monday if we can 'generate sufficient heat' on socials before then."

"'Heat,'" I echo. "Is that what we're calling it now?"

She doesn't smile. "You know what Sarah is like. She wants drama. Conflict. A little bit of scandal, ideally with a side of emotional nudity."

"I'm not taking my clothes off in a café again. There's a restraining order."

"Let's just get it done. I made a list of possible angles." She slides her notebook towards me. I resist the urge to doodle on it.

Angle 1: The psychology of performative relationships—Instagram couples, fauxmances, etc.

Angle 2: The emotional fallout of pretending—are we all faking it, or just the ones who get caught?

Angle 3: Case studies from our own lives (*see below*).

She's written "see below" in italics, as if it's a secret message.

I tap the list with my pen. "You missed one. Angle 4: Just tell the truth for once and see if anyone dies."

She raises her eyebrows. "That's your suggestion?"

"It's a working title."

She sits back, folds her arms. "Fine. How would you pitch it?"

I think for a second. "Start with the premise that everyone is lying, all the time. Especially the people who say they aren't. Then trace it back—childhood, social media, school, uni. All the relationships we faked to survive. Then pick one and blow it up in the final paragraph, like a controlled demolition."

She considers this, nodding slowly. "It's bleak."

"Bleak is authentic. Authentic is viral."

She jots something on her agenda. "What about a counter-point? A defence of honesty, or at least the attempt?"

I lean in. "Isn't the counterpoint the punchline? That nobody can tell the difference anymore?"

She gives me a look I can't quite decode—half admiration, half exasperation. "You should have gone into politics."

"I did. Journalism is just politics for people who can't keep a straight face."

We volley ideas for the next twenty minutes, the conversation so fast it's almost anaerobic. Every time she tries to steer us towards something actionable, I swerve back into chaos. She's not above playing dirty, either; twice, she pretends to agree with my point just to see how I'll sabotage myself. It's the closest we get to flirting.

My coffee finally arrives, ostentatiously topped with gold leaf and a drizzle of something I assume is edible. I stare at it, then at Grace, then at the price written in biro on the receipt. "You know," I say, "when this is all over, we should open a place like this. Call it Schadenfreude."

She doesn't look up from her screen. "Too on the nose."

"I'm nothing if not literal."

She smiles at that, just a fraction. "You're impossible."

I sip my drink, then lean back in my chair. "You know what the real scam is?" I ask, apropos of nothing.

She types without pausing. "Other than capitalism?"

"Other than that. The real scam is how easy it is to pretend you're not still mad about something that happened years ago. You just talk enough, drink enough, fuck enough, and eventually you almost believe it."

She stops typing. The silence is sudden, heavy.

I push on, unable to help myself. "Do you ever think about it? About us?"

She's motionless for a second, then closes the laptop and folds her hands on top. "Paul—"

I hold up a hand. "Sorry. Ignore me. It's the gold leaf. Toxic at high doses."

She sighs, long and thin. "What exactly are you asking?"

I look at the floor, then at her. "Were we ever not pretending?"

The question hangs there, ugly and real. I can see her measuring the space between us, calculating the emotional blast radius. For a moment, she looks like she might answer.

Then, she opens her notebook again, flips to a fresh page. "Let's get back to the column. We have a deadline."

"Sure," I say, but the word tastes like old pennies.

We work in silence for a while, each in our own bubble of self-justification. I keep wanting to say something else, to pull the pin on the whole thing and see if we both survive, but I don't. Instead, I watch her write, the way her hand tightens on the pen, the way her mouth moves when she's searching for the right phrase.

Eventually, she breaks the silence. "If we're being honest, you're not the only one who wonders."

I blink. "About what?"

She doesn't look at me. "Whether it was real. Whether any of it was."

I want to say, "It was." I want to say, "I'm sorry." I want to say, "Let's try again, this time without all the lies and the caution." But I make a joke, something about Stockholm syndrome and deadlines.

She laughs, but it's brittle. The moment's gone.

We finish the outline, agree on the first draft deadline, and pack up in synchronised silence. On the way out, I see she's left a sticky note on my laptop: "Don't be late again." She's underlined "late" three times.

I watch her leave, her heels echoing on the polished concrete, and wonder how many more times I can pretend we're only pretending.

Probably just this once.
Maybe not even that.

The journalism corridor at Sheffield always smelled of instant coffee and panic. The walls were a petting zoo of department flyers, protest posters, and faded satirical cartoons nobody had bothered to take down since the Brown government.

I'm late, because I'm always late, but I know the lecturers won't care as long as I show up with a snappy headline or a half-decent hangover. My bag is half-open, the last third of a chicken wrap poking out, and I've not bothered with a coat because the walk between Halls and the Media Block is three minutes, tops.

I'm halfway to the end of the corridor when someone— Matt? Max?—claps me on the back so hard I nearly choke on the last mouthful of chicken. He's grinning, shirt untucked, fist clutching the neck of a two-litre bottle of Tango like it's a trophy.

"Congrats, mate!" he says, eyes glinting with the thrill of gossip. "Didn't think you and Hampton would make it through the final round, but the staff are loving the drama."

I swallow, then wipe my hand on my jeans. "What?"

He laughs, shaking his head like I'm playing hard to get. "Don't act dumb. It's all over the group chat. She's in, yeah? Thought you'd be celebrating already."

I feel a weird stutter in my chest, a mechanical misfire, but I let it pass. "Yeah, well. I'm waiting for the official word."

He shrugs. "Go check the board. They put it up early." Then he's off, two-steps-at-a-time, shouting "legend" at a girl he's never spoken to sober.

I know damn well her name's on the board, I saw it there

yesterday myself and then I'd ripped the notice into tiny pieces.

I wait until he's rounded the corner, then finish the wrap, stuffing the foil in the nearest bin. My hands are sticky, and the corridor feels colder all of a sudden, but I brush it off, blaming the recycled air.

The air outside is raw. It takes me a minute to realise I've started walking towards her block, the route so well-worn it's practically muscle memory. I should have said something to her, instead of just barging past her like a toddler having a tantrum. I think about stopping, about texting her instead, but the idea of "congratulations" via WhatsApp makes my skin crawl.

Her building is red brick, post-war, the kind of architecture designed to crush dreams gently. The main doors are propped open with a fire extinguisher. I climb the stairs three at a time, and knock on her door before I can psych myself out.

It's her flatmate, Zoe, who answers. She's in a dressing gown, one eye rimmed with last night's mascara, mug of tea in hand.

"Hey," she says, blinking. "You're looking for Grace?"

I nod, swallowing the burn in my throat.

Zoe sips her tea, then gestures to the empty corridor behind her. "She's gone."

I stare, not comprehending.

"She left this morning," Zoe clarifies. "Early. Said she was off to her mum's place. Left a note, I think." She disappears for a second, then comes back with a slip of lined paper. She doesn't hand it to me, just reads it aloud, voice flat and unbothered.

"'Sorry, Z. Needed a change of scenery. Will message when I get to the house. Don't let Paul eat my Weetabix.'"

I hear my name, but only as background noise.

"She's not coming back?" I ask.

Zoe shrugs. "Doubt it, term's pretty much over. She was pretty wound up last night. Went through a whole bottle of cheap plonk and started quoting poetry at the kitchen tiles. You know how she gets."

I don't know how she gets. Or maybe I do, but it doesn't fit the story I've always told about her.

"Thanks," I say, and leave without waiting for more.

Back outside, I walk until the cold is so sharp it feels like it's carving out the inside of my mouth.

I build the narrative in my head as I walk: She must have applied behind my back. Maybe she never even wanted me in the first place, just the proximity to the thing she really wanted. Or maybe it was all a game to her, and I was the last to get the joke.

I could text her. I could call, or even get a train and turn up at her mum's place. But that would mean admitting I care, that I need her to explain. It would mean accepting a version of the story where I'm not the hero.

So I don't.

Instead, I walk home, and tell myself that I'm over it. That it doesn't matter. That the next time I see her name, it'll be on a byline I won't bother reading.

Back in my room, I lock the door, kick off my shoes, and sit on the end of the bed. I stare at the cracks in the ceiling for a long time, counting them like they're days on a prison wall.

Eventually, I pull out my phone, type her number into a new message, then delete it before it can become anything.

Somewhere in a part of my brain I can't shut off, I replay the scene at the noticeboard. Every time, I expect it to end differently. Every time, it doesn't.

I wonder if this is what faking it feels like: knowing the truth, but choosing the better lie.

I tell myself I'll never give her the satisfaction.

I lie so well, I almost believe it.

NINE

GRACE

There are only two ways to enter a newsroom after going viral: with the casual arrogance of a Roman emperor returning from Gaul, or the tight-faced resignation of someone approaching the public stocks. I have always preferred the latter.

This morning, I walk in dead on time, flat white in hand, eyes fixed just above the horizon line of my own desk, and step over a nest of electrical cables with the grace of a condemned woman making her last journey. The open-plan office is at full volume—phones ringing, keyboards clattering, the Features team already in their daily state of controlled combustion—but the second I cross into their airspace, there's a momentary lull, like the hush before a minor celebrity face-plants on ice.

It's not that anyone stops working, exactly. It's just that their attention recalibrates, tilting fractionally towards me, the way houseplants bend to the sun. Even the interns—never slow to sense blood in the water—are suddenly hyper-diligent, pretending to ignore me while memorising every detail for their next WhatsApp group post.

I lower myself into my chair, an ergonomic punishment device with a lumbar support like the barrel of a gun, and log on to the world's slowest PC. The screen takes a full thirty seconds to boot, affording plenty of time for the social theatre to play out. From my right, I sense a deliberate throat-clear; on the left, the heavy sigh of someone who wants me to know that my mere existence is causing a backlog in their critical work. The guy at the neighbouring desk (tall, tanned, wore a fake bandage for six weeks after a minor cycling accident) glances over his monitor and gives me a smirk so lopsided it's almost an act of aggression.

"Morning, Grace," he says. His tone is syrupy, but there's a glint of actual malice in it.

"Morning," I reply, calm and professional. I make a point of aligning my notepad to the desk's edge, uncapping my pen with a practised flick. I have already checked the day's schedule—two planning meetings, one phone interview, and a brainstorm for the "viral vertical"—but I go through the motions anyway. Today of all days, I crave routine, the comfort of a system with no room for error or humiliation.

I sip my coffee, which is now too bitter and too cold, and try not to listen as a small cluster of junior writers stage-whisper about "the next Brangelina." My name is used, but not in a way that invites direct response.

At 9:03, the Editor appears. She stands at the front of the bullpen, the fluorescent lights reinforcing her suit's inhuman shade of green. Sarah is, as ever, perfectly poised for maximum psychological intimidation: hair scraped back to the point of fascism, tablet held out like a holy relic, voice calibrated to reach the back row without ever breaking a sweat.

"Morning, team. If you could all pause your doom-scrolling for ten seconds?"

The room complies. Phones are palmed, tabs minimised. Every set of eyes swings to the front, except one pair.

Paul Callaghan is sitting dead-centre in the first row of desks, legs kicked out in front of him, arms folded like he's watching a magician saw someone in half. He is dressed in the standard Paul uniform—ill-fitting black jeans, a wrinkled shirt that was probably clean this month, and a battered rain coat thrown over the back of his chair. He is not, at first glance, paying attention, but I know better. If there's one thing Paul is good at, it's watching the room without looking at it.

Sarah launches into her standard opening: numbers, engagement stats, the existential threat of "content fatigue." There's a quick, staccato review of last week's viral success. She gestures at the screen, where a bar graph is ascending so steeply it looks like a stock market crash in reverse. "Our Modern Romance column is a runaway. Page dwell time is still over three minutes, shares are double last week's, and our organic reach among under-thirties is officially 'industry-leading.' So, congratulations once again, Grace and Paul." She doesn't say our surnames together, but the implied hashtag hovers in the air, radioactive and immortal.

There's a round of applause, but it's the sarcastic, golf-clap variety. I smile, small and contained, and fight the urge to just go home.

"Next," Sarah says, "we want to keep the momentum. We're on the agenda for the board briefing, and it's been strongly suggested that we follow up the chemistry of the last two weekly columns with something even more... engaging." She looks at me, then at Paul, then back at me, like a tennis match where I am always the losing player.

At this, a ripple goes through the room. The smirk from the cycling guy returns, amplified by the giggle of the social media editor, who leans across her desk with the predatory grace of a cat stretching before the kill.

"Can we expect more of your 'unfiltered takes' in this one, Grace?" she asks, voice honeyed but loaded.

I keep my expression neutral. "I'm sure the office will have plenty of feedback, as always," I reply, then add, "Let's hope the comments section doesn't outpace the actual piece this time."

She's about to reply, but from the back of the room comes a loud, unfiltered snicker. "At least you two are finally admitting it," someone says, just loud enough for me to hear.

I feel my face flush, a quick hot bloom of embarrassment. This is the problem with going viral: you become everyone's property. Every joke, every private glance, every pixel of your life gets meme'd and dissected. I look up at Sarah, expecting a shut-down, but she's already moved on to the next item on her agenda. For her, my humiliation is just another engagement metric.

I chance a glance at Paul. He's looking at me now, directly, a half-smile on his face that could be interpreted as either solidarity or sabotage. He does a little salute with his mug, then mouths: "Surviving?"

I want to roll my eyes, but I just nod. It's the closest we'll get to intimacy in a room full of jackals.

The meeting drones on. Assignments are doled out, deadlines shuffled, resources "re-aligned." None of it matters; the only thing anyone in the room will remember is the way Sarah said our names together, the implication of a relationship so transparent it could be used as a window.

By the time she dismisses us, my jaw is tight enough to crack a tooth. I stand, gather my things, and make for the kitchen area, desperate for a moment of silence and maybe a fresh cup of coffee that doesn't taste of bile. As I pass the Features desk, the intern—one of the ambitious ones, with a CV longer than her skirt—leans over and whispers, "Congrats, by the way. You guys are, like, office royalty now."

"Thanks," I say, not trusting myself to add anything else.

In the kitchen, the new coffee machine is already broken,

leaking a thin brown puddle onto the laminate. I stare at it for a second, then decide it's as good a metaphor for my morning as any. I rinse my mug, fill it with tap water, and count to ten. My hands are steady, but my heart is not.

The noise from the bullpen swells and recedes, punctuated by the occasional shout or nervous laughter. I hear my name again, then Paul's, and then the phrase "will-they-won't-they" uttered in the sort of mocking tone reserved for soap opera recaps and political scandals. I wonder if anyone actually believes the column is fake, or if they've already decided that every relationship is half-performance anyway.

I lean against the counter and close my eyes, just for a moment. When I open them, Paul is in the doorway, arms folded, watching me with an expression I can't decipher. He doesn't say anything, just raises his eyebrows as if to ask, *Well?*

I shake my head. "You'd think people would have better things to do with their time."

He snorts. "You know better than that. It's a slow news week. We're all they've got."

We stand there in silence for a beat, neither of us willing to give ground. Then he pushes off the wall and comes to stand next to me, shoulder to shoulder.

"You okay?" he says, voice lowered.

I force a smile. "Never better."

He gives me a long, searching look, then says, "Don't let them get to you. They'll move on when the next thing blows up."

"Yeah, well. Maybe next time it'll be your turn," I say, aiming for light but missing.

He grins. "Doubt it. You're the interesting one."

I want to argue, but the truth is I'm too tired. Instead, I refill my water, nod at him, and head back to my desk. As I sit, I catch the tail end of another conversation—someone speculating on how long it'll be before HR has to step in and issue a "fraternisation memo."

I set my jaw, open Word, and begin drafting the next piece. The cursor blinks at me, patient and unjudging. I think about what Sarah said—about chemistry, about engagement, about the relentless need for spectacle—and wonder if maybe, just this once, I could write something honest enough to outlast the meme cycle.

Probably not. But I start typing anyway.

By noon, the whispers have faded. The news cycle lurches forward, dragging the office's attention with it. I am, once again, just another part of the scenery.

But the whole time, I can feel their eyes on me—waiting, measuring, daring me to slip.

I won't give them the satisfaction.

At least, not yet.

By the afternoon, my desk is an island of controlled chaos. I have three open notebooks, all in different stages of nervous breakdown, and a stack of advance copies from the Books desk, all marked with Post-its in my own private system of triage and shame. The glare from my monitor is a persistent ache at the base of my skull, and the office air is thick with the scent of burnt filter coffee and half-hearted deodorant.

Somewhere in the background, the click of the Features team's group Slack is like a digital woodpecker boring holes in my concentration. But I keep my eyes on the screen, writing and rewriting the opening line of our next "Modern Romance" column until every variant sounds either passive-aggressive or faintly obscene.

I'm two sentences deep into the third rewrite when my phone vibrates. The notification glows up from the desk: "Prof

Harlow." It's just a text—Hey you, saw the latest column, hope the Big Smoke isn't eating you alive. If you want to talk, I'm always around. x H.—but the effect is immediate and seismic.

I stare at the message, thumb poised to reply, but can't bring myself to type anything. Instead, my brain cycles through a highlight reel of every bad decision I ever made at uni, every seminar where I bluffed my way through a reading I'd only skimmed, every offhand compliment Harlow ever paid me that I'd secretly written on my dorm wall. I can smell the mildew from the Media Block seminar room, hear the faint metallic whine of the radiators, feel the dry heat of his gaze as he told us we were the future of British journalism.

I want to text back—something bright and self-deprecating, maybe even a joke about media Stockholm syndrome. But I can't. I have a column to write, a reputation to build, and a carefully-cultivated façade to maintain. So I lock the phone and shove it face-down into my drawer, then pretend to myself that it's not there.

A shadow falls across my screen. I look up, startled, and see Paul, mug in one hand, battered Moleskine in the other.

He doesn't sit, just leans against the side of my desk, invading my personal space by an amount measurable only in nanometres. "You free to talk logistics?"

I arch an eyebrow. "Isn't that your code for 'procrastinate and undermine the agenda'?"

He grins, undeterred. "Not this time. Sarah wants us to do the next one as an actual date—just us, dinner, drinks, maybe something embarrassing with karaoke if we're lucky. She thinks the readers will go mad for it."

I groan, dropping my head into my hands. "I'd rather coat myself in raw bacon and run through the dog park."

"Can't rule out that being next week's assignment," he says. "But for now, we just have to look like we're trying. Apparently, there are 'expectations.'"

He air-quotes the last word, and for a second, I catch myself almost smiling.

Then he says, "If it's any consolation, we get to expense the drinks. And the food. And, according to Sarah, any dry cleaning that results from 'creative differences.'"

He gives me a look, the sort that's meant to disarm, but instead it sets my teeth on edge.

"We should probably pick a night," he says. "Make a booking, agree on an alibi, rehearse our lines."

Something about the way he says "alibi" needles me. "Are you incapable of taking anything seriously, or is it a choice?"

His face goes blank for a beat, then the cocky smile flickers back. "Didn't realise we'd shifted into Method acting already."

The words are out of my mouth before I can stop them. "I just assumed you'd prefer to improvise your way through, then blame me when it goes wrong."

He blinks, taken aback. "That's not fair."

"Neither is any of this," I snap, and now my voice is high and thin and echoing in the dead air between us.

For a second, Paul doesn't move. He looks down at his mug, then at me. His eyes narrow—not angry, just tired, as if he's heard this script before and always hoped for a better rewrite.

"Why do you always assume the worst of me?" he asks quietly.

I freeze. For one irrational, heart-stopping moment, it feels like the entire office is holding its breath, waiting to see which one of us will cry first.

I want to apologise, but the habit of self-defence is too deeply ingrained. Instead, I say, "Because the worst is usually what I get."

He opens his mouth, then shuts it. The silence stretches, taut and ugly.

Then, without warning, he straightens, tosses the notebook

onto my desk, and turns away. "Fine. You handle it. I've got another article to work on. Let me know what night I need to show up."

He's gone before I can even process the sentence. I stare at his notebook, the pages dog-eared and peppered with ballpoint sketches of angry animals. For a moment, I want to rip it in half, just to feel something other than this dense, aching guilt.

The Features team is suddenly, ostentatiously, not watching me. Even the cycling guy is pretending to have a spontaneous, life-changing interest in tax law. I feel the old, familiar urge to run—out of the office, out of the city, back to that first moment at the noticeboard when nothing had been decided yet.

Instead, I pick up my pen and grip it so tight the plastic bends. I try to get back to the column, but the words keep blurring, the letters rearranging themselves into old arguments and unfinished apologies.

Eventually, I open my phone, read Harlow's message again, and almost—almost—type out a reply.

Then I close the app, lock the phone, and stare at the half-moon imprints the pen has left in my palm.

For the rest of the day, I keep my head down and my words to myself.

But every so often, I catch myself glancing at the empty space where Paul's coffee mug used to be.

I want to believe it means nothing.

I want to believe I'm over it.

But the marks on my hand don't fade, and the words keep coming, harder each time, until all I can do is let them pile up and hope one day I'll be brave enough to say them out loud.

TEN

PAUL

If I stare at the blinking cursor for another second, I'll have to call a priest. The *Chronicle's* "collaborative workspace" is an exercise in mutual destruction: open-plan desks laid out like a chessboard, every move visible and liable to be countered, the air tinged with desperation and second-hand deodorant. My screen is set to the lowest brightness, but the document still glares at me like a searchlight.

I type, "The problem with love is," then backspace it out so fast the letters don't have time to lodge in memory. Next try: "In the algorithmic age, relationships are—" I lose interest before the sentence completes and jab at delete until nothing's left but white. If productivity is measured in keystrokes per hour, I should be eligible for a promotion.

Across the quad, Grace's desk is vacant. She's probably in a meeting, or maybe she's hiding out in the stairwell, a known haunt for the emotionally afflicted. I tell myself I don't care, but my peripheral vision is tuned to her absence. The chair is pushed in, her water bottle half full and sweating on a Post-it.

There's a single, perfect circle of condensation, the kind you see in adverts for bottled water and wish you could taste.

The column is due in less than twenty-four hours. Every time I scroll back, the opening paragraph looks smaller, as if the act of rereading is whittling it down to a splinter. The editorial Slack keeps vibrating my phone closer and closer to the edge of the desk: "Let's keep it spicy, Paul!" "Great first draft, but can we get more... friction?" "Don't forget team drinks tonight!" I mute the thread, then immediately unmute it, because silence is worse.

I've gone two hours without speaking, a personal best since year eleven at school. This does not go unnoticed. I can feel the side-eye from the Social team, the Notting Hill boy with the statement glasses, the interns who treat every day as a live audition for *The Apprentice*. Usually, I provide background noise—sarcasm, deadpan fact-checks, a running commentary on the idiocy of modern media. Today, I am a vacuum.

Into this void steps Jamie. He navigates the newsroom with the easy grace of a man who knows he can return upstairs to the Finance department whenever he wants, and is only slumming it down here with the worker bees for the drama and gossip. He's holding two coffees, the cardboard tray abandoned for a more dramatic, single-fisted delivery. He deposits himself at the edge of my desk, leans against the divider, and waits for me to acknowledge his existence.

"An entire three weeks. Didn't think you'd still be here," he says, pushing a cup toward me. "Thought you'd have cracked and thrown yourself out the window by now."

I take the coffee but don't look up. "Was waiting for a more receptive audience."

He surveys the battlefield: the blank screen, the angry red margin on the Google Doc, the low, constant hum of my leg bouncing under the desk.

"You look like a man who's either in love or constipated."

I manage a half-smile, all jaw, and swallow half the coffee at once. It's burnt, and better for it. "Not mutually exclusive," I say, then immediately regret saying anything at all.

Jamie sits next to me uninvited, and stretches his legs under the desk, knocking the frame in the process. He is the only person in the office who can pull off this level of intrusive comfort without anyone calling HR.

"Grace out today?" he asks, voice pitched for maximum plausible deniability.

"She's in," I say. "Just not here." The distinction feels important.

He nods, scanning the room for her as if she might materialise from the thin air. "You ever going to tell her?"

I feign ignorance. "Tell her what?"

He shrugs. "That you're incapable of writing a nice thing about anyone except her. That you stalk her Instagram on weekends. That you've still got her old birthday card taped inside your laptop case. Take your pick."

I consider lying, but the effort is more than I can muster. "She knows," I say. "She's not stupid."

"No, mate," he says, "but you are. For thinking that doing nothing is the same as not caring."

This is a more honest take than I'm ready for at eleven-forty in the morning. I look at my hands, which are shaking slightly, then at the mug, which reads "WORLD'S OKAYEST WRITER." It was a joke, but the joke has curdled.

Jamie glances at the screen, where the cursor blinks in a field of snow. "Stuck?"

I nod. "It's supposed to be a hot take on fake relationships, but I can't even fake the hot take."

He laughs once, hard enough to make the intern at the next desk jump. "If anyone can, it's you, mate. You've been fake since you started growing facial hair."

I allow a small, mean smile. "You're projecting."

He shrugs, unconcerned. "Maybe. But at least I finish what I start." He checks his phone—always vibrating, never not in crisis—and stands. "You coming to the pub after?"

I hesitate. "Maybe."

"Don't say maybe," he says, "say yes. You're more fun when you're two pints deep and not thinking so bloody hard."

He walks off, a storm front moving on to more interesting terrain.

I stare at the screen for a while longer, then try again.

"The problem with love is that it's a story we tell ourselves. The truth is what comes after the story ends, when you have to live with the version of yourself you made up just to get through it."

I read it three times, then delete it.

From somewhere in the office, a laugh rises, cuts through the hum, and dies. I wait for the sound to fade before I start again.

I'm not sure if I'm constipated or in love, but either way, the result is the same: a head full of nothing, a heart not even in the right postcode, and a column that refuses to write itself.

The dog café is so on-the-nose it feels like a setup. "Paws & Pause" sits on the corner of a street that can't decide if it's Shoreditch or Hackney, the frontage painted eggshell blue, the windows already misted up from the body heat of fifty Instagrammers and their canine accessories. Inside, the air is an emulsion of coffee, wet fur, and the base note of low-key panic you get wherever more than three creatives are forced to make small talk.

I'm early. Not intentionally, but that's how it shakes out. I claim a battered sofa near the window, order the cheapest black coffee on offer, and try not to look like the sort of man who sits alone in a dog café and waits. It's not easy. There are at least seven dogs in the room, each with an affectation more ridiculous than the last: a Whippet in a tartan jacket, a Shih Tzu with pink bows, a Corgi whose owner is treating him to a "puppuccino" while narrating every move on TikTok Live. The only other unaccompanied human is a man in a fleece, hunched over a dog-eared copy of *Infinite Jest* and sipping mineral water with the caution of someone who's been burned before.

I pass the time by rewriting the intro to the column in my head. "Modern romance is a competition to see who can be least themselves, for the longest amount of time." Too bleak. "Dating in the twenty-first century: it's all fun and games until someone gets doxxed." Too topical. The coffee arrives. It's not hot, but it's bracingly bitter, which seems appropriate.

Grace is ten minutes late. She materialises in the doorway in a tailored navy blazer, hair scraped back, glasses glinting in the sickly overhead bulbs. For a second, she looks straight at me, the old laser-guided targeting system in full effect. Then she zeroes in and threads her way through the obstacle course of leashes and over-caffeinated Schnauzers.

She sits, smooth as always, and doesn't bother to shed the blazer even though it's a full five degrees warmer inside. She looks more out of place than the man with *Infinite Jest*, and somehow that makes her seem even more in control.

"Hi," she says.

"Hi," I echo, raising the cup as if to toast our mutual suffering.

She glances around, lips pursed, taking the place in with a single scan. "Is it just me, or does it smell like hospital in here?"

I think about it, inhale. "Could be the antiseptic. Or the dog flatulence."

She writes something on her phone, thumb moving fast. I try not to imagine the notes: "PAUL: SHAMBOLIC, DOG

CAFE: ALSO TRAGIC." She orders a tea, then folds her hands on the table, posture so rigid she could be auditioning for a West End revival of 'Statue.'

"So," she says, "we're doing this."

"Apparently."

"We need some photos," she says, as if it's the most natural thing in the world.

I grimace. "I'd rather stick my head in the ball pit."

She doesn't laugh. "You know the drill. The readers eat it up."

I suppose I do. There's a camera on every surface in the room, including the one in my own hand, recording this for posterity and/or HR compliance.

She lines up her phone, angles us in a way that crops out most of the awful décor, and snaps three pictures in rapid fire. I make a face in all of them, but she picks the least awful and posts it to the joint column's Instagram with a caption that would make even the algorithm wince.

"Smile," she instructs, though it's already too late.

We lapse into a silence that is almost companionable. A Labrador sidles up to our table, sniffs my knee, and then lays its enormous head in Grace's lap. She doesn't flinch, just pats it absently, the same way you'd tap an elevator button. The owner, a woman in oversized headphones and a sweatshirt that reads "GRL PWR," flashes us a thumbs-up and returns to her oat latte.

"So," I say, "how's it going?"

She shrugs, not breaking eye contact with the dog. "Fine."

I try again. "You get any feedback from Sarah?"

She nods. "She wants more banter. And maybe more on-location shots, if we can fake not hating each other for five minutes."

"I don't hate you," I say, too quick.

She looks at me, really looks. "You don't?"

I shake my head. "If I did, this would be easier."

The dog lifts its head, bored with the lack of snacks, and trundles away to lick the hand of a child who's clearly allergic.

Grace watches it go, then checks her phone. "We have to make this look good," she says. "We're on the homepage next week."

"Wouldn't want to let down the fans," I say, and instantly wish I hadn't.

She must sense it, because her voice softens. "It's just a job."

It isn't, but I let her pretend.

A waitress in a polka-dot apron brings Grace's tea. The cup is shaped like a Pug's face, which is either on-brand or a hate crime, depending on your view of novelty crockery. Grace sips, then grimaces.

"They put cinnamon in it," she says, setting it down like evidence.

I smile. "You could complain."

She shakes her head. "I don't do complaints. Just action items."

"Classic," I say, and it's meant as a joke, but it lands flat.

I try to steer the conversation somewhere less awkward, but every road leads back to the thing we're not saying. She's still scrolling on her phone, probably triaging emails, but every so often she glances at me over the rim of her glasses, as if she's waiting for something to happen.

It does.

A Golden Retriever puppy, barely more than a sentient mop, barrels into the side of our table and yelps in surprise. The owner—a man with the look of someone who once worked in finance and now sells essential oils—apologises profusely, then immediately pivots to cooing at the dog in baby talk. The puppy shakes it off, then licks my hand in solidarity.

Grace laughs, a real one, sharp and unexpected. It cuts through the haze like a starting pistol.

"You used to hate dogs," she says, still smiling.

"I hated the metaphor," I correct. "Loyalty, unconditional love, all that. Always seemed like a setup for disappointment."

She nods. "You're good at that. Seeing the disaster in everything."

"It's a skill," I say.

"You should put it on LinkedIn."

For a moment, we're back in the student newsroom, surrounded by deadlines and instant noodles and the certainty that everything matters. I almost say it, but the puppy has found a stray bit of pastry and is devouring it with the intensity of a convict on death row. The moment passes.

A woman at the next table leans over, smiling at us. She's middle-aged, silver streak in her hair, wearing a scarf that costs more than my monthly food budget. "Excuse me," she says, "but you two are just adorable. Are you married?"

The question lands with the weight of a thrown brick. I open my mouth to answer, but Grace is quicker.

"Not yet," she says, voice bright and cold as tonic.

The woman claps her hands together. "Oh, how lovely! You remind me of my daughter and her fiancé. University sweethearts. They're having a dog-themed wedding next month. You should see the invites."

She rummages in her purse, fishing out her phone, and starts scrolling through photos. Grace's hand is suddenly on my forearm, a warning or a lifeline, I can't tell.

"We met at university," I say, and the words are true enough. "We worked on the student paper together."

"Oh, so romantic!" the woman beams. "Rivals to lovers, then?"

I glance at Grace, who holds my gaze longer than I can stand.

"Something like that," she says.

We leave it there. The woman shows us three pictures of Pugs in tuxedos, then turns her attention to the Labradoodle at her feet. The background noise swells, then settles.

Grace lets go of my arm, but the ghost of her hand stays.

She drains her tea, then sets the cup down, aligning it perfectly with the edge of the saucer. "We should go," she says.

I nod. "I'll get the bill."

At the counter, the barista rings it up, then asks if we want to buy a branded mug for charity. I say yes, because it's easier than saying no. Grace waits by the door, arms crossed, lost in her phone.

Outside, the air is sharp, and the sky is just starting to bruise. We stand there for a minute, neither of us ready to move on.

"You know," I say, "we could just write the truth."

She arches an eyebrow. "About what?"

"About why we're really doing this."

She considers it, then shakes her head. "No one would believe us."

"Maybe that's the point," I say.

She laughs again, softer this time. "You're impossible."

She hails a cab, and I watch as she disappears into the city, leaving me holding the mug, the bill, and the memory of her laugh.

I walk home. The streets are full of dogs, and for the first time in a while, I don't mind.

I get back to my flat, open my laptop, and start typing.

"The thing about modern love is, it's not the lies that get you. It's the moments when the truth slips out, raw and unscripted, and you have to pretend you didn't hear it. That's what keeps you coming back for more."

I don't delete it.

I just keep going, word after word, until the truth is the only thing left.

ELEVEN

---♥---

GRACE

A new week and I arrive at my desk to find two new cables and a fresh Post-it from Facilities warning me to "avoid socket #6—possible sparks." I tuck my bag under the desk, plug in anyway, and begin my daily ritual of synchronising four calendars, five inboxes, and an ever-growing graveyard of embargoed press releases. The only evidence I exist, other than the sodium-glow of my monitor, is a coffee cup from the Pret in the foyer, still too hot to drink.

The air is already charged. You can smell the viral moment coming, like the metallic ozone before a storm. Today's running joke—besides the fact that no one has seen HR in weeks—is that "Modern Connection," our once-parody dating column, has now overtaken the entire Politics desk in unique users. The headline on the wall, in magnetic letters: "Sex Sells, But Only If You're Sad." I wrote that. Sarah stuck it up. Paul added a penis drawing with a Biro.

I flex my hands, open Slack, and begin methodically working through the overnight pings. There's the usual crop of corrections, a running sub-tweet about the state of my hair ("the eternal ponytail"), and three separate reminders from the publisher about the "content alignment" session at 10:30. I reply with a passive-aggressive emoji, then move to the day's briefs.

This week's column will be "Conflict in Relationships: Why We Love to Fight." I scan through the outline I typed up last night. My notes are meticulous, almost pathological, and I read them the way a patient reads a prescription label—seeking reassurance, but mostly expecting side effects. The first draft is half-finished and twice-revised; I hate it already.

The noise in the bullpen ratchets up a notch, and I hear my own name. Not directly, but in the dog-whistle register of journalists who know how to gossip without attribution.

"She's got a call with Legal at eleven," says the woman from Finance, loud enough for the Features desk to register. "Apparently, it's to do with the—" she glances around, lowers her voice, "the Payout Scandal."

"Is that the same as the Divorcegate thing?" asks a junior from Data.

"No, that's a different legal nightmare. This one's got NDAs and some shadow donors involved. Could be a charity scam."

They both laugh, the kind that's more about warding off doom than actual amusement. I keep my face blank, eyes on my screen. The cup is now at optimal temperature; I take a sip, and burn my tongue anyway.

A notification pops up in the corner of my screen: #legal-hotfix. The message is from Sarah, but it's tagged to me and Paul.

URGENT: Drop whatever you're working on—case just broke re: charity scam, but source is redacted. Potential huge scoop. See if Callaghan's contacts can dig up donor's ID.

I'm about to dig right in and then stop. Why should I lead?

If Paul's going to share the byline, he can do some bloody work for once. I message Paul, ask him to send over his initial thoughts, grab my bag and decide now's as good a time as any to go and visit Mum.

The journey back to Surrey is exactly as I remember it: two hours of suburban crawl, forty minutes of pure M25 hell, then the long, gashed lanes through villages with names that sound like a middle-class sigh. I pull up on the driveway, tyres sinking into the same muddy divots that ruined my first pair of white trainers in year seven. The house looks smaller every time I come home, shrinking in sympathy with the bones of my mother, who is waiting at the door with a tea towel over one shoulder and the local newspaper in the other hand.

"Grace, darling, you look exhausted," she says, pulling me into a hug that leaves a dusting of icing sugar on my blazer.

I want to protest, say it's just the light, but there's a mirror in the hall and I can see the smudges under my eyes, the ponytail already rebelling against the hours of suppression. I follow her into the kitchen, the true heart of the house, where the oven is always on and the fridge is held together by charity magnets. The table is set for two, tea brewing in the pot with the crack down the side.

She sits, gestures for me to do the same. "I hope you like lemon drizzle. Your father's got high cholesterol, so I substituted the butter, but don't tell him. He's at golf, he'll be sorry to miss you." She slices with clinical precision, slides the plate my way. The lemon icing is so tart it makes my gums ache.

We do the usual dance—small talk, the news, the weather, local politics: "Disgraceful, the council," she says, "absolute corruption." She asks about my job, the new column, whether I'm getting on with "the team." I tell her it's fine, that the new regime is "innovative," that I'm enjoying the challenge. All the lies are easy, the grooves worn smooth by years of practice.

She narrows her eyes, the way she always does when she senses blood in the water. "You're working too hard again. I can tell. It's in the jaw."

I touch my face, surprised. "I'm just tired. Deadlines."

"It's always deadlines with you, Grace." She pours more tea, the liquid the colour of old pennies. "I read your last article, you know. The Modern Romance one."

My face goes hot, then cold. "Did you?"

"I did. I thought it was clever, the way you and Mr. Callaghan sparred. Very sharp, very lively. Is he still a—what's the word—menace?"

I laugh, for real this time. "He's a professional liability, but they pay him to be one."

She nods, satisfied. "Well, he's got a way with words. Not as clever as you, but entertaining. I always said you needed someone to keep you on your toes."

I go for a second slice of cake, mostly to have something to do with my hands. "Mum, please."

She ignores me, starts fussing with the post on the counter, then doubles back. "I worry about you, you know. You don't have to be perfect all the time. Nobody does."

I make a noncommittal noise, pretending to read the headlines on her newspaper, but she's already moving in for the kill.

"There's a box in the hall," she says, voice casual. "I found it in the attic. It's got some of your old things—school reports, those awful birthday cards, photos from university. I thought you might want to look through it before I throw it all out."

She says, "throw it all out," but I know she'll keep every scrap, and we'll go through this same dance in about four years' time. I nod, willing her to drop the subject.

She doesn't. "There's a photo of you and Paul in there, actually. The one from the Ball. You remember?"

I do. I remember everything about that night: the cheap wine, the lost shoes, the way Paul made me laugh so hard I choked on a vol-au-vent. I remember the picture because it was the first time I saw myself happy in a photo, not just posing for it. I also remember how I'd deleted it from my old Facebook the day after we broke up—if you can call it that—like a surgeon excising a tumour.

"Mum, I really don't—"

She gets up, returns with the box, and sets it on the table between us. "Just look through it, Grace. For me."

I sigh, open the lid. Inside: a mess of pastel cards, all written in my mother's perfect French cursive; a handful of school merit certificates (mostly "Effort" or "Attendance"); a battered copy of *The Catcher in the Rye* with my name and school year written on the inside cover. The photo is at the bottom, face down, as if it snuck in when no one was watching.

I flip it over. There we are: me in a navy evening dress, Paul in a rented tux, hair three inches too long, and a smile wide enough to be mistaken for sincerity. His arm is around my shoulders, my hand on his chest. We're both looking at the camera, but I remember we were laughing at something else—the photographer's disastrous attempt at flirting, maybe, or the memory of the drinks we'd just stolen from the bar.

My chest tightens. I don't want to feel anything, but the feeling is there anyway. Nostalgia, maybe, or its malignant cousin, regret.

"He was a handsome boy," my mother says, peering over my shoulder. "Even with that ridiculous hair."

I snort, then tuck the photo under a stack of old birthday cards. "We're not exactly friends now, Mum."

She shrugs, unconcerned. "That's life. You lose people, but you never really forget them."

I want to argue, to say I've forgotten plenty, but instead I just trace the edge of the photo with my thumb, the cardboard soft from years of handling.

She pours the last of the tea, sits back, and surveys me. "You'll be all right, Grace. Just stop trying so hard to prove it."

I smile, the polite kind, and say nothing.

After lunch, I make an excuse to "check emails" and retreat to the guest room. The air is thick with the scent of lavender sachets and the faint, ghostly trace of my father's aftershave. I sit on the bed and stare at my phone, but all I can see is the picture of Paul and me, laughing at something only we understood.

I run a hand over my hair, smoothing the ponytail, then pull it loose. It falls in a wild, tangled curtain, the way I used to wear it at uni. I stare at myself in the mirror, trying to find the girl from the photo. She's there, but faded, like someone turned the saturation down to zero.

For a long time, I just sit, the box open on the bed, the old life and the new one separated by nothing more than a thin membrane of time and denial.

When I finally go back to the kitchen, my mother is putting away the cake, humming along to the radio. She glances up, eyes bright. "Did you find anything worth keeping?"

I shake my head, but I slip the photo into my bag anyway.

"Just old stuff," I say.

She nods, as if that answers everything.

We spend the afternoon weeding the garden, a silent truce between generations. She tells me about the neighbours, the dog that keeps escaping, the new vicar at St. Mark's. I listen, half-present, my mind still turning the past over like a worry stone.

When I finally leave, the sun is low over the hedgerows. My mother hugs me at the door, then stands on the step, waving until I turn the corner, out of sight.

Before I join the motorway, I pull over to check my phone. There's a message from Sarah ("legal wants a rewrite on the romance draft") and one from Paul ("need to catch you up. charity scam's breaking wide. call me if you have time.")

I don't reply to either, not yet.

Instead, I open my bag and look at the photo again. I trace our faces, the awkward tangle of arms, the wide, wild, unguarded smiles.

Then I tuck it away, safe and secret, and promise myself that one day I'll figure out what to do with it.

For now, I just let myself feel the ache, the familiar bruise, and drive with it on my lap all the way back to London.

TWELVE

PAUL

I can always tell when I'm about to do something idiotic by the taste of my breath. This morning it's copper, wet coins, and cold tea—a flavour that means I'm walking into a trap, but not yet sure who's set it.

I've been working on this story for weeks—feeding scraps of my life into it like coal into a dying furnace. Late nights, off-the-books calls, a dozen leads that went nowhere until one finally did. Grace thinks I've been slacking off, not pulling my weight on the column, but she doesn't know. Couldn't. This isn't something you share. Not until it's real. Not until you've got something no one else does.

Except now, someone else does.

The whispers started yesterday: another reporter, different paper, same target. The charity story—my charity story— wasn't mine anymore, not unless I moved fast.

So here I am, chasing ghosts, hoping my contact still has what he promised. Proof. Paper. Something tangible before the whole thing slips away. I should tell Grace. I should tell

Sarah. Hell, I should tell someone. And I will, if I have the proof to back it up.

The print shop is exactly where it's always been: back end of a railway viaduct in Hackney, the bricks mottled with a century of coal smoke, the sign above the steel shutter so faded it could be in any language. You only find this place if you're already looking for it, and you only look for it if you're desperate, deranged, or a freelance journalist with too much time and not enough fear.

Inside, it's forty degrees and airless. The press is running, and the whole unit smells of scorched plastic, ancient oil, and that bitter, chemical tang you get from toner left to stew. There's a fluorescent overhead that buzzes like it's prepping for its final performance. The only source of ventilation is a tilt window wedged open with a gnarled offcut of wood, through which I can just about see the feet of a man having a smoke on the pavement above. I close the door behind me, and the noise doubles, like a threat.

The man at the press doesn't look up. He never does; not until you're close enough to grab or be grabbed. He's wiry, bent in the middle from a decade at the platen, hands tattooed with old chemical burns and fresh ink. He's wearing a T-shirt with the sleeves hacked off and a slogan about unions that would get you blacklisted from three-quarters of Fleet Street. His name, for the purposes of my notebook, is "Stan," but nobody has ever called him that in my hearing.

I wait for him to finish whatever delicate operation he's pretending to do, then clear my throat in what I hope is a casual, unbothered way. It comes out a bit ragged. He doesn't react at first, just slaps the side of the press with the back of his hand and lets the machine shudder to a halt. The silence is immediate and so loud it's actually painful.

He turns, wipes his hands on a rag that might once have

been a Union Jack, and inspects me through the smeared Perspex of his safety goggles.

"Callaghan," he says, drawing out the syllables like he's tasting blood. "Didn't think you'd show."

"Slow news week," I reply. "And I was in the area."

He grins, showing a row of teeth that look like old ivory chess pieces. "You're never in the area, mate. Not unless someone's paid you to be."

He's not wrong, but it stings more than it should. I wonder if he knows about the freelance gigs drying up, or if he just assumes everyone is hustling now.

"You got the thing?" I ask, because small talk is the enemy.

He nods toward the battered metal desk at the back. "Over there. Envelope, just like you said. But you didn't say why."

I do my best impression of a man with somewhere better to be. "You know how it is. *The Chronicle* needs proof of concept. Editor wants paper. Maybe they'll pay me this time."

He shrugs, and his shoulders make a sound like crumpling tinfoil. "It's all digital now, you know. No one gives a shit about hard copies anymore. Except..." He gives me a look that's less curiosity and more post-mortem.

"Except people who know how easy digital is to scrub," I finish for him.

He laughs at that, a dry smoker's hack that goes on too long and ends with a wheeze. "You ever get tired of being clever, Callaghan? Or does it just get you laid?"

"Neither," I say. "But it keeps me alive."

He shakes his head, like he's giving up on a bad rescue. Then he walks over to the desk, fumbles in a drawer, and retrieves a manila envelope that is so saturated with finger oil and printer dust it might as well be a biohazard. He sets it on the desk, but doesn't let go.

"Look," he says, voice lower now, "I know I'm just a

middleman, but I hear things. I heard about the last guy who poked into this one. The charity scam. The offshore bit."

I try to play dumb, but my body betrays me—a twitch of the thumb against my jeans, a white-knuckle clench of the hand I didn't even realise was fisted. "Yeah?"

"Yeah." His eyes narrow, and I remember the time I saw him break a man's index finger for missing a payment. "Bloke from one of the broadsheets. Used to come in all the time, flapping his gums, buying round after round at the Lion. Proper journo, not a hack like you."

"Flattered."

"He stopped coming round. Word is, he took a job in Sydney. Word is, he didn't want to go, but someone persuaded him."

I meet his eyes, which is a mistake. "You think I'm going to Australia?"

He shakes his head slowly. "I think you should stop asking about charities that don't want to be questioned. I think you should take the envelope, walk out, and never come back."

We both look at the envelope, which now seems less like an envelope and more like a dead rat, delivered as a warning.

"Is this a threat, Stan?"

He smiles, but there's nothing behind it. "I don't do threats. I do printing. And I don't want blood on the press, if it's all the same to you."

My hand is sweating, but I reach for the envelope and slip it into the pocket of my jacket, trying to look casual. "Some stories are worth it," I say, which is a line I've lifted from a film and immediately regret.

He shakes his head again, this time with something close to pity. "Not this one. Some stories eat the people who write them."

I want to laugh, to make a joke about journalism and cannibalism and the time the *Express* sent me to cover a vegan food fight in Ealing. But I don't. Instead, I say, "Good thing I've got nothing to lose," and head for the door.

He calls after me, voice flat, "Some stories ain't worth the byline, Callaghan. Remember that."

I step out into the daylight, which is a mistake. My eyes sting, and the street seems louder, the traffic more insistent. I duck into the first corner shop I see, buy a bottle of water and an energy bar, and stand in the aisle like I've forgotten how food works.

My hand is still trembling, so I take the envelope out and hold it against my chest for a second, just to feel something solid and real. Then I stuff it back inside my jacket pocket, pay for the water, and cross the road, headed for the tube station. My phone buzzes twice, both from Grace: "Where are you?" and then, two minutes later, "Sarah wants us in at three. Don't be late."

I reply, "On my way," then delete the message before it's sent, and keep walking. The whole way, I can feel the sweat in my armpits and the blood pounding in my ears, as if I've already been chased and caught.

Maybe I have.

When I reach the newsroom, the envelope is still warm.

I think about what Stan said about the other journalist, and wonder if anyone would bother sending me to Australia.

Then I think about Grace, and Sarah, and the story I'm holding in my pocket, and decide it doesn't matter. Some stories eat the people who write them. Maybe I'll get a byline out of it first.

I walk up the stairs, one at a time, and try not to look over my shoulder.

I hit the newsroom at peak density, the whole Features bullpen humming with the sound of semi-lucid people trying to type themselves out of irrelevance. It's the hour when everyone's caffeine is peaking and the temperature is climbing, the air is a soup of budget deodorant, and the faint, burnt-caramel note of instant coffee reheated in the microwave. The overhead fluorescent tube lights are running a sweepstake to see which will explode first, and the only relief comes from the windows, which have been cracked open just enough to let in traffic noise and the occasional bit of rain.

Grace is already at the desk, which means I'm late even though I'm technically early. She's in full battle array—hair back, blouse buttoned to the throat, her arsenal of gel pens and marker tabs deployed like a colour-coded Maginot Line. I can't tell if she's angry or just focused, but the way her jaw flexes as she chews her thumbnail tells me it's both, plus a third thing she'll never admit.

"Nice of you to join us," she says, without looking up.

"Wouldn't want to ruin the streak," I say, sliding into the chair opposite. The seat cushion is the same one we had at the *Express*, except with less gum and more ambition.

She glances at the envelope poking out of my jacket pocket. "That the big scoop, then?"

I nod. "Printer's copy. Original is long gone, but the scans survived. We get one go at this before they realise what's out."

She picks up a Post-it, then puts it down. "I've already traced the payment flow. It's mostly circular—donor to shell, shell to the charity, then out again. Only thing missing is a signature."

"That's where this comes in," I say, tapping the envelope like it's an explosive device. "Stan says there's an authorisation form in there. Signed. Dated. We run it, it'll go nuclear."

She doesn't react, but I see the flicker of her eye as she

recalibrates. "Or it'll bring Legal down on our heads, and the whole piece will be buried under a stack of NDAs."

"We go public first," I say, pulling the envelope all the way out and setting it on the desk. "Force them to respond."

She leans forward, voice low. "This isn't the *Express*, Paul. We have a process. I'm not putting my byline on something that'll get us sued into oblivion before it even prints."

"You think *The Chronicle* isn't *The Express* now? We've merged. Name and process," I mutter, too loud. A couple of the freelancers look over, then go back to pretending they aren't listening.

Grace stares at me, hard. "I think we owe it to the source not to blow up their life without at least a day of fact-checking. You want a scalp, fine. I want a story."

"Don't act like you're the ethical one here," I shoot back, and now my heart is properly racing. "You're just as desperate as the rest of us. You just want to get there without getting your hands dirty."

She goes pale, then red. "At least I don't burn every bridge on the way."

"Oh, please. You're the queen of plausible deniability." The words are coming faster than I can stop them. "You never do the dirty work yourself; you just let someone else light the match."

She sits back, folds her arms, and looks away. "You done?"

"Not even close," I say, but the edge is off now, replaced by a sick hollowness in my stomach.

There's a pause, filled only by the sound of the intern dropping a mug on the tiles and the head of Social swearing in Mandarin. I try to breathe, but the air feels thick.

Grace picks up her pen again, but she's not writing. "Look. I know you're good at this. You see angles nobody else does. Christ, you saw the whole story before anyone else had a sniff.

But you can't keep pretending you don't care who gets caught in the crossfire."

"You know what?" I say, louder this time, so the whole desk can hear if they want. "Not all of us had the luxury of broadsheet backing, Grace. Some of us did the rounds. Three months behind on rent, eating beans out of the tin, chasing dead-end stories because no one would return our calls. Some of us had to print our own CVs in the library because we couldn't afford a new ink cartridge."

She's looking at me now, and it's not anger. It's something else, something I don't want to name.

I press on, because it's either that or letting myself implode. "You want to know what tabloid theatrics are? It's getting paid seventy quid to ghostwrite a think piece for someone who doesn't even read the finished article. It's knowing you could break a story wide open if someone would just give you the time of day. It's—" My voice catches, and I pretend it's a cough.

Her hand is flat on the table, knuckles white. She says, "I didn't know it was that bad."

I snort. "Nobody knows. That's the point."

The bullpen is silent. Even the Socials team is pretending to be on a lunch break, but they're all tuned in. I can feel my face go hot.

Grace doesn't flinch. "Let's open it, then. Together."

I nod once, and we both reach for the envelope. My hands are shaking, hers steady as always. She slits the seal with a nail and fans out the contents on the desk.

There it is: a payment trail, some bank statements, a forged receipt. But at the bottom, a letterhead—official, pristine, with an actual wet signature. It's not just a story. It's a bullet.

She traces the name with her finger. "That's the CEO. That's—"

"The end of the line," I finish, the words a lead weight in my mouth.

We both sit there, staring at the page like it might explode. I realise I haven't exhaled for a full thirty seconds.

Grace speaks first. "We need to call Legal."

"Yeah," I say. "We do."

She looks at me, eyes softer than I've ever seen them. "Paul. I mean it. You're not alone. Not with this."

Something in my chest tries to uncurl, but I kill it before it gets anywhere. "Don't go all therapy-hour on me now. We've got a job to do."

"Okay, then."

She gathers the papers, stacking them with that mechanical precision she applies to everything, and stands. "I'll get the brief to Sarah. You want to draft the lede?"

I nod, still not trusting myself to speak.

She hesitates, then says, "You're good, you know. Really good. Even when you're an arse."

I can't help it—I smile, just a bit. "Takes one to know one."

She shakes her head, and for a split second, I think she's going to touch my arm or say something that will break the spell. Instead, she just leaves, the papers clutched to her chest.

I sit there, jaw clenched, hands braced on the table. The room is filling up again—phones ringing, people arguing over headlines, the day's scandals chasing each other around the screens. I watch the space where she just was, and wonder if maybe, just maybe, I haven't ruined everything yet.

Maybe this is how it starts. Not with the story, but with the truth of it.

I look at the blank document on my laptop and start typing, letting the words come, fast and raw and unedited.

This time, I don't delete anything.

THIRTEEN

GRACE

My assignment is to untangle a year's worth of charity money-laundering in a few hours. No pressure. I have colour-coded spreadsheets for every suspected donor, Post-its breeding across the keyboard, and a Word document so heavily commented it now scrolls like a conspiracy theorist's blog. It should feel like control, but all it does is amplify the terror of missing the obvious, of screwing up one connection and killing the story before it even gets to print.

I start with the payment trails. The donor records are a horror show of fake addresses, round-number transfers, and the sort of errors that either mean someone is laundering money or that British clerical workers have never encountered the spellcheck function. Each name is more generic than the last—Smith, Jones, Patel, a few double-barrelled disasters with a whiff of minor aristocracy—and each one is connected, by the world's most infuriating daisy chain, to a shell company on a beach in the South Pacific. Paul was surprisingly close with a lot of his guesswork, and his list of possible suspects is proving right more often than not. I triple-check the figures, then cross-reference them against the charity's own accounts, just in case I've lost my mind and am now inventing conspiracies for the hell of it.

It takes thirty-two minutes to confirm what we already knew: the numbers don't add up, and someone is lying. Probably several someones.

I jot a note—"follow up: Bexley Trust, March Q2 anomaly"—then realise I've written it in the margins of an unrelated brief. There's no time to fix it; if the world ends, I'll go down with my paperwork properly misfiled.

The Features team is louder than usual. I hear my name, then Paul's, in a volley of banter that manages to sound both admiring and savage. I resist the urge to look up, but the urge is strong. Paul's desk is a shrine to creative chaos: coffee rings, torn-up drafts, a tangle of charging cables like a nest for some rabid metal snake. He isn't there, which is both a relief and a challenge, because I can't triangulate my progress against his. He has a way of making every assignment look like child's play, even when he's barely clinging on.

Pen tapping on the notepad. Rapid, staccato, too loud even for me. I can't stop. The evidence refuses to line up, the gaps growing wider the more I fill them in. I try a breathing exercise I read about in an airport magazine: inhale, count to four, exhale, count to six, pretend you're not drowning. It works for exactly one breath before the panic returns, full-force.

"Grace," says a voice behind me. Sarah, in her usual green power suit and heels. She leans on the divider so hard the whole desk vibrates, then peers over my shoulder at my screen.

"Tell me you're close," she says, not unkindly, but not kindly either.

I drag the cursor down and highlight the key figures, hoping colour will compensate for the lack of substance. "Getting there. Payment trails are a swamp, but I've found at least three instances where the same money gets recycled through five different charities before winding up back with the original donor. It's"—I gesture helplessly at the mess—"an ecosystem of fraud."

Sarah is not impressed by metaphors. "I need a draft for Legal by five. And I need it tight, or it'll get bounced to the *Mail* and you'll have to live with the shame of being scooped by someone with a cartoon avatar."

I nod. "I'll have it. Just want to make sure it's—" I almost say 'perfect,' then catch myself. "—bulletproof."

She straightens, a satisfied glint in her eye. "Good. Because the Board is already prepping a back-pat for themselves, and if you trip, they'll pin it on you. Or me. Neither option is acceptable."

Sarah waits a half-beat, scanning the surface of my desk, then leans in closer, her perfume somehow medicinal and a little bit frightening. "We can't afford to lose this scoop to someone hungrier, Grace. I need you in kill mode. Can you do that?"

My hand is still tapping, but I force it to stop. "Yes," I say, with what I hope is conviction.

She gives a crisp nod, then glides away, leaving a cold trail of adrenaline in her wake.

I count to four. I exhale. I try to think about the numbers and not the way my stomach is turning itself into origami.

The phone rings again. Not mine—mine never rings, because the only people who want to talk to me are in this room, and they prefer to do it by shouting across the aisle. But the ringing is contagious; I check my mobile just in case, hoping for a miracle, maybe a text from a whistleblower from inside the charity who can help me figure it all out in the next hour or so. Nothing.

I go back to the master spreadsheet, but the columns are

swimming. I can't focus. The pressure is building behind my eyes, a dull, familiar ache.

I remember last week at the dog café, Paul saying, "The system is rigged, Grace. You can't beat it by playing nice."

At the time, I thought he was just being his usual self—cynical, charming, doomed—but now I hear the echo in every cell of my body. I want to believe it's not true, that the work matters, that we're more than just fast-twitch meat in a digital sausage grinder. But the numbers refuse to back me up.

My phone buzzes. This time it's an unknown number, and my heart leaps in hope before the fear sets in.

I answer, voice hoarse. "Hampton."

On the other end: static, then a woman's voice, low and urgent. "You need to stop. They're watching the comms."

Before I can even process that, the line goes dead.

I stare at the phone, thumb hovering over recall, but there's no point. Number withheld, just like always. The first time it happened, I assumed it was a prank, but now I know better. It's part of the dance, the warning that you're closer to the truth than anyone wants you to be.

I jot another note: "OPSEC. Check Signal." Then I realise I have no idea what I'm supposed to be checking for.

The room has got quieter. I glance up. Paul's desk is still empty, but the Features team is deep in conference, faces close, voices low. Every so often, someone glances in my direction, then looks away.

It should make me feel important, but all it does is raise the temperature another two degrees.

I force myself to drink some coffee. It tastes like chemical warfare, but I swallow anyway. My fingers tremble just enough to spill a drop on the trackpad. I wipe it away, then start again, line by line, forcing the data to align.

By four p.m., I have a draft strong enough to survive the

first round of Legal. I attach it to an email, type and retype the subject line, then just hit send before I can lose my nerve.

The adrenaline surge lasts exactly six seconds, then the panic returns, worse than before. I stare at the sent folder, waiting for a reply, knowing it'll be another hour before anyone gets back to me.

Across the office, the Editor is in her glass-walled sanctum, talking animatedly into her headset. Every so often, she stabs at her keyboard with two fingers, like a sniper picking targets. I watch, waiting for the moment she signals for me. In my head, I imagine the phrase: "We're going to press," and my name in the byline, and for a brief, traitorous second, I feel proud.

Then I remember Paul's warning, and the panic resets.

I check his desk again. Still empty, but a mug with his name ("Best Writer, Worst Human") is upside down on a pile of draft pages.

I try to get back to work, but the numbers blur. The phone buzzes again—this time a text from my mother, asking if I've eaten. I ignore it.

The second hand on the office clock ticks so slowly, I want to smash the face and set the hands free.

Forty minutes later, the Editor leans out of her glass box and barks, "Grace. My office. Now."

I don't stand; I unfold, like someone climbing out of a trench after a bombardment. My legs are wooden. I cross the floor, aware of every eye tracking my movement.

Inside the office, Sarah waves at a chair, and waits for the door to click shut.

"We're running your copy first thing tomorrow," she says without preamble. "Legal hates it, which means it's good."

For a moment, I don't register the compliment.

She steeples her hands, then fixes me with that predator gaze. "I need you to know something. This story is going to get ugly before it gets pretty. The donors will push back. The charity, and those implicated, will try to bury it. But if you hold your nerve, you could blow this open in a way that matters. Are you ready for that?"

My mouth is dry. I want to say yes, but what comes out is, "I don't know."

Sarah doesn't blink. "No one ever does. That's why it works."

She hands me a printout, already marked up with the sub-editor's red ink and lawyerly caveats. "Go home. Get changed and see what more you can find out tonight. Tomorrow is another day; you'll be famous or fired. Either way, you get a story out of it."

I take the printout and nod, trying to look like the kind of person who deserves this. I'm not sure I am.

Back at my desk, I gather my things, careful not to leave a trail of nerves behind. The room is mostly empty now; people vanish fast when the work is done. I scan the horizon for Paul, but he's not here, not even a sign that he ever was.

I sling my bag, drain the last of the coffee, and walk out, leaving the empty mug as a totem.

The anxiety stays with me all the way down the lift, out into the evening air, and onto the city street. It's only then, with the lights of the office receding, that I let myself wonder if Paul was right.

Maybe the system is rigged. Maybe we're all just waiting for the moment it eats us alive.

Or maybe, just maybe, I can be the one to change it.

I walk quickly into the darkness, my hand white-knuckled on the strap of my bag.

The venue is a monument to bad taste and excessive disposable income. Faux-Grecian pillars line the entryway, each one shrouded in white fabric and backlit with mood lighting the colour of haemoglobin. At the threshold, a quartet of violinists churns out "Rolling in the Deep" with a straight face. The effect is so perfectly ridiculous it makes me want to applaud or run for the fire exit.

My invitation said black tie, but no one told the dress code about inflation: every other woman in the lobby is poured into couture that could feed a developing nation for a year. I opted for the safest option in my wardrobe—a black sheath dress, nothing fancy, not too short, not too tight, just the sort of garment that says "I'm here to do business, please do not ask me to dance." My shoes are two inches high and one degree more sensible than the competition. The only hint of personality is the battered clutch, bulging slightly with my notebook, three pens, and an emergency tenner for the cloakroom.

There is a check-in desk at the entrance, flanked by twin ice sculptures of *The Kidz Trust* charity logo. Each guest gets a name badge with their organisation and a colour-coded lanyard—red for media, gold for "patrons," white for everyone else. The young woman manning the desk gives me a once-over, notes the bag, and smiles with the neutral competence of someone who's trained to spot a gatecrasher at fifty paces.

"Hampton? *Chronicle?*" she asks.

I nod, hand her my invitation, and try not to sweat through the dress.

She slides the badge across and whispers, "Bar's to the left. Canapés in the garden room." She makes it sound like the two will never meet.

Inside, the event is already at capacity. Every conversation is at maximum decibel, every glass refilled before it's empty. Waiters in black bow ties ferry trays of *amuse-bouches*—micro-blinis, pipettes of something that might be gazpacho, spoons of luminous roe—while the guests circulate in tight little swarms. I spot at least three MPs, two media columnists I'd sell a kidney to ghostwrite for, and a quartet of minor celebrities, all pretending not to recognise one another. The head of the charity is holding court near the stage, flanked by an entourage of aides and what looks like a human rights barrister in Versace.

I make a circuit, working the perimeter. The plan is to blend, observe, identify the power brokers and the weak points in the herd. We'll publish with or without it, but if I can get a whistleblower on record...

Every so often, I pause to scrawl a note: "Donor w. cuff-links, deep tan, accent South African. Seated w/ potential wife, not listed on sheet. Possible shell co.?" or "Lobbyist, female, 60s, Prada. Talks to everyone, forgets names." I'm not the only journalist present, but the rest stick together like a feral pack, swapping tips and biting at the open bar. I avoid them, for now.

I down a flute of Cava (not *actual* Champagne; I can taste the supermarket aisles), then another, just to get the edge off. My stomach is in a knot, a mixture of social dread, anticipation over the article that's a matter of hours away from publication, and the persistent knowledge that I do not belong in this room. If anyone here remembers my byline, it will be because of the Divorcegate exposé, or the time I accidentally called a senior party advisor "sexually extinct" on live radio. Maybe it will be different after tomorrow morning's headline.

The first three conversations are predictable: one man pitches me a piece on "crypto-philanthropy," a woman from a rival paper tries to interrogate me about what I'm working on ("just human interest, the usual, you know how it is"), and a man with the teeth of a shark tells me he loves my columns but never reads them. I smile, nod, collect a business card, then ghost all three the second their attention turns elsewhere.

"Grace," says a voice behind me. I flinch.

It's Sarah, somehow appearing out of thin air. She's

dressed for the occasion—satin suit, hair glossy, eyes doing their best not to roll at the spectacle. "You're meant to be networking," she hisses. "Not lurking by the coat check."

I force a smile. "Just surveying the terrain."

"Good. Survey it while talking to donors. Get some quotes. And for God's sake, try to look like you're enjoying yourself." She flashes a diplomat's grin, then vanishes, absorbed into the crowd.

I attempt another lap, this time more assertively. I shake hands with a man who runs a homelessness charity, trade barbs with a *Sun* reporter, and end up locked in a three-way debate about "impact journalism" with a pair of new media influencers who have more Instagram followers than I have brain cells. All the while, I'm scanning for someone—anyone— who looks even remotely like an insider, or a source.

At the bar, I finally locate my mark: the finance director of the foundation, one of the key signatures on the suspect documents. She's small, sharp-featured, and wears her stress like a badge of honour. I sidle in, order a glass of white, and time my opening line perfectly.

"Busy night," I say.

She laughs, hollow. "Busy year."

I lean in. "Bet it's tough, keeping the books straight with all these new regulations."

She gives me a look that is both calculated and a little bit desperate. "You have no idea."

We make small talk, the surface stuff. She's good at it, professional, never letting the mask slip. But every so often, her eyes dart to the side, like she's afraid of being watched.

I steer the conversation toward the audit. "I heard there's some kind of review coming up."

She freezes, just for a second, then recovers. "Standard procedure. These days, you have to prove everything three times over."

"Red tape," I say, commiserating. "The hoops they make you jump through."

She shrugs. "It's a job." Then, softer, "Honestly, I just want to help people. It's not always like this, you know."

I nod, and for a second, I almost believe her.

"Excuse me," she says, and slips away, glass in hand. I watch her join the oversight chair and the tech bro, heads bent close. It's going to be difficult to get one of them alone and comfortable enough to speak.

I retreat to the edges, heart pounding. I'm about to pull out my notebook and start synthesising when I see him.

Paul, in a tuxedo.

He is across the room, leaning against a pillar like he owns it. The hair is combed, the stubble trimmed, the shirt actually ironed. He is talking to a man in a dinner jacket, but his eyes are not on the conversation—they're scanning the crowd, doing the same reconnaissance I am.

For a moment, he doesn't see me. Then he does, and the change is instantaneous: a flicker of recognition, then the old, insolent half-smile. He gives a micro-nod, then turns his attention back to the mark.

I should feel triumphant, seeing him out of his element, but all it does is trigger a fresh wave of annoyance. He disappeared for the whole day, and didn't contribute to the article at all. If he's here, it's because he's working the same angle. And if he's working the same angle, he's either about to blow the story open or burn it down for both of us.

I duck into the corridor leading to the terrace, needing air, needing to regroup. The night is cold, and the city lights are fractal through the cheap glass doors. I stand there, hands clenched on the railing, trying to plan my next move.

It doesn't matter, because a second later, Paul joins me.

"Didn't expect to see you here," he says, his voice lower than I remember.

I pretend not to care. "It's a free country."

He laughs softly. "Not in this crowd."

I glance sideways. "Nice tux."

He shrugs. "Rented. Like most of the people in that room."

We stand in silence. It's not comfortable, but it's less dangerous than talking.

Finally, he says, "How close are you?"

I don't pretend to misunderstand. "Have enough to make some noise. Legal are happy to publish. Just missing a quote or an admission on the record."

He grins, but there's no malice in it. "You always were better at this."

"Then why do you always get there first?" I shoot back.

He looks at me, really looks, and I feel the familiar current —irritation, admiration, something else. "Maybe I'm just better at sniffing out the bullshit because I've spent longer wading through it."

We lapse again, watching our breath fog in the cold.

Inside, the party surges, oblivious to the two of us freezing to death for the sake of professional pride.

He turns. "You want to work together on this, or keep doing the Cold War thing?"

I hesitate. I want to say yes, but I'm still pissed off that he abandoned his post after delivering the evidence. I wanted to work with him this afternoon, not now, after I've already written the damn article.

I look at him, the black of his suit almost blue in the neon spill from the function room. For a second, I remember the uni parties, the debates, the arguments that ended in laughter or, occasionally, a broken glass. I remember what it felt like to trust him, and what it felt like when that trust broke.

I say, "You first. What do you have?"

He grins. "Not a lot. Yet."

I laugh, despite myself. "So, business as usual."

He puts a gentle hand on my shoulder. "But I'll find something."

I nod, and he drops his hand, the contact lingering as heat.

We go back inside, side by side. The party is in full spate; the music has shifted to seventies disco, and most of the guests are line-dancing near the silent auction table.

Paul and I head for the bar. He orders a whisky, neat. I go for another Cava. We stand close, arms almost touching, surveying the chaos.

I whisper, "We need to talk to the oversight chair."

He nods. "She's slippery."

"She's hiding something," I say, keeping my voice low.

He turns to face me, and for a second, we're the only two people in the room. "What do you think it is?"

I shake my head. "Money, always. Or power. But I don't think she's the brains."

He grins. "You're the brains."

I flush, unbidden.

There's a commotion near the silent auction—someone has knocked over a tray of glasses, and the sound ricochets off the marble. People look up, drawn to the drama. In the confusion, I spot the finance director slipping out toward the rear staircase, phone to her ear, moving fast.

I nudge Paul. "Now or never."

He nods, and we move together, weaving through the crowd like we've been doing it for years. At the stairwell, we catch up just as she ducks into a side corridor.

She turns, startled to see us both.

"Oh, hi," she says, voice brittle.

Paul smiles, easy. "Didn't mean to intrude. Just wanted a word."

She eyes us. "About what?"

I pull out my notebook, pen ready. Paul produces his phone, voice recorder already rolling.

"We just want to understand the process," I say. "How the audits work. Who signs off. Where the oversight comes in."

She sighs, leaning against the wall. "Look. I don't know what tree you're barking up—"

"We're barking up the tree of truth. When this all comes out. And it will come out," Paul says slowly, pausing for effect. "Who do you think they'll blame?"

"I have no idea what you're talking about. Now, if you'll excuse me."

Paul stands aside to let her pass, holding out a card. "If you want to go on the record—"

She shakes her head. "Not yet."

We thank her, and she vanishes, leaving us in the echo of our own hubris.

"Pity. I thought she'd crack." Paul says.

"She'll wish she did."

Back in the ballroom, the noise has reached a fever pitch. The CEO is on stage, introducing the charity's "next great initiative." I can feel the phones coming out, the hashtags already trending.

FOURTEEN

---♥------------------

PAUL

There's no amount of cheap cologne or editorial cynicism that prepares you for a charity gala at the Savoy. The lights are calculated to flatter the richest, oldest skin; the glassware glints with that particular malice reserved for things you could never afford to break. Every surface is polished, every chair upholstered in the nervous flesh of a thousand dead cows. I stand with Grace on the periphery, shoulder to shoulder but never quite touching.

The charity's donors float around us like jellyfish—impeccable, translucent, stinging in ways you don't notice until it's too late. Half of them are called "Lord," the other half "Lady," and every conversation opens with the phrase, "Oh, a journalist, how quaint."

Grace has already gone a shade paler; she wears stress like a fine perfume, invisible but room-filling. Her dress is navy, severe, immaculately fitted, and I suddenly wish I'd spent more than three minutes flattening my hair or picking out cuff-links that didn't look like they came free with the tuxedo hire—which they did. In my defence, I did iron my shirt.

She says, "You look like you're plotting to rob the place."

I sip the whiskey, which is the second-best thing I'll drink tonight. "You look like you're going to buy it, bankrupt it, then have it condemned for health and safety transgressions."

Her mouth does the thing where she wants to smile, but is morally opposed. "That's not very progressive of you, Paul."

"It's not very progressive in here," I say, gesturing at the room. The bar is twenty-deep with men who make a million a year pretending to care about poor kids, and the canapés are so minimal they might as well be theoretical.

We hover near the edge of the main ballroom, both keeping a line of sight on the nearest exit, as if at any moment a fire alarm will sound and we can sprint for freedom. I check my phone, just to feel tethered to a world where I'm not a prop, and there it is: "Remember to SMILE!" from the Features Editor, with three grinning emojis that make me want to commit an act of violence against my own screen.

As if on cue, the charity's Social Media team materialises. They travel together like they're joined at the hip, and smell of nervous sweat and organic dry shampoo. Their leader—a man who made a name for himself overhauling the social media strategy of one of the budget airlines and describes himself as an "influencer whisperer"—approaches with the rigid energy of someone who's been mainlining Red Bull since puberty.

"Paul! Grace! *The Chronicle*, right? Perfect, perfect. We just need a quick photo for the 'gram—can you, ah, stand a little closer? Maybe put your arm around her shoulder? Great, thanks."

Grace's lips barely move. "I'd rather be shot."

I say, "It's for a good cause," and let the words hang, souring in the air like off-brand Prosecco.

The social guy lines us up in front of a flower wall that

looks like it cost more than my flat. The photographer—an actual professional, with a complicated-looking camera—positions us, adjusts my bow tie, and says, "A little less murder, Paul. Think 'friendly.'"

Grace leans in, but only just. I feel the heat of her shoulder, and it takes real effort not to close the gap. The camera clicks, flashes, and it's done. The Social guy checks his phone, smiles too wide, then shows us the post. "*Chronicle's* new golden duo," it reads, above our faces, side by side, caught mid-blink and half-grimace. I look like a hostage. Grace looks like the negotiator who's just about to pull the trigger.

It goes live before we can protest. My phone vibrates, and I see the likes stacking up—first from charity supporters, then from the rest of the newsroom. My jaw locks on instinct, an old muscle memory from the last time my face was used as clickbait.

Grace makes a sound, low and tight. "They're going to run this everywhere, aren't they?"

"Already done," I say. "We're trending for all the wrong reasons."

She swears under her breath, the word tight and economical. "Brilliant. Just brilliant." She downs the rest of her wine in a single swallow, then nods toward the kitchen corridor. "I need air."

I follow, partly because I want to, mostly because I'm not letting her out of my sight with this many enemies in the building.

We slip through a half-open door into a service corridor painted with that off-white shade you only see in places that fear liability more than death. The hum of the main room drops to a distant murmur; in here, it's the slow, comforting whirr of refrigeration and the clatter of staff prepping a fresh army of canapés.

Grace leans against the wall, arms crossed so tightly she

could probably arrest her own circulation. She doesn't look at me, just at the floor, where a single cocktail napkin has been crushed under the heel of a size-nine brogue. The silence is palpable.

She looks at me, really looks, and there's something in her face that I can't name without ruining it.

"Do you ever wish we could just... stop?"

"Stop what?"

She shrugs. "Stop pretending. Stop performing. Just be, for a minute."

I want to say yes, to admit that the only time I'm not rehearsing my own lines is when I'm talking to her. But I don't, because there are some truths you don't say out loud if you want to keep living in your own skin.

Instead, I say, "You know that's not possible. We're only as real as the next story."

She closes her eyes, as if that's the answer she expected but hoped she wouldn't get. "You're impossible."

"Not true. Just very, very consistent."

Her mouth twitches, and the silence grows lighter, more like the quiet that follows a storm. She looks past me, out to the main room, where the drone of conversation has reached a fever pitch. "We should get back. We need to get someone on record."

I nod, but neither of us moves.

A waiter glides past, a tray balanced on one hand, eyes flicking between us like he's stumbled upon a lovers' quarrel or the prelude to a staff mutiny. I catch the judgment in his glance and almost laugh.

Grace straightens, smooths her hair. "Ready to be the golden duo again?"

I say, "Only if you promise not to stab me with a mini-satay skewer."

"No promises," she says.

We step back into the glare of the ballroom. My phone buzzes again—this time a WhatsApp from Jamie: "You two are everywhere, mate. Might as well kiss on the dance floor and get it over with."

I show Grace. She reads it, then hands it back. "You're not my type."

I grin. "You don't have a type. You just have a very elaborate vetting process."

"Which you failed, spectacularly."

We let the crowd swallow us, but there's a thread between us now, invisible but tensile, and I know that if I tugged on it she'd probably follow. For a while, we mingle, we banter, we play the roles expected. But every time our eyes meet, the rest of the room blurs into static.

It's almost honest, in its own way.

I stand next to her in a hired suit I'll return tomorrow and pretend that being part of this golden duo isn't the best worst thing that's happened to me in years.

By the end of the night, everyone in the building has seen us together, and for once, I don't mind being watched.

The worst rain in London is not the biblical stuff, the kind that makes headlines and floods the Underground. It's the sideways, mean-spirited drizzle that turns umbrella canopies into concave swimming pools and makes every loose pavement slab a deathtrap. We stand under the portico—me, Grace, and a woman I think used to be the Home Secretary—all three of us marooned by the weather and the unavailability of affordable Ubers. The Savoy awning offers no protection, only the false hope that someone will eventually remember us out here and send for rescue.

Grace huddles deeper into her shawl, eyes narrowed at the

pelting rain. She's silent, which is never a good sign, and when I offer my jacket, she gives me the look reserved for men who have entirely missed the point of feminism. I shrug, hang the jacket over my arm, and watch the other guests squabble over the single black cab that's just pulled up.

In the end, it's one of the waiting staff, clearly keen to get home herself, who sorts the queue. "You're both heading east, yeah?" she says, pushing us towards the open cab. "Share, or we'll be here until the Thames recedes."

The driver clocks us and sighs, already bracing for a zero-banter fare with a side order of cold war. We pile in, Grace first, me after, and there's a moment where I think she might slide all the way to the far door, instead she parks herself dead centre, knees almost touching mine.

The inside of the cab is a greenhouse: damp, steamy, windows already filmed with condensation from a thousand wet nights before this one. The city outside is a wash of red and gold, tail lights and street lamps bleeding together in streaks. The seats are sticky with rainwater and I'm not sure what.

I give the driver my address. Grace mumbles hers, then corrects it, then says nothing more. For three whole minutes, we don't speak. I count the seconds on the digital clock, watch the beads of water race down the glass. The wipers beat a rhythm that is either comforting or funereal; I can't decide.

Grace is rubbing her shoulder, fingers kneading the muscle just above the collarbone. She does it absently, as if she's forgotten I'm there. But I haven't.

"Still gets you, does it?" I say quietly, like it's possible to keep a secret in the back of a London taxi.

She blinks, hand pausing mid-rub. "What?"

"Your shoulder."

She snorts, but it's not unkind. "You remember that?"

"I remember you played the last five minutes of the hockey

match with it hanging out of the socket. And still scored." I watch her face in the flickering streetlights, the way the memory tries to fight through the mask.

She shrugs, which is probably agony, but she's not going to admit it. "Reckless stupidity. You called it that."

"I was right," I say. "But it was impressive."

She glances at me, eyes searching for mockery, finds none. "You carried me off the pitch. Didn't think you'd remember that, either."

"Hard to forget the smell of mud, blood, and Head & Shoulders shampoo."

She laughs, short and sharp, and the tension in the car shifts from hostile to something else. Nostalgia, maybe. Or the first stage of grief.

The cab hits a pothole, and the memory shatters. We lurch in our seats, and her shoulder knocks into mine. For a second, she doesn't pull away. I can feel the heat of her through the wet cotton, and I want to say something that isn't a joke or a challenge.

Instead, I watch the window, where the city is blurring by too fast to make sense of any one detail. I wonder if this is what it's like inside her head: everything coming at speed, no time to process, just react and survive.

We hit a standstill on Hackney Road, traffic bunched up in a way that only happens when every other road in London has been shut for a royal visit or a charity fun run. The driver sighs and flicks the radio on, some late-night call-in show about the government's latest "initiative." Grace cracks her knuckles, a nervous habit I'd forgotten until just now.

At the next light, she looks over, voice low. "Why didn't you apply for the *Chronicle* Internship the next year?"

I hesitate, then answer honestly. "After slumming it as a freelancer for a year, I didn't feel like I belonged anymore."

She chews that over. "You always belonged, Paul. You just hated admitting it."

I want to argue, to point out all the ways I didn't fit, that I still don't, but it seems pointless now. "Maybe you're right."

She leans back, eyes closed, head against the rest. In the reflection, I see her mouth twist, not in pain but something like regret.

The cab finally pulls up outside my building, a 60s council block with the lights blown on half the entryway.

"You want to come up?" I ask before I can think better of it.

She raises an eyebrow. "For what?"

I don't have a good answer. "To dry off. Or... I don't know, drink tea."

"Sure," she says, paying the driver before sliding out of the cab, my jacket clutched over her head, and stands in the rain waiting for me to lead the way.

I do.

The rain is heavier now, soaking my shirt and running down my neck in cold sheets. The lights in the lobby are out, but she's already found the lift call button. I unlock the door, and we step into the darkness together, footsteps echoing off the tile.

I don't know why I offered, or why she said yes. I only know that her hand brushes mine as we walk along the corridor, and this time, neither of us pretends not to notice.

We reach my door. I fumble with the keys, wet and clumsy, but she waits, silent, watching me like she's not sure what happens next. Neither am I.

I push the door open, and we stand on the threshold, two drowned rats with nothing left to lose.

She says, "After you."

So I lead on.

The flat is cold and dim, the only light comes from the

streetlamps outside. She drops her wet shawl and my jacket to the floor. I go to the kitchen and put the kettle on because there are protocols for this, and I can't think of anything better.

She leans against the counter, arms folded, watching me with that same old laser focus.

"We're not done," she repeats, and now it's clear she means all of it: the work, the argument, the story, maybe even us.

I pour two mugs, hands still shaking. I don't ask if she wants sugar.

We stand in the silence, rain hammering the glass, steam rising from the mugs and from the surface of our skin.

There's a story here, somewhere. Maybe I'll write it down someday.

For now, we just stand in the dark, not done.

FIFTEEN

— ♥ —————

GRACE

There are three ways to justify turning up at your ex's flat after midnight, none of which stand up in court. One: You need to debrief on a breaking story. Two: You need to return the phone charger you stole. Three: You need him, and if you say it out loud, the world will collapse into a pit of self-parody from which it may never recover.

The flat is not just messy, it's in active rebellion—piles of print-outs on every surface, the floor a graveyard of highlighter pens, takeaway cartons forming a load-bearing wall by the sofa. There's a whiteboard propped against the radiator with the words "Motive, Opportunity, Apathy" circled in blue. I remember the handwriting from a hundred nights in the student newsroom, the way he always turned the most pedestrian of deadlines into a matter of existential despair.

The case files we're supposed to be working on together are scattered across the surface in a collage of misery: screenshots of social media posts, bank transfer records, a blurry photo of a fundraiser where everyone is grinning except the person at the centre of the story. There's a list of names written in block capitals down the side of one page: three are highlighted, one is crossed out, and the rest are annotated with a dense margin of insults and speculation. He's been working hard on this, but hasn't said a word, or more importantly, written a word.

"Nice place," I say.

Paul snorts, a sound halfway between agreement and apology. "Didn't have time to tidy for the surprise audit."

I sit on the edge of the sofa, careful to avoid the worst of the loose papers. He throws me a towel and sits at the far end, legs outstretched, then shifts them aside when it becomes clear I need more space than that. I realise, belatedly, that he's now barefoot. The last time I saw him barefoot was the holiday we took in Brighton, where he spent the entire weekend making fun of my SPF habits and then got sunburned so badly he couldn't wear shoes for a week.

For a moment, I don't say anything. The rain is louder now, slamming the glass with the kind of determination that only London in February can manage. I watch the droplets race each other down the pane, willing myself not to make a metaphor out of it.

"Do you ever stop?" I ask, pointing at the investigation materials all around us.

He considers this, running a hand through his hair until it sticks up in new and interesting directions. "I tried. Didn't stick."

We both look at the whiteboard, at the chaos of notes and arrows. Then back at each other.

I want to tell him that I'm proud of him, that I admire his tenacity. But the words snag in my throat. Instead, I say, "You're going to burn out before you get anywhere, you know."

He laughs, but it's a soft, tired sound. "Old news. You going to try and save me, Hampton?"

"Not my job," I say, but we both know it's a lie.

I remember nights in the student newsroom, arguing until two a.m., neither of us willing to give ground. I remember, too, the one time we ran out of things to argue about and just sat in silence, his head on my lap, my fingers combing absentmindedly through his hair until he fell asleep.

I shake the memory away.

Paul takes the damp towel from me and dries his hair. He stands to stretch, arms above his head, shirt riding up just enough to show the pale line of his hip. I make a noise that is definitely not a whimper, then cover it with a cough.

He grins at me, and for a second the look on his face is so open, so completely without artifice, that I feel something inside me twist.

I retreat to the kitchen under the pretext of needing more tea. The state of the place is dire, but I manage to find the teabags.

Paul comes in after, leans on the counter next to me. "You remember when we used to do this every night?"

"Which?" I ask. "Staying up until dawn chasing dead leads, or ruining perfectly good relationships with our mutual obsession?"

"Both," he says, laughing. "Mainly the second one."

I pour the tea, focus on the swirl of milk until the liquid turns the precise shade of beige that means I'm avoiding the question.

He reaches out, a hand hovering just over my shoulder. For a moment, I think he's going to touch me, and every cell in my body waits for it. Instead, he plucks a stray hair from the back of my dress, holds it up in triumph.

"You shedding already? It's not even spring."

I flick the hair from his hand, but not before my fingers brush his palm. The shock is electric, embarrassing in its intensity.

I clear my throat. "Personal space, Callaghan."

He's close, so close I can smell the aftershave on his skin. "You never used to mind."

"I do now," I lie, but it doesn't land.

He studies my face for a beat, eyes searching. Then he steps back, arms folded, giving me the space I demanded. I feel colder for it.

We drink our tea at the kitchen counter, the silence broken only by the rain and the soft clink of ceramic.

After a minute, he says, "Why did you come tonight?"

I swallow hard. "The story. We're supposed to be working on it together."

He nods, but I can tell he doesn't buy it.

I stare at my mug, then at him. "What about you? Why are you still doing this? You could walk away, you know. Get a job somewhere that pays more than sandwiches and doesn't make you go speed dating on Friday evenings."

He looks out the window, the city lights smeared by water and distance. "I don't know how to do anything else," he says. "And even if I did, I wouldn't want to."

It's too honest, too raw. I want to make a joke, but the air won't let me.

Instead, I reach for the kettle to top up my mug, desperate for something to do with my hands.

Paul reaches for it too, and our fingers collide, knuckle to knuckle. Neither of us moves. For a long second, we just stay there, hands overlapping, the heat rising and falling in equal measure.

"I should go," I say, but I don't move.

He tilts his head. "You could stay. Just until the rain stops."

I look at him, at the line of his jaw, at the scar on his wrist from the time he'd defended my honour in a student union brawl. I want to say yes. I want to say, "Let's forget the last seven years and start again, right here, over terrible tea and a table full of evidence." I want to say, "I never stopped missing you."

But I don't.

"You ever think about what we'd be doing if we weren't here?" he asks.

I want to say, "We'd be in bed, and you'd be making up conspiracy theories about the duvet industry," but the words jam up in my throat. Instead, I say, "Probably be asleep," and the moment passes, but only just.

He grins, but it doesn't reach his eyes. "Liar."

I glance over, and he's watching me—really watching, the way you look at an open wound or a poem you hate but can't stop rereading.

Our faces are inches apart. I don't know who moves first, but suddenly I'm close enough to count the lines around his mouth, the flecks of blue in his eyes that only show when he's about to say something important.

He does.

"You can stop pretending now," he says, and the words are a challenge, a dare, a confession.

I want to laugh, to fire back something glib and damaging, but the inside of my chest has gone soft and unarmoured. He leans in, slowly, the way you approach an animal you think might bite.

For a moment, I let him.

Then, with the speed of a panic attack, I pull back. "We shouldn't," I say, and it's less a decision than a reflex.

He blinks once. "Why not?"

"This feels too familiar," I say, voice barely audible. "And we both know how it ended last time."

His jaw flexes, and for a second, I see the old anger, the version of him that would have slammed a door or started an argument just to avoid being the first to break. But he doesn't.

He just stands there, hands flat on the counter, as if he's afraid to touch anything else.

"Maybe it ended that way because you never gave us a chance," he says, and his voice is small, unguarded.

I want to say something, anything, but the air is thick with things that can't be fixed by words.

"I have to go," I say louder than intended. I pull my hand away, and recover my sopping wet shawl from the hallway floor. "I've got an early meeting," I say. "And if I show up looking like I haven't slept, Sarah will assume we're sleeping together and fire me out of spite."

He grins. "You don't need to worry; she thinks the sun shines out of your arse."

I'm at the door before I realise I'm moving. I turn, hand on the knob, and say, "Don't forget to update the Google Doc if you find anything. And try not to fall asleep on the sofa."

He salutes, the gesture perfectly ridiculous. "Copy that."

I open the door, letting the sound of rain fill the corridor. For a moment, I think he'll follow. But he just stands there, watching, the light behind him turning his face to shadow.

"Goodnight," I say, and it's all I can manage.

Outside, the air is sharp, the rain somehow colder than before. I huddle under the entrance to the block, breathe in the smell of damp concrete, and try to convince myself that I'm still in control.

I check my phone. There's an email from Sarah, subject line: "Are You Still Alive?" and a missed call from my mother. I ignore both.

Instead, I stand there, alone, and watch the city flicker in the darkness, every window a story, every streetlight a promise.

It's almost enough.

Almost.

SIXTEEN

PAUL

The flat is so quiet I can hear my heart beating, which is new. Usually there's some distraction—the hum of the fridge, the odd siren, the upstairs neighbour practicing her tonal murder of the piano. But right now there's only the percussive tap of keys and the aftermath of Grace's exit, which is louder than any music.

The cursor blinks, insistent. I've been staring at the same paragraph for twenty minutes, trying to will it into coherence. "Modern romance," it begins, then dies a wet, unremarkable death. I try a different approach: "If you ask anyone who's ever tried to date in the era of surveillance capitalism..." That's worse somehow. I delete, rewrite, delete again.

Every time I look up from the laptop, I half-expect to see Grace on the other end of the sofa, hair wet, a navy evening dress, finger tapping in time with her thoughts. Instead, there's only a scatter of loose printouts and my reflection in the blank TV, which looks like someone who's just realised he's been outplayed by a better opponent.

I try to write about love, but all I can think about is loss. Specifically, the way she left: not dramatic, not even angry, just done. Final, like the click of a phone going dead. I replay the last conversation in my head, as if there's a director's cut where I say something clever enough to keep her from walking out. There isn't. The whole scene is so familiar I could stage it from memory—down to the way she doesn't look back when the door swings shut.

I pull up the draft of our column, the one Sarah still wants completed, even though the big story is the charity scandal. The Google Doc is a graveyard of comments, mostly hers. "You're leaning too hard on the metaphor here," she's written. "Try cutting the last sentence. Or the whole paragraph. Actually, start over."

I want to argue, but she's right. There's a hollow in the writing now. It reads like two people holding a conversation through a pane of glass, pretending not to see their own reflections. I scroll back through our old work, columns from when we were still at university, fighting over commas and footnotes, drinking supermarket wine out of plastic cups at three in the morning. The words back then crackled, full of life and spite and the thrill of being cleverer than everyone else. Now it's just noise.

The night outside is a study in nothing. The rain has stopped, leaving the city streets slick and anonymous. I should go to bed, but the thought of sleep is laughable. I haven't managed more than three hours in a row since the "Modern Romance" column started. My brain is running on caffeine and nostalgia, and both are running out.

I close the laptop and try to pace it off. The flat is small, so this involves a circuit from the kitchen to the bathroom and back, avoiding the growing debris field of paperwork and unwashed mugs from earlier. I catch sight of myself in the bathroom mirror. It's not good. I look like someone who's spent a week locked in a casino and lost every hand.

I splash water on my face and towel off with the least dirty towel I can find. The cotton is stiff, smells faintly of bleach and defeat. I run a hand through my hair, which is already sticking up at odd angles, and consider shaving. I don't.

Back at the table, I check my phone for messages. Nothing from Grace. Not that I expect one.

I open the Doc again, determined to at least pretend I'm a functioning adult. I manage two lines before the urge to check her profile wins out. It's a sickness. There she is: still up, still green-lighted on WhatsApp, probably still working. Probably writing the piece herself offline and not waiting for me to catch up.

I want to send a message. Something short, direct, impossible to misread. Instead, I type, "Modern Romance draft's up to date. Let me know if you want to take the next section." I delete it before I hit send. I can't decide whether this is self-control or cowardice.

I get into bed and stare at the ceiling, counting the cracks in the plaster and all the ways in which I am, and will always be, a disappointment to the people I care about.

It takes a long time for sleep to come. When it does, it's shallow and crowded, full of broken sentences and images of her in that dress at the charity gala.

SEVENTEEN

GRACE

I wake at five, which is a personal best for failure to switch my brain off. My flat is thick with the smell of last night's panic coffee and a hint of burnt toast that even three open windows can't fully shift. I drift the perimeter, mug in one hand, phone in the other, doing the dance of the severely under-rested: scroll, sip, reload, repeat.

The Chronicle's homepage is still running last night's lead —something about a city council member caught faking disability claims, which on a regular day would make me snort. Today, it barely registers. I swipe back to Twitter, check the notifications, then loop around to WhatsApp in case the editors have decided to pull the article at the last possible minute. They haven't, but I check again anyway, just in case.

The clock ticks past six. The neighbour's toddler is already screaming, and there's a rhythmic thud from above, as if the woman upstairs is deadlifting her furniture again. I lean over the kitchen counter, forehead pressed to the faux-granite, and will the universe to just get on with it.

It drops at 06:30 on the dot.

The new front page loads with a shudder, pixels rearranging to reveal a headline so large it nearly eats the screen: "CHARITY FRAUD UNCOVERED: POLITICIANS AND CEOS IMPLICATED IN £12M SCAM." Underneath, my name. All caps. GRACE HAMPTON. In the body copy, all the ugly evidence Paul had been building and what I unearthed from the financial records. Some of it, admittedly, is conjecture rather than fact, but where there's smoke...

I read the whole thing once, then again, looking for signs of neutering. Legal has sanded down the edges, added a brace of "alleged" and "the *Chronicle* understands," but the meat of it remains. I'm waiting for the moment when it starts to feel like victory, but mostly I just feel cold and a little bit sick.

My phone vibrates so hard it almost leaps from the counter. The newsroom WhatsApp group has gone nuclear: one of the sub-Editors sends a parade of screaming emojis, followed by "WAKE UP AND SMELL THE FRONT PAGE, BITCH," then a screenshot of the headline circled three times in pink. Max chimes in with, "Omg did you actually spell 'malfeasance' right on first try?" and a GIF of an elderly woman fainting. Even ex-colleagues now working at other papers pile in, their texts a blend of admiration and thinly disguised jealousy.

There's a text from my dad, who normally never puts finger to keypad unless someone is dead. His message is short: "Proud of you, love. Don't forget to eat."

There's a pulsing ellipsis for a moment, as if he's weighing up whether to write more, then nothing.

On Twitter, the fallout is instant and glorious.

By eight, the charity's CEO has "stepped away from the role to spend more time with his family," the finance director is being led into a police car, and a junior minister who'd been happy to pose with oversized cheques only a month prior is suddenly "on extended leave." I allow myself the minor thrill of watching the hashtag trend, my phone hissing with mentions, insults, conspiracy theories, and the occasional "well done."

The story is picked up by every other outlet. The *Evening Standard* reframes it as a "crisis of confidence," the *Mail* calls it "Hampton's hammer blow to City Hall," and *The Sun*, the paper that once called my writing "shrill," runs the entire second paragraph verbatim, complete with the typo I asked the sub-editor to leave in as a trap for lazy aggregators.

I make a note to thank Tess for that suggestion.

By ten, my inbox is a battlefield. There are requests from TV producers, three different radio shows, and a message from Legal reminding me not to post on social about "ongoing investigations." There's also an email from HR, but I delete it without opening it. If it's about the employee satisfaction survey, they can bite me.

I finally get dressed, which is to say I swap pyjama bottoms for the cleanest jeans I can find, and drag myself to the mirror. There's a line on my face I've never seen before, running from the edge of my left eyebrow all the way down to my cheekbone. It's not a scar, just a trench worn in by six months of clenching my jaw. I rub at it, but it doesn't go away.

I eat toast. I drink more coffee. I watch the numbers on the *Chronicle's* "most read" sidebar rise in real time, the little progress bar slamming forward with every refresh. I know I should log off, take a walk, or at least wash my hair, but I'm rooted to the spot, unable to shake the feeling that if I blink, the story will vanish, and so will I.

At 09:02, Sarah calls. I answer on speaker, hands shaking only a little.

"You did it," she says, voice thick with satisfaction and, if I'm honest, a bit of awe. "You absolute machine. Did you see the statement? The CEO went full Boris Johnson."

I grin, the muscles in my face protesting at the sudden movement. "He'll be in Málaga by Monday. I give it six hours before he blames it on a rogue intern."

Sarah cackles, then sobers. "Seriously. This is the best work you've done. I mean, you're still a nightmare, but you might actually get a raise for this."

"Or sued."

"Or sued! But at least you'll be famous. Or infamous. Depends who you ask."

She pauses, the line filled with the sound of her biting into something crunchy. "Anyway, can you come in? Miriam wants to do the debrief at two, and she's bringing pastries."

"Yeah," I say, staring out the window as the city plods on below. "I'll be there."

"Wear something that says 'investigative journalist,' not 'on remand.'"

I hang up and spend a full five minutes wondering what that even means. Then I throw on a blazer over my T-shirt, jam my feet into boots, and prepare to face the world as the person who, for one morning, broke it a little bit.

If there's a crackle in the air when I step into the newsroom, it's because the collective tension could set off an explosion. The place thrums like election night. Not just the old *Chronicle* diehards, but *Express* staffers, too—most pretending to be annoyed at having to share desk space, but all side-eyes and micro-smirks when they think no one's watching. There's a queue at the office coffee machine, and someone's already broken the "two items per person" rule, leaving the intern to mop up a small lake of oat milk.

My desk today is at the centre of everything: two seats down from the Digital Politics team, three from the Features pod, and almost perfectly positioned for maximum exposure to anyone who wants to snipe at or congratulate me. I get both before I even log on.

Sarah materialises, thrusting a Tupperware of homemade muffins at me, her eyes so bright I suspect performance-enhancing drugs. "Have you seen the comments? Fucking legend," she says, voice pitched low but carrying. "Also, don't eat the canteen muffins, they taste like carpet glue."

I thank her, then triple-check my desktop for emails from Legal before daring to crack my inbox. It's bad, but survivable. Five requests for comment, seven thank-yous, three strongly worded complaints from people I've never met but who apparently think I ruined their lives. The ratio is flattering, though, so I let myself enjoy it.

I'm halfway through a muffin when I notice Paul, propped against Sarah's doorframe like a bouncer who's only just remembered he's off duty. He's got his arms folded, chin down, eyes hidden behind a fringe that says, "I haven't slept" more eloquently than any actual confession. When he sees me, his mouth doesn't move, but his posture shifts—barely, but enough. He's waiting for something.

I raise a hand, a tentative wave. He doesn't return it. Instead, he turns, steps into Sarah's office, and lets the door click shut behind him.

I stare for a second, muffin halfway to my mouth, then take a breath and start typing. If this is a call-in, I want my own side of the story at the front of my mind.

Fifteen minutes later, the door opens, and Sarah leans out. "Grace? Can I see you a sec?"

I stand, dust the crumbs from my jacket, and do the walk. The whole newsroom is watching, but pretending not to.

Inside, Sarah's office is arranged to keep the power dynamics ambiguous: three chairs, all identical, facing each other over a tiny table that holds a single, unopened water bottle. Paul is pacing, hands in pockets, the same way he did in uni before a big debate. Sarah sits, already typing something invisible on her phone.

"Close the door, please," she says, then looks up, all professional smile and no warmth. "Let's keep this brief. I just want to hear about the process."

I sit, meet Sarah's eyes, then glance at Paul. His expression is carved from wood. I remind myself I don't have to fill the silence. I do anyway.

"I sent the final to Legal at 02:30," I say. "They bounced it back at 05:15, so I made the amends and loaded it to the CMS. I was hoping we would have got someone on record last night at the gala, but it would have required a follow-up with no guarantee of anything juicy. With the leak risk and the CEO already making noises, I figured we needed to get out in front of it."

Sarah nods, tapping a nail against her phone. "You didn't flag it to Paul?"

The answer is no, and she already knows it, but I try for dignity. "I'd been waiting all week for Paul. I know he was working his own angles, he was doing the work, but he didn't actually contribute to the shared document. I didn't want to risk another delay. We were first on the evidence, and I wanted to keep the lead."

Paul cuts in, voice cool. "Translation: she didn't want my input."

Sarah holds up a hand, as if swatting away a bee. "This isn't about point-scoring. It's about trust. We merged the teams for a reason, and it wasn't so we could run two parallel operations. If the *Express* side gets wind that you're freezing them out, they'll throw a fit—and if Legal thinks we're not managing process, they'll make us do everything in triplicate."

I nod, but I can feel my jaw clenching.

Paul stops pacing, stands behind the chair opposite me.

"Can I just—" He stops, glances at Sarah, then back at me. "The story's good. Better than good. But you didn't need to rush it. You just wanted the win."

I want to argue, but he's right, and the proof is all over my inbox and my face.

Sarah sighs, a performance of fatigue that's only slightly exaggerated. "Look, I don't care who gets the byline. What I do care about is that we don't implode before the next cycle. You're both too good to waste on office politics, but if you can't work together, we're all fucked."

I swallow the comeback, and instead say, "Noted."

Paul says nothing. Just stands there, radiating tension.

Sarah's phone buzzes, and she glances down. "Minister's just released a statement. Grace, can you prep a reaction piece for digital? Paul, follow up on the charity's board. Who knew what and when? I want this running all week, not just as a flash-in-the-pan."

She stands, signalling that we're done. I get up, ready to leave, but Paul lingers, eyes fixed on a point over Sarah's head. For a second, I think he's going to say something, but he just nods, almost to himself, then steps aside so I can go first.

The newsroom is louder than before. More clicks, more voices, the caffeine surge hitting critical mass. I duck back to my desk, try to focus on the screen, but my heart's racing and the words blur together.

I watch Paul at his desk, head down, fingers tapping at his keyboard. Every so often, he glances up, catches me looking, then looks away before I can read his face.

My frustration boils over. "Look—"

"Busy." Paul continues to type. He doesn't even bother to make eye contact with me.

Fine. I puff out my cheeks, counting to three before I turn to the draft for the next piece, the words coming in fits and starts. The newsroom hums, alive with the myth of teamwork and the reality of individual ambition. I type, delete, retype, the story unspooling in two directions at once.

I delete it all, and allow myself a single minute of nothing, hands limp in my lap, eyes closed against the white noise.

Then I start again, chasing the next story, the next headline, the next reason to keep moving. On my own. As always.

Maybe one day I'll learn how to stop.

But not today.

EIGHTEEN

PAUL

Stepping out of Sarah's office, I make it to my desk without looking at her.

This is a tactical choice: one part self-preservation, two parts calculated offence. The merged newsroom is still new enough that no one's quite sure where the best seats are yet, so Grace and I are parked together at a table meant for four, the other chairs orbiting in and out as needed. Today, it's just us. She's already at her laptop, sleeves rolled, hair up, the universal sign of "I'm busy, but also aggressively available for conversation." I ignore her.

My jaw aches before I've even logged on, a low, grinding pain that started somewhere around Bermondsey, when I saw the article live on the homepage, and has been working its way into my left temple ever since. I clench harder, just to check if it's possible to shatter a molar with sheer willpower. It is.

She starts with, "Look—" but I'm ready for it.

"Busy," I say, and fire up my email. The word comes out brittle, but it does the trick. Silence.

The office is humming, the main floor flooded with the kind of energy that comes from caffeine, mild hangovers, and the awareness that Grace's article is a *really* big scoop. Phones ring. Printers rattle. Someone in Ad Ops is playing a TikTok at top volume, probably out of spite.

Grace is making herself small. Not the easiest trick for her —she's got a presence, even when she's not trying, which is why the morning's news cycle is full of her name and not mine. I scroll the homepage again, just to punish myself: there it is, top story, her photo by the byline. The headline is a model of restraint—no exclamation marks, no cheap shots, just the cool certainty of "The Chronicle Uncovers £12M Fraud." It's good. I hate how good it is.

People keep stopping by her side of the desk. Some are genuine—"Great work, Grace," "How'd you even get that document?"—but most are here to take her measure, sus out whether she's about to be the new golden child or just struck it lucky and will be like the rest of us again next week. Every compliment lands like a flicked paper cut. She accepts them with a smile, but I can see the tension in her neck, the way her hand doesn't quite leave the keyboard. She's braced for something, probably from me.

What she gets is nothing.

Sarah's already sent me my assignment for the day: "local hero profile," the kind of puff piece designed to pad out the Sunday supplement and keep the advertisers happy. On a normal week, I'd fight it, or at least sandbag the deadline until someone higher up intervened, but today I'm grateful for the busywork. I open a fresh doc, write the headline "BAKER'S DOZEN: THE WOMAN FEEDING DEPTFORD'S HOMELESS" and then sit back, waiting for the anger to settle into something more useful.

It doesn't. It simmers.

The keyboard on my laptop has a slight rattle in the space

bar. I never noticed it before, but now every word sounds like I'm drumming out a warning. I make it louder, just in case Grace needs reminding that I'm here, that I'm not sulking, that I'm actually doing my job. I can feel her watching from the corner of her eye, but I refuse to look up.

A text from Jamie comes through: "u okay? saw the article. if you want to get trashed later, I'm buying." I ignore it, even though I know he'll follow up with a meme or a photo of his breakfast. He means well, which is the problem.

At eleven-thirty, someone from Features brings Grace a cup of tea. They don't bring me one. She tries to offer it my way—"You want?"—but I shake my head without breaking stride. I'm on paragraph three and already have half a page of quotes, none of which I intend to use, but it's the illusion of momentum that matters.

The air around our table is thick with everything we're not saying. She keeps opening her mouth, then closing it, then opening it again, like a fish that's been yanked out of the tank and can't decide whether to fight or just suffocate. It would be funny if it weren't so familiar.

I finish the rough draft, attach it to an email, and send it to Sarah with a subject line so perfunctory it could serve as its own eulogy: "Here." Then I close the laptop and sit, arms folded, staring straight ahead.

For a second, I think maybe this is how it ends: two people, side by side, each one trying to outlast the other in a contest neither of us signed up for.

But then she says very quietly, "You're not even going to critique the article?"

I look at her finally, and the look on her face is raw enough to make my teeth hurt.

I want to say yes. I want to say I read it twice, that it was flawless, that I'm not even mad, just jealous, and that I wish, just once, that it had been me on the other side of the byline. I want to say all that, but the words just clog up behind my tongue.

Instead, I stand, pick up my laptop, and head for the far end of the newsroom, where the Wi-Fi is worse but at least the company is optional.

As I walk away, I hear someone from the Social team call out, "Nice work, Grace!" over the partition. Her reply is too soft to carry.

I keep moving, but the ache in my jaw doesn't let up, and neither does the noise of all the things I'll never say.

At 13:58, Jamie appears with a cup of coffee and an expression I'd describe as "benign concern" if I thought he was capable of either. More likely, he's just bored. Either way, he hovers over the edge of my borrowed desk until I acknowledge him, which takes longer than it should.

"You gonna talk to her," he says, "or keep acting like a sulky teenager until HR brings in a therapy dog?"

His voice is just loud enough to catch the attention of the woman at the next table, who glances over and then away with professional indifference.

I don't answer, just stare at the screen, scrolling through an article about the Wandsworth bin strike as if it holds the secret to existence.

Jamie sighs, then sits on the edge of the desk, making it creak in protest. "I'm serious, mate. Isn't this exactly how you two self-destructed last time?"

I cut my eyes at him, sharp enough that I hope it draws blood. "I'm working."

"Yeah, you're working," he says. "You're always working. But you're also not eating, not sleeping, and"—He leans in, voice low—"not winning."

He means it as a jibe, but it lands as a dare. I let it linger, then shut my laptop with a snap.

"What do you want, Jamie?"

He shrugs, sips his coffee, and surveys the room like he owns it. "Nothing. Just thought you should know she's not the only one who got a brief from Sarah. They're planning a 'point-counterpoint' thing for Sunday. Digital's going to run a poll. Best comment wins a bottle of Tesco gin and a column slot for a week."

I snort, but it's mostly air. "Real journalism, that."

He grins. "The future, apparently. Maybe you could try not fucking it up for both of you this time."

I open the laptop again, the screen's blue glare lighting up every vein in my hand. "She'll be fine."

"I know she will," says Jamie. "Question is, will you?"

He stands, stretches, and lopes off, leaving a ring of coffee at the edge of my workspace. I wipe it with my sleeve, just to see if it'll come off. It doesn't.

I check my email—nothing urgent, just a running thread about parking passes and an all-staff reminder not to microwave fish in the breakroom. My next assignment is a sidebar for the "Modern Romance" feature, the one Sarah wants as a double act. I'm supposed to be collaborating with Grace, but the idea of "us" as a team is so risible I nearly delete the brief on principle.

Instead, I open a fresh doc and type, "Modern Romance: Why It Never Works."

The title is a provocation, and I leave it in bold at the top, just in case anyone is looking over my shoulder.

I look up, finally, over to Grace, her headphones on, eyes fixed on her screen. She's probably three drafts deep already, fingers a blur. There's a small furrow in her brow, a wrinkle that says she's deep in the machinery of it, building something mean and beautiful. I should hate it, but I don't. Not really.

The newsroom is an echo chamber of rising voices and deadlines. At the main cluster of desks, someone is arguing with IT about a password reset, while the Features pod is locked in a deathmatch over whose phone keeps going off. The nearest printer jams and starts shrieking; the guy from Editorial thumps it until it resumes spitting out pages, all slightly off-kilter and misaligned. I let the white noise build, then fade.

I type:

"Every relationship is a contest. Even the good ones. Especially the good ones. Some people win, some people break even, but most just try not to lose."

I pause, then delete *"most just try not to lose."* It's too soft.

I start again, this time sharper, harder, aiming every word at the invisible spot just behind Grace's left shoulder.

The thing about being in second place is, you never get tired of fighting. You get used to the blood in your mouth, the knots in your stomach, the way your heartbeat becomes a metronome for every regret and almost. It's not noble. It's not tragic. It's just what happens when you can't bear the idea of finishing last.

I keep typing, faster, letting the lines run jagged and raw. Each sentence is a flex, a jab at the invisible audience I imagine is watching, waiting for me to trip or falter. I can't give them that satisfaction. Not today.

Grace's head tilts, just for a second, as if she's caught my stray thought in the air. Then she goes back to work, her face unreadable.

I write:

"In the end, there's no such thing as a tie. Someone always gets the last word."

I set it in italics, then hit save.

The act of writing feels like breathing underwater—tense, necessary, dangerous if you linger too long. I lean back, roll my shoulders, and for the first time all morning, there's a faint hint of a smile. Not a happy one, not even close, but the kind that comes when you know exactly what you're about to do, and you're going to do it anyway.

Across the room, Grace is typing, oblivious. The line between us is clean, sharp, and exactly where it belongs.

Let the best byline win.

NINETEEN

GRACE

The day begins with the cold, reptilian blink of my phone—
6:14 a.m., the blue light carving a trench through the dark.
The flat is at its most honest at this hour: silence, the smell of
last night's pizza box, my dressing gown leaking heat onto the
duvet. In the half-light, my own limbs feel borrowed, too heavy
and not quite attached.

I pick up the phone, thumbprint laggy from sleep. There's
an email from Paul Callaghan, subject line: "Draft for Sarah,
per deadline." No preamble. No "Morning," no handshake, no
recognisable human emotion.

This should be a relief. But my pulse has already ratcheted
up, the anticipation of disaster familiar enough to make my
stomach clench before I've even opened the document.

I tap the screen, and it loads with the speed of a hand crank.

There's an attachment. Nothing in the body, nothing at all.

For a moment, I stare at the header, waiting for my brain to
supply the hidden meaning, the context I've somehow missed.

There isn't any. Paul has always been allergic to unnecessary words, but this is a new level of brevity.

I download the file. It opens in Pages, defaulting to a typeface I'd banned from all *Chronicle* submissions, just to annoy him. The title is a placeholder: "Modern_Romance_4_vFINAL." I skim the first paragraph, and the ground opens beneath my feet.

My name isn't on it. Not at the top, not in the byline, not even a parenthetical in the first footnote.

I scroll, scanning for a hint of my own existence. Nothing. Not even a "thanks to my colleague," not even an "as my co-author argues." The piece is laser-precise, every argument honed to a point, every section echoing debates we'd had at three a.m. in the ancient, tequila-stained student newsroom. The words are his, but the structure—the intellectual rigour, the sniping cadence of the opening salvo, the entire midsection about "algorithmic dating and the myth of authenticity"—is mine. My notes, my outline, my lifeblood.

I check the email again. The address is the same as always. No "cc," no hidden bcc to Sarah or Liam or the freelance pool. I search for a follow-up, a text, an explanation. There's nothing. I want to believe this is a mistake, a technical glitch, but the pit in my stomach is already crowded with the ghosts of every old betrayal.

I open my own draft, the one I spent five hours finessing last night. It's smarter. It's more original. It's also just sitting in the "Drafts" folder, unsent, because I wanted to do one more pass before sending.

The flat has gone cold in the hour I spent reading and rereading. I can see my breath when I open the fridge for milk, and the bottle is nearly empty. I try to dress like I'm not about to walk into an execution: green dress, hair up, subtle lip. I consider leaving the house without my rings, just to see if anyone notices. In the end, I put on every single one, the familiar silver and gold bands biting into my fingers.

The tube is murder. Someone's thrown up on the platform, and the train is packed with commuters in various states of despair. I grip the handrail, knuckles white, and watch the city strobe past. At Liverpool Street, two schoolgirls get on and immediately start dissecting a boy called Seb, who is "a total narc" and also "fit, but with an unfortunate eyebrow situation." I want to say: "He won't remember your name, even if you haunt his dreams for a decade." Instead, I get off at Moorgate, nearly lose a shoe to the gap, and power-walk the three blocks to the office.

The Chronicle's façade has been repainted since last week, but the logo is already peeling. The security guard gives me the nod, the one reserved for "faces that have been in the news." The reception desk is littered with packages—PR mailers, dead plants, a single helium balloon with "CONGRATS!" that's started to wilt. I punch the lift button and wait, staring at my reflection in the gold-flecked panel. There are dark smudges under my eyes. My collar is already askew.

Upstairs, the newsroom is in full howl. The Features pod is arguing about whether you can legally call a cocktail "Negroni Sbagliato" if you don't use the right kind of vermouth. The Podcast team is running a test call with a source, so every other word is "fuck" or "cut that."

I scan for Paul. His desk is empty. The mug is there, the battered old laptop, a notebook with his signature scrawl ("Corrupt to correct to collapse" in biro). But no Paul.

For a second, I think: *Maybe he's on deadline. Maybe he had to leave early to chase a lead. Maybe this is all some elaborate gambit to keep me off balance.*

I dump my bag at my desk, boot up the laptop, and open the group chat. There's already a thread going—Sarah, me, Paul, and the entire Features desk. The message at the top:

"Need the FINAL FINAL for legal by 10 a.m., otherwise we lose the slot." There are exactly four minutes left.

I look at my draft again, then at the one Paul sent. There's no time to finesse, no time to plead my case to Sarah or to anyone. I send his draft along with my own, with a single line: "Attached."

I open the document. I highlight every single line that originated from my outline, every phrase that is so precisely, so unmistakably mine that even a first-year journalism student would spot the overlap. I want to email it to Sarah, to attach a long, annotated list of grievances. But I don't. I'm not a victim. I'm not going to let him win that easily.

I walk to the kitchen, my legs shaky from adrenaline. I pour the last of the coffee and stand by the window, watching the city wake up through the fog. The sun is coming up over the river, the buildings picking out light one by one, like a nervous smile.

I think about the last time we did this—eight years ago, a different paper, a different deadline, the same sense of impending doom. Paul beat me by twelve minutes. It was the last day of the term of our second year, and I didn't speak to him for the entire summer break. He sent a postcard from Berlin, no words, just a badly drawn skull and crossbones.

I run my thumb over my rings, twisting them until they bite. I close my eyes. I breathe.

When I get back to my desk, the email from Sarah is waiting. She's sent it to both of us.

"Going with Callaghan's version. More focused, sharper. Sorry, Grace—yours was solid, but this one has more 'voice.' Next time, CC each other on all changes so we don't get another byline drama. You're both too old for this."

I stare at the screen, willing myself not to cry. I won't. Not here. Not now.

Instead, I open a new document. Title: "Losing Grace."

I write the first line: "Modern romance is a blood sport, and I keep forgetting which side I'm on."

The words come fast. They always do.

By the time Paul returns to the office, I'm three paragraphs in and rising. I don't look at him. I don't have to.

He sits, the old chair creaking under his weight. I feel his eyes on my back.

I type, and type, and type, until the world blurs into nothing but words.

By mid-morning, my inbox is an ice bath of "urgent" subject lines, each more desperate than the last. I stare at the screen and try to hold the shape of myself together, but I keep thinking about the way Paul's name looks alone, the way Sarah's verdict landed like a slab of concrete. "Too old for this." If she meant heartbreak, she's right. I don't have the cartilage for it anymore.

I need to know—need it confirmed, on the record, so I can carve the feeling into bone.

Sarah is a goddess of the corridor, always in motion, always on the brink of a more important meeting. I catch her as she's striding toward the glass-walled "strategy pod," phone to her ear, heels merciless on the tile.

"Sarah—can I grab you for a minute?" I ask, careful to keep the desperation in my voice on the far side of audible.

She mutes the call and lifts an eyebrow, equal parts "shoot" and "you've got thirty seconds."

"I just wanted to clarify about the byline. For the Modern Romance thing." I say it lightly, like it doesn't matter, like it's just another line on my weekly self-flagellation report. "Was it a Board thing, or...?"

She frowns, genuine confusion softening her face for the first time since the merger. "Board thing? No. Why?"

"I just—Paul sent his in solo. I thought we were supposed to, I don't know, collaborate." The last word is bitter on my tongue.

Sarah checks her phone, then the calendar on her wrist. "You are. Were. In fact, I was going to tell you this morning that the joint stuff you two were doing was working. Didn't expect separate drafts."

My brain stutters. "So, no one said—?"

She shakes her head. "No. I told you both to run with the story. I wanted the classic bickering, the 'will-they-won't-they' energy. Board loves that shit. But solo? That's not what we want. I mean, we'll run Paul's this time, but—" She shrugs, all business again, and glances down the corridor, clearly seconds from rejoining the call. "I thought you two were finally working it out."

I don't answer. I can't.

She holds my gaze a second longer, then says, "If there's a problem, you fix it. Don't make me referee."

"Of course," I say, voice neutral as air. "No problem."

She walks off, already back in boss mode. The silence left in her wake is clinical.

It takes a minute for the realisation to percolate. He did this. He alone. Whether to sabotage or to save himself, the result is the same: my name left off the record, my work digested and shat out under someone else's signature. Retaliation for my single byline for the charity scoop.

For a second, my chest hurts so much I can't move. The next, I'm walking, high-speed, back to the desk cluster. Paul is there, tie already loosened, mug in hand, chatting to Liam about some Premier League fuckery neither of them actually cares about. He's smiling. Not a real smile, but the one he uses for crowds, the one that never reaches his eyes.

I don't say a word. I log in, open the draft he submitted, and print the whole thing—double-sided, ten-point font, as economical as you like. The printer hiccups, then coughs it out, warm and smelling faintly of ozone and recycled hope.

I take a red pen from the admin desk, the one with the needle-point nib, and go to work.

Every misjudged comma, every sentence that could be tighter, every lazy transition or recycled metaphor: I mark it. I make a point of annotating in the margins, the way I used to do when we were both still students and he claimed to want honest feedback. I write fast, with the conviction of the newly vengeful. By the time I'm done, the paper looks like it's been shot at close range.

I leave the pages on his desk.

I pack my laptop, my bag, my rings—one by one, twisting them off my fingers and lining them up on the desk before sliding them back on. I don't speak. I don't need to.

I walk out. Past the Podcasts and the Features hub, past Sarah and her phone call, past the mural on the wall by the reception desk that's supposed to "inspire innovation."

I don't look back.

Not once.

TWENTY

PAUL

It's waiting for me. A printout, face down and already dog-eared, resting on top of my laptop like a death threat from the past. I pick it up, and the first thing I notice is the colour—red ink, not Biro blue, not the soft pencil I know Grace prefers for line edits, but surgical, arterial red. It's everywhere. Every margin, every header, whole paragraphs autopsied in the margins, sentences spliced open with little arrows and triple underlines and exclamation points that only ever mean pain.

The top page is my draft. "Modern_Romance_4_vFINAL." The one I emailed to Sarah last night, thinking—no, convincing myself—that this would be the time I beat Grace at her own game. That she'd see it and maybe respect the effort, or at least find something to sharpen her teeth on. Instead, it looks like she's spent the entire morning feeding it through a wood chipper.

A whisper ricochets over from the Design desk. Something about "Callaghan" and "massacre." I pretend not to hear, but the blood in my face is climbing fast.

I leaf through the pages, a private gallery of my own incompetence. The comments start professional—"Too many clauses, watch the structure," "Cliché, see attached meme," "You realise this is just a paraphrase of what I said in Sheffield?"—but quickly spiral into something else. On page three, a line in the margin: "Do you ever read your own work, or just send and pray?" On page five: "This is actually good— why did you hide it under all the bluster?" There's a Post-it on the seventh page that just says "LOL," underlined twice. By page ten, the line between editorial and existential is gone entirely.

I can feel people watching me now, not directly, but in that way journalists do when there's a live feed of professional violence. Grace isn't at her desk—she's vanished, maybe to the kitchen or maybe to the rooftop to scream at the Thames—but her presence is everywhere, inked into the bones of my draft. The Layout team pretends not to glance up every time I flip a page, but their eyes are stuck on the margins. One of the Features guys, two pods over, is actively narrating the blow-by-blow to a freelancer who has never met me and, from the look on her face, never wanted to.

I read every single comment. It's the only way to survive the Inquisition. I read them slowly, because some of them sting and some of them, worse, are completely fucking right. On page six, she's caught a logic jump I thought I'd buried so deep no one would ever find it. On page seven, she's written: "You missed the point here, but it's not too late to try again." That's the one that gets to me. Not the brutal notes, not the pointed sarcasm, not even the all-caps "NO" scrawled over an analogy I'd stolen from a pop psych book. It's the patience in that line, the invitation. Like she actually wants me to do better.

I get to the last page and there it is, the final diagnosis: "You could have just asked. But you never do." The "just" is underlined, and so is "never." There's a full stop after each, as if she's dictating the terms of my own execution. Below that, in smaller print: "Try again, or don't. Either way, it's over."

I close the printout. My fingers are tight on the paper, the skin on my knuckles a weird, unhealthy white. For a second, I want to tear the whole thing up and scatter it over her desk like confetti. Then I want to crawl under the table and die there, or at least wait out the next media cycle until someone else is the office pariah. Instead, I just sit, letting the fluorescent lights burn little holes in my vision and the sound of a hundred angry keyboards fill my skull.

The thing about getting dressed down by Grace is that she never raises her voice. She doesn't need to. Her edits land hard. It's the economics of it that hurts. The absence of any performance. When other editors rip me to shreds, it's a power trip—a show for the room, or a shot at climbing the food chain. With Grace, it's different. It's personal, but not in the way I always think. It's personal because she wants it to mean something. Because she thinks I can take it.

My jaw is locked, my teeth grinding a slow, deliberate rhythm. I try to relax, but the muscles won't let go. I flex my hands, shaking out the ache, and pick up the draft again, searching for a way to reassemble what's left of my dignity. Instead, all I can see is her handwriting, looping and crisp and impossible to ignore. It's in my head now, every note and correction replaying like the world's most passive-aggressive voicemail.

I stare across the open plan, at the rows of screens and coffee cups and the slow, relentless churn of news cycles. For the first time since I started in journalism, I wonder if maybe I am the problem. If maybe, just maybe, the reason we keep colliding is because I'm so convinced I'm the only one steering. That if I just drive fast enough, I'll outrun the things I don't want to admit.

I flip through the pages one more time, slower now. I start

to see the shape of what I did wrong—not just in the writing, but in the way I assumed the only way to win was to go solo, to box her out, to finish first or not at all. The edits aren't just a professional critique; they're a record of how I keep missing the point. How I keep doing the thing that ends with her handing me back my own words, rewritten as a warning.

I put down the pages, hands flat on the desk, and try to breathe through the humiliation. The newsroom is still humming, but it's just background radiation now, a white noise to the pulse in my ears. I stare at the spot where she usually sits, waiting for her to return, to say something, to do anything that will let me off the hook. But she's gone, and the absence hurts.

I wonder if I should seek her out. I wonder if I even have the right.

Instead, I sit, and read the last line again: "*You could have just asked. But you never do.*"

And for the first time in months, maybe ever, I realise she's not talking about the story at all.

I sit still at my desk for forty seconds, which is longer than it sounds. Long enough to let the shame congeal, long enough for the newsroom's attention to shift elsewhere, long enough for me to convince myself that I have a choice in the matter. I don't. I stand, the chair snapping back with a sound that draws eyes, and walk. I don't bother with my jacket, or my phone, or the half-finished mug of tarry coffee. Just the printout, rolled up and white-knuckled in my fist.

She's not in the kitchen. Not by the printers or the stairwell or the little glass pod labelled "Privacy Booth" that everyone uses for phone sex and panic attacks. I circle the floor, doing my best not to look like I'm hunting, but the adrenaline makes my feet slap the tile with double-time intensity. There are people everywhere, too many witnesses, the air heavy with the smell of old toner and instant noodles. The exit corridor is a long, bright strip of nothing—just a handful of last year's Christmas cards taped to the wall and a series of floor-to-ceiling windows looking out on the grey, damp city.

I find her halfway down, back to me, arms folded, the outline of her hair a dark flame against the glass. She's not alone: a tech guy is talking at her, both hands in the air, gesturing at something on his tablet, but she's not seeing it. She's looking past him, at the horizon or the river or whatever it is that people see when they can't stand to look at the person next to them.

The corridor amplifies everything. My footsteps sound like an execution squad. The tech guy glances up, clocks my approach, and abruptly finds a reason to be elsewhere.

Grace stands her ground. She's in full defensive mode—posture perfect, chin high, that micro-expression at the corners of her mouth that means: *I've already decided how this ends.* She doesn't speak first. She never does.

I start, because someone has to. "You didn't have to go nuclear," I say, which is not the opening I planned, but it's the one that comes out.

She watches me, unmoving, like she's waiting for a better line. When I don't supply one, she says, "You started it."

I hold up the draft, still bleeding red. "This wasn't personal."

"Everything's personal, Paul," she says, quiet but level. "You make sure of it."

I want to tell her she's wrong, that I did what I did for the story, for the deadline, for Sarah and the Board and the twelve other layers of management who want to see us eat each other alive. But she's right, and we both know it.

I take a breath, try to steady the tremor in my voice. "I thought—"

She cuts me off with a raised hand. "No, you didn't. That's the problem."

The corridor is cold, the windows steaming at the edges, and she stands between me and the light. She's waiting for me to say something real, something true, and the only things I can think of are all the wrong ones.

I say, "You always said it was about the work. About the truth."

She shakes her head, hair falling loose around her face. "It is. But you think the only way to get there is by going it alone. Like you're the only one who can do it right."

"That's not fair," I say, and even as I do, I can hear how weak it sounds.

"Isn't it?" she asks. There's nothing in her voice, no tremor, no bite. Just air. "You left me out of the process. So I wrote it and published."

It's a perfect hit. Not mean, not dramatic—just exact. I feel the blood rise in my face, the heat curling into my ears.

"But instead of learning from that," she continues, "you double down and write your own version of our joint column, ignoring my draft completely."

I try again. "Look, I panicked. The deadline was tight. I wanted something, but—" I hesitate, lose the thread, and she's already ahead of me.

She says, "You didn't ask. You decided for both of us, and now you want me to tell you it's okay. That's what you want, isn't it?"

I want to say no. I want to say yes. I want to say something that will erase the way her eyes are burning through me, but I can't.

The corridor is full of other people now, but none of them matter. She's the only person in the world, and she's leaving.

She steps past me, the scent of her perfume spiking in the cold. As she passes, she says, "You didn't think. Full stop."

The tap of her heels on the tile is the only sound. I stand there, watching her walk away, and for once, there's nothing clever left in me. Nothing to say, nothing to fight for, nothing but the slow, cold realisation that this is exactly how we always lose each other: me, running ahead, her, left behind.

I let the silence fill up the space she's left, and try to remember the last time I didn't need to win.

Outside, the city is grey and endless, the sky a blank page, waiting for someone better to write the next line.

TWENTY-ONE

♥

GRACE

The night is so quiet when I get in that for a moment I wonder if the world has ended while I was in transit. My flat—tiny, underheated, all corners and grudges—smells faintly of the two-day-old burrito on the counter and the deodorant I impulse-bought last week, thinking it would make me a better person. It didn't.

I dump my bag, step over a tangle of shoes and the basket of clean laundry that's still waiting to be put away, and ignore the creeping army of unopened post under the letterbox. The kitchen is an active crime scene: three half-empty wine glasses on the table (all mine, all different evenings), a scattering of notebooks with the kind of margin doodles that would get you referred in primary school, and an overflowing bin of failed meal deals. In the sink, the remains of a heroic attempt at risotto—mostly mushrooms and salt, stuck to the pan like cement.

I should shower, or at least change into pyjamas that don't look like I mugged a cartoon character. Instead, I stand in front of the microwave, holding a Sainsbury's chicken tikka ready meal in one hand and my phone in the other. I don't remember buying it. I don't remember most of today.

The anger is a constant, like an earworm or a pressure system. Even now, standing here in the soft, off-white humiliation of the energy-saving bulb, I'm running through the argument again, every word from Paul echoing in my skull. "You didn't have to go nuclear." As if he's ever done anything else.

The ready meal goes in. Two minutes forty-five seconds on high. I press the buttons harder than strictly necessary, the plastic wrap squeaking under my thumb. The phone is already in my other hand, the contact list blinking up at me: Zara, top of the feed, her icon a photo of the two of us at graduation. I hit call and put her on speaker, tucking the phone under my chin while I grab a fork and a plate from the cupboard.

She picks up on the third ring, still breathless from whatever workout or subterfuge she's running. "Tell me you're not at your desk."

I snort, tug at the plastic wrap. "I'm home. I'm microwaving something that technically qualifies as food."

She makes a noise that's equal parts relief and disgust. "I'll pray for your colon. How was the murder scene?"

"Worse than expected." I sit on the edge of the table, nudging aside a wine glass to make space. "He did it, Zara. He went full Lord of the Flies. Wrote his own version and sent it without telling me. Then acted like I'd forced his hand."

"Please tell me you set him on fire," she says, with a sincerity I can only admire.

I let out a breath. "I wanted to. But Sarah had already picked his version. 'Sharper voice,' she said. 'Next time CC each other, don't make me play referee.' Like I'm the problem."

She's silent for a beat, which is rare. "Did you tell him what you really think?"

"Ha. Not really." I jab the fork into the chicken, watch the sauce ooze. "I called him out for being a selfish bastard, if that counts. But it's pointless. He doesn't care."

"That's not true," Zara says, voice dropping a register. "He cares too much. That's why he acts like such a bellend."

"I'd prefer if he cared less," I say, mouth full of microwaved rice. "Or at least cared in a way that didn't involve destroying my career for the sake of his ego."

She laughs. "Grace, your career is the only thing more indestructible than your taste in men."

"If he were just a colleague, I'd probably have just slapped him by now. But it's—" I break off, chewing the inside of my cheek. I can feel the old resentment pooling in my chest. "It's complicated."

"You mean, you still fancy him," she says, in the tone of someone diagnosing a treatable illness.

"Don't," I reply. "It's not— It's just unfinished business. That's all."

Zara makes a noise, the kind she reserves for people who deny needing therapy. "Look. You were always the smarter one. The better one. He knows it, and it scares him shitless. That's why he keeps trying to get one over on you."

I pace, meal in hand, a hot trickle of tikka sauce burning my thumb. "Why does it always have to be a competition? Why can't he just—" I remonstrate to an empty room. "Why can't he just say, 'Nice work, Grace, let's do it together'?"

There's a pause, the hiss of her boiler in the background. "Because he thinks you'll say no."

I stare at the food on my plate, sauce dotting my knuckles, and for a moment I am so tired I could sleep standing up. "I wouldn't. I mean, I— Not now."

Zara's voice is soft. "You want him to see you. That's all."

I laugh, but it's a brittle, empty sound. "He sees me every day. That's the problem."

She lets me hang in silence. Then, as I'm wiping sauce off

my hand with a paper towel, she says, "Maybe you're not mad because he wrote it. Maybe you're mad because you still want him to ask permission first."

"That's not—"

"It is. But don't let the truth get in the way of a good martyr story. Eat your dinner, Grace. Love you."

I hang up before I can process the implication, the phone still pressed to my cheek, the words echoing in my ear.

The flat is silent again. I stand by the table, and try to decide if I want to throw the phone, or just throw up.

The anger hasn't gone, but now it has company—a slow, crawling shame, the kind that lodges in the hollow of your throat and won't move no matter how much you swallow. I set the phone down, slide into the chair, and stare at the mess of wine glasses and empty notebooks.

I want to call her back, to tell her she's wrong, that I don't care what Paul Callaghan thinks or says or does. That he's just another footnote in a long, undistinguished career of men who didn't get it.

But I can't. Because, for the first time in months, maybe ever, I know she's right.

I spoon up a mouthful of congealed rice, the flavourless orange sludge, and feel the humiliation of the day condense into a single, burning point behind my eyes.

It's not the story. It never was.

I want him to see me.

And he never, ever does.

The past lives in blue light and second-hand smoke.

I close my eyes and I'm back in the student newsroom at Sheffield, the ceiling barely a foot above my head. There are two dozen computers and maybe half as many chairs, but only one really matters tonight: the battered Mac at the news desk, where Paul is slouched with a bottle of Beck's in one hand and a layout proof in the other, legs splayed like he's daring the furniture to collapse under him.

We've done it. We've actually done it. The students' union president bribery story—two weeks of fake names, burner emails, and rummaging through bins behind the admin building—has gone live, and the inbox is already full of threats, corrections, and three separate invitations to fight. It's nearly one in the morning. The only people left in the building are us, a security guard who sometimes sleeps behind the front desk, and the ghost of every writer who ever thought they'd end up at the *Guardian* before the world set them straight.

Paul grins at me over the rim of his bottle. There's ink on his jaw, and his hair is all wrong, and the only clean part of his shirt is the patch where he's wiped off his hands.

"Did you see that email from the vice chancellor?" he says, voice low so it won't echo in the emptiness. "He actually used the phrase 'disgruntled element.' That's a real thing. I thought it was just in Cold War films."

I let out a cackle, spin my own chair until it hits the desk and nearly takes out the waste bin. "He also called us 'juvenile anarchists,' which is basically a compliment at this point."

Paul beams, the gap in his front teeth visible for the first time since yesterday's all-nighter. He leans in, waving the page. "We're going to get so sued."

"Only if we're wrong," I say, grabbing for the proof and missing, which means I have to half-climb the desk to reach it. My knee lands against his thigh, but he doesn't flinch; if anything, he shifts a little to make more space for me. The warmth of his leg seeps through my tights. I ignore it, or pretend to.

We scan the page together, heads bent so close that if I turn even a fraction, I'll catch his aftershave—cheap, citrus, somehow sharper than his wit. The silence is a blanket, thick and private, broken only by the distant hum of the ancient wall heater.

I run a Biro down the column, hunting for typos. "Did you actually fact-check this bit about the funding, or are you just hoping no one will notice?"

He shrugs, which is as close to an admission of guilt as he gets. "Technically, there's a source. Whether he was sober at the time is a different question."

I try to glare, but end up laughing instead, and it goes on longer than it should. I nudge his shoulder with mine, hard enough to nearly tip him off the chair. He retaliates by bumping my arm, which smears a line of blue ink across my knuckles.

He looks down at the stain and grins wider. "Now it's a blood pact."

"Gross," I say, but I don't wipe it away. We go back to the page, this time reading slower, the laughter softening into something like pride. Two hours ago, we were at each other's throats about whether to run with the allegations or bury them until the university's executive team forced our hand. Now, there's no question. We're the story, and everyone knows it.

Paul's voice drops, suddenly serious. "You know this is going to make a mess, right?"

I nod. "Always does."

He glances over, eyes brighter than the halogen tubes overhead. "Wouldn't want to do it with anyone else."

I feel the words hit, a physical thing just under my sternum. I want to answer, to say something that isn't a punchline or a self-own, but the words get stuck behind my teeth. Instead, I let the moment sit, long enough for the screensaver to flicker on and paint the ceiling with shifting blue squares.

We sit there, beer between our knees, page between our

hands, and for a second the whole city is silent, holding its breath.

He breaks it first. He always does.

"Applied for an internship at *The Chronicle*, by the way," he says, like it's nothing. "Figured it was time to see if I could hack it with the big kids."

The laugh escapes me before I can stop it. "You? In a real newsroom? You do realise you'd have to work office hours, and get dressed?"

He barks a laugh, loud and sharp. "Yeah, I'm not really looking forward to that bit."

We finish reading the page. He makes a mark in the margin, and I do the same, our hands colliding. For a moment, neither of us pulls away. His fingers are warm, steady. I let mine linger longer than I should.

The silence comes back, thicker now. I look up, and his eyes are on me, direct, unblinking. For the first time all night, I don't know what to say.

He does. "Why don't you apply?"

I snort, but the words come out quiet. "Interning at *The Chronicle*? No, I want to travel for a bit. Get it out of my system before, you know, having to face the reality of work for like, the rest of my life."

He smiles, but it's softer now, the edge gone. "Probably for the best. If you did apply, they'd pick you over me for sure."

"That's not true."

It's late when we finally pack up and notice the security guard's snores echoing from the foyer. We fumble with coats and laptops and the bundle of proofs, the shared energy crackling even as the night gets colder. Outside, the rain has started —sharp, icy, blowing straight in from the Pennines. I shiver, and Paul shrugs out of his jacket, drapes it over my shoulders with a theatrical flourish.

"Chivalry's dead," I say, "but thanks for the corpse."

He laughs, and for a second I think he's going to say something else, something important. Instead, he just stands there, hands in his pockets, watching the streetlights flicker through the rain.

We part ways at the tram stop.

He says, "See you tomorrow, chief."

I say, "Bring your own snacks next time."

The city is empty, slick with water, and for once, the walk home feels lighter, like I could float above the pavement if I let myself.

The flat is dark when I get in. My housemates are either out or unconscious. I go straight to my room, kick off my boots, and dump the proofs on my bed. The adrenaline is still there, sharp and sweet, refusing to let me sleep. I pace, turn on the lamp, and reread the margin notes until my eyes blur.

There's a letter waiting for me on the desk. I recognise the typeface—University of Sheffield, official and unwelcoming—but it's addressed to me, which is rare enough to make my hands shake a little as I open it.

Inside: a single sheet, letterhead crisp, ink barely dry.

Dear Miss Hampton,

We are pleased to inform you that your name has been submitted for consideration to the internship programme at *The London Chronicle*...

I stop reading. The words are swimming.

I never applied. I never even thought to.

The realisation is a punch, not to the gut, but to the soft space just behind my ribs, where hope usually hides. I sit down, the mattress sagging beneath me, and stare at the letter until the words resolve into a single, unanswerable fact.

Paul will think I went behind his back.

He'll find out tomorrow, or the day after, and when he does, everything we've built together—articles, ink, laughter, the quiet touch of hands on proofs—will be gone. It will change nothing, and it will ruin everything.

I lean back, let the page fall from my hand, and stare up at the ceiling, where the blue afterimage of the newsroom is burned into the plaster.

I wish, for a second, that I could go back to thirty minutes ago, when we were only worried about lawsuits and cold rain and the thrill of beating the odds together.

But I can't.

Instead, I sit there, listening to the storm build outside, and know that tomorrow I'll have to start all over, alone.

It's almost funny, in its own way.

Almost.

TWENTY-TWO

♥

PAUL

If you ever wanted a demonstration of late capitalism in action, you could do worse than standing outside Miriam Levin's glass office at nine in the morning, watching the new Editor-in-Chief eat the last remnants of your dignity with a smile. The glass isn't soundproof, but it may as well be; everything she says is calibrated to a register that's both condescending and plausible, and everything I say gets stuck, raw, somewhere at the back of my throat. Behind her, the newsroom pulses and shrieks—phones, printers, the thrum of collective despair— while she sits at her desk lording it over the riffraff.

She doesn't even offer me a seat. I take the chair anyway, out of spite.

Her desk is an ocean of negative space. Not a single pen out of line, no errant Post-it, just a brand-new MacBook, a Montblanc, and a pad of A4 perfectly squared to the grain. It's so aggressively clean I half expect her to start surgery on me right here, skipping anaesthetic.

She looks up, glasses perched low, the frames so thin they

could be a hallucination. "Paul," she says, all liquid consonants. "Thanks for coming in early."

I nod. I've got nothing else.

She gestures to the chair I've already occupied, a small frown at my initiative.

"I wanted to talk about your current... productivity cycle."

She says it like it's a chronic illness, or maybe a regrettable kink.

I keep my jaw tight, but the fingers of my right hand start tapping, the first metronome of the inevitable spiral. "If this is about the copy desk, I—"

"It isn't," she interrupts, which is the same as saying it absolutely is. "It's about your output on the Modern Romance project." She flicks her wrist, and the laptop screen rotates with the precision of a guillotine. The open tab is a Google Doc with my name and Grace's in the header, and a highlighted note from Sarah that says, simply, "MORE COHERENCE PLZ."

Miriam never raises her voice. She doesn't need to. "The column is supposed to be collaborative, Paul. Not a live-fire exercise."

"Grace and I have a working dynamic," I say, and my voice comes out flatter than intended. "The bickering is part of the brand."

She glances over the top of her glasses. "The only brand I'm concerned about is the *Chronicle's*. I brought you over from *The Express* because you're supposed to have an edge. Instead, you're stuck in a loop of"—she checks the notes, as if confirming a diagnosis—"personal vendetta and performative sabotage."

I smile, but only with the left half of my face. "That's called journalism."

She doesn't blink. "I want a final, publishable column on my desk by Friday. With *both* your names on it." She leans in, steeples her hands. "If not, I'll have to consider strategic realignment."

There it is, the velvet-covered threat. They teach it at Management School, module one.

I bite the inside of my cheek. I can see Grace's edits in the margin, and I know exactly which words will end up in print and which ones will end up in the bin. "You want it, you'll get it."

She nods, writes something down with the Montblanc, a flourish of blue so sharp it's almost a wound. "I'm glad we understand each other."

There's nothing left to say. I stand, careful to make it look casual, and reach for the door handle. The glass distorts my reflection into something slick and haunted.

"Oh, Paul?" she says, just as I'm halfway out the door.

I pause. My shoulders are so tense I can hear the vertebrae grinding.

She tilts her head just a few degrees, like a chess player checking a gambit. "This is your last warning. We do need to make cuts. Don't make that decision easy for me."

"Understood," I say, because anything else would be career suicide.

She offers a smile so thin it could slice ham. "Good. See you at the standup."

I walk out, pretending not to care that every eye in the newsroom tracks my progress across the open floor. I make it to the end of the corridor before my hands start shaking. I clench them tight, but the tremor just migrates upward, nesting somewhere behind my left eye.

I can already hear Grace's voice in my head, mocking me: "Got another motivational seminar from the suits, did you?" The worst part is, I couldn't argue.

I tell myself I'll write the column. I tell myself I'll make it brilliant, and angry, and as sharp as the day we left a legacy at the student newspaper with our last joint byline. I tell myself a lot of things.

There's work to do.

There's always work to do.

The trick to living alone is to pretend the mess is temporary. You can forgive anything if you tell yourself it's for the sake of efficiency, or hygiene, or (my favourite) "creative flow." This is why the inside of my flat looks like the forensic aftermath of an unsolved homicide. The radiator's on, but it only heats the air directly above it, so the rest of the room is locked in a kind of permafrost.

I set the laptop on the table, pushing aside a pyramid of unopened post and a tangle of charging cables that no longer connect to anything I own. The screen blinks awake, and there it is: the column. "Modern Romance" top of the doc, followed by two hundred words of pure cringe. I read it, then read it again, hoping something will jump out and slap me across the face. Nothing does.

My fingers hover over the keyboard, but the only thing I can summon is the memory of Miriam's threat: "The Board expects results." The Board. The mythical pantheon that sits above us all, hands clean, waiting for the next human sacrifice.

I try to type, but the words come out clotted, lumpen, dead on arrival.

I get up and pace the room, stepping over a pile of laundry so dense it might actually have tectonic plates. I run my hands through my hair, which is already at maximum chaos, and then stop in front of the bookshelf. It's full of old textbooks I never sold or took to the charity shop, the spines broken and margins scrawled with insults—mostly from Grace, in her handwriting, which is impossible to misinterpret. There's a box on the bottom shelf labelled "Sheffield." I pull it out and thumb through the contents, half-expecting to find an answer in the debris.

There's an old student card with a photo so embarrassing I nearly put it through the shredder: me, eighteen, hair down to my ears, face so thin I look malnourished. I set it aside. There's a handful of battered notebooks, the corners chewed, pages filled with deadlines and doodles and, on one, a list of "Best Column Titles Never Used." I flip through, and the last page is just a single line: "Make it matter."

At the bottom of the box, folded and yellowed, is a photo from the university paper. Grace and I stood in the student newsroom, both mid-laugh, cheeks flushed, ink on our hands. She's got her hair up and is making a rude gesture at someone off-camera. I'm looking at her, not the lens. The photo is so honest it hurts.

I close my eyes. The air feels thinner than before.

Something else is on the bookshelf: a tri-fold leaflet, bright blue, NHS logo in the corner. "Understanding Your Heart Attack." It's from three months ago, when my dad finally lost the fight with his arteries and landed in hospital. I'd spent a week sleeping in the ward waiting room, mainlining vending machine chocolate and trying not to think about the world outside.

When he came to, the first thing he said was, "Did you bring the paper?" The second thing was, "Don't tell your mum."

I never told anyone, not even Jamie, who's supposed to be my best mate. I shoved it all into a box, like I do with everything, thinking I'd deal with it later.

Back at the table, the column is still waiting, blank and judgy. I force myself to sit. My chest feels tight, but I ignore it.

I type, "*Modern romance is a game of mutual destruction. The only way to win is not to care.*" I delete it. I try again: "*In the age of radical transparency, the only thing we're afraid of is being known.*" I delete that, too. Every sentence is a hostage note, and I can't figure out who's holding the gun.

I scroll up and see Grace's comments from last week, each more devastating than the last. "*Unfocused,*" she wrote, next to a paragraph I thought was brilliant. "*Try harder,*" she typed in the margin. There's one near the end that just says, "*This is why you're not happy.*"

I lean back and let the chair tip until my head hits the wall. I stare at the ceiling, counting the hairline cracks.

Maybe this is why I'm not happy. Maybe I really am allergic to my own feelings.

The phone buzzes again. I don't answer. I can't.

Instead, I open a new window and search "chronic stress symptoms." The first hit is an NHS page, the same shade of blue as the heart attack leaflet. I close the tab, then open another. I don't know what I'm looking for, but I keep looking.

The room feels smaller by the minute. The walls are moving in, slow and silent, ready to press the breath out of me.

I pick up the photo of me and Grace, hold it up to the window. Outside, the city is smudged and lifeless, a hundred thousand people pretending they've got it figured out. I press the photo flat against the glass. It leaves a grease mark.

I think about calling her, just to hear her voice, but I know exactly what she'd say. She'd say, "You're an idiot." She'd say, "You could have just asked." She'd say, "It's not too late, unless you want it to be."

The air is so thin now that I can barely breathe.

I set the photo down, close the laptop, and slide out of the chair. My legs are numb. I shuffle to the window and watch the traffic crawl by, headlights smeared into comets by the rain.

I tell myself I don't need anyone. I say it out loud, just to make it real. "I don't need anyone."

But the echo in the room sounds like a lie.

My phone lights up again, and I let it ring.

I'm still staring out the window when the sun sets, washing the city in orange, then red, then the grey of total failure. I let the darkness come. I let it in.

For the first time in months, maybe ever, I know that I'm not okay.

I just don't know what to do about it.

The phone rings again.

I let it ring.

TWENTY-THREE

GRACE

The thing about turning up at a man's flat unannounced is that you get exactly the reaction you deserve. Namely: the look of a startled dog who expected the postman and instead found God at the door, bearing tandoori chicken and two cans of Polish lager.

I stand on the landing, a foil bag sweating grease in one hand, a six-pack (minus four) in the other. The corridor is the colour of old nicotine, and the overhead bulb is flickering in a way that makes my shadow vibrate on the concrete walls. I can hear Paul's TV through the door, something football-shaped and angry, the commentator's voice rising and falling in waves. There's a second where I think, *Don't do it, Grace, just bin the food and call it character growth*, but then I remember the alternative is going back to my flat and the thousand-watt silence of a fridge full of nothing.

I knock. Three raps, even, the way people do in old movies before they get murdered.

The TV cuts off mid-sentence. Muffled footsteps, then

the scrape of the chain, then the door cracks open. Paul peers out, hair at maximum entropy, T-shirt reading "YES, I'M STILL SAD" in a font that looks like it was designed by a man with strong opinions about IPA. He blinks twice, sees me, and does this microscopic flinch like the air just changed pressure.

"Didn't order anything," he says.

"Yeah, I know. Thought I'd chance it." I hold up the take-away and the cans, do my best not to look at the slice of flat visible behind him: chaotic, familiar, maybe more so than when I last saw it. "You looked like someone who needed carbs and company."

He stares at the food like it might bite him. "This a mercy mission, or are you here to salt the earth?"

"Can't it be both?" I ask, already stepping past him. The hallway smells of dust and something faintly medicinal, like plasters or paracetamol. I hear the door click shut, the lock turning.

The living room has the look of an animal nest: newspapers in islands across the carpet, takeaway cartons forming a sort of archipelago on the coffee table, laptop open and humming at one end of the battered sofa. There are three mugs in play, all half-full of tea in various states of abandonment. I put the food down, nudge aside a pile of unopened post, and start unpacking.

Paul lingers by the door, hands deep in his tracksuit bottoms. For a moment, neither of us says anything. I remember all the nights we spent co-writing in the student newsroom, arguing over which headlines would definitely get us sued and which would just earn us a strongly worded letter.

He clears his throat. "You didn't have to—"

"I know," I say. "But you left my copy of *The Journalist's Guide to Personal Ruin* in your bathroom, and I want it back."

He almost smiles, but only at the corners. "That's in the

pile marked 'evidence.' Don't touch, or it'll break the chain of custody."

I dig out two tinfoil trays, hand him the one with the red dot on the lid. "Tandoori chicken, extra chips, a Keema Naan that's already gone flaccid. I got the good stuff."

He takes it, eyeing the food and me with equal suspicion. "You really sure you don't want to just kill me and be done with it?"

"Give it time," I say, cracking open a can.

The sofa is technically big enough for two, but the detritus means I take the armchair, which is weirdly lopsided. The springs poke through the upholstery in a way that encourages excellent posture or permanent spinal injury. Paul slides onto the sofa, tucks his feet up under him, and opens the tray with the care of a man handling radioactive material.

The first ten minutes are wordless. I eat, alternating between naan and lager, and watch as he shovels food with the mechanical efficiency of someone who hasn't eaten all day. I don't press for conversation. The windows are cracked just enough to let the sound of rain in, and the smell out.

I let my eyes wander around the room. His whiteboard is now propped against the wall, dense with scribbles: names, arrows, the word "MOTIVE" circled and underlined. There are two piles of books on the radiator, one fiction, one non-, and a sheaf of printouts that looks suspiciously like our last column draft, annotated in red and blue.

Every so often, Paul glances at me, as if to check I haven't morphed into a snake mid-bite. Each time I catch him, he goes back to the food, chewing in silence.

We finish eating at the same time, synchronised like animals raised in the same lab. I stack the cartons, wipe my fingers on the napkin, and crack my knuckles, one at a time, just to fill the space.

"So," he says, finally. "What's the real reason you're here?"

I reach for my can, swirl the dregs. "Maybe I just didn't want to eat alone."

He snorts. "Sure. Because what this flat needed was more awkward energy."

"It was a coin toss," I say. "Awkward here, or awkward on my own. At least here, the heating sometimes works."

He slumps back into the sofa, wipes sauce from his lip. "You ever think we were better when we hated each other?"

I think about the newsroom, about the red-inked pages and the line he drew—no, the line I drew, daring him to cross it. I think about what it cost to be the better writer, and whether that's a thing you get to keep forever, or whether every win comes with a tally of people you left behind.

"I never hated you," I say quietly.

He looks at me then, really looks, as if seeing what's left after you sand all the surface down to bone. "Could've fooled me."

The TV is still paused, a smear of frozen motion on the screen. I want to ask if he's okay. I want to say, "You look like shit," but it's obvious. The colour's gone from his face, and there are lines at the corners of his mouth that weren't there last week.

"Are you—?" I start, then abort the sentence. "Do you—"

"I'm fine." He says it so fast it's automatic. "Just tired. Deadline, you know. Miriam is allergic to my face."

"She's not," I say. "She just expects you to give a shit."

He laughs, low, and the sound is almost human. "Maybe she's the only one left, then."

We end up sitting on the carpet, backs pressed to the sofa, knees drawn up. The city is dark now, save for the smudges of light leaking in through the single-glazed window, and the room has that thick, post-takeaway silence where you can hear the blood moving behind your own ears. Paul balances his beer on one knee, fingers tapping the can not quite in time with the clock. My own can is long empty, condensation pooling on the carpet where I've set it down. Neither of us wants to move, not even to queue up the next distraction.

There's a lamp on the end table, the kind that casts dramatic shadows and makes you look older, or tired, or both. I watch as the light bends around the bones of his face, the half-healed nick on his chin, the hollow under his left eye that never filled in after uni. He stares at the wall, as if expecting it to blink first.

My hands are restless. I peel at the ring on my thumb, rolling it up and down, the friction burn familiar. It would be easier to talk if I were drunk, but I'm not—not enough. The words just bunch and knot behind my teeth.

He breaks the quiet, voice softer than the rumble of traffic outside. "Did you ever think it would turn out like this?"

I consider the question, letting it hang. "What, the byline slap-fight, or the general drift into mediocrity?"

He gives a thin, horizontal smile. "Either. Both."

"Not really. I thought I'd be dead by thirty."

"That's optimistic." He drains the can, sets it next to mine, and picks at a frayed thread on his joggers. "When we were at Sheffield, I thought you'd be the next Marina Hyde. Or at least get famous enough to be cancelled."

I laugh, but it's a weak sound. "I peaked in second year. Everything after that's been a slow glide down the other side."

He nods, and we let the quiet settle again, two embers cooling on opposite sides of a dead fire.

I fidget, dig my nail into the soft wood of the coffee table next to me. "Paul."

He doesn't look up, but I know he's listening.

"I didn't lie to you," I say, voice smaller than intended. "Not about the copy, or the edits, or any of that. About the internship. At *The Chronicle*. The one that started all this."

Now he looks at me, side-on, a flicker of wary confusion. "What are you talking about?"

I wrap my arms around my knees, chin tucked in. "My tutor submitted the application. I didn't know until they emailed the shortlist. I thought it was a joke at first. I wasn't even going to go to the interview, except Zara made me come back early from Thailand—she said it'd be good practice, that no one from our year had a shot."

He says nothing, but his jaw tenses.

"I had planned a full twelve months in Southeast Asia," I say, a half-confession. "I thought if I just tanked the interview, I'd be free. But I got there, and—" I stop, remembering the sudden slick of sweat in the lobby, the way the Editor-in-Chief's handshake crushed my fingers, the impossible logic that said if I made it look like I didn't care, I wouldn't be hurt if I failed. "I thought you'd get it. I wanted you to get it."

He shakes his head once, sharp, like he's clearing water from his ears. "That's bullshit."

"It's not," I say. "I never wanted it. Not really. But I didn't know how to tell you. You were so angry, and it felt like—if I tried to explain, you'd just think I was rubbing it in."

He stares at the carpet, eyes tracking the pattern like there's a code in the synthetic fibres. "Why are you telling me this now?"

I make myself look at him. "Because if I don't, I'll be stuck here forever, replaying every version of what could've happened if we'd just—" I gesture, helpless, at the air between us. "If we'd just talked."

He's silent for a long time, and I can see the calculation in his jaw, the slow grind of teeth against tongue. When he does speak, it's a half-whisper.

"I built my whole adult life on the idea that you fucked me over. That you saw your chance and took it." He lets that sit, ugly and raw. "I spent years pretending I didn't care, but every time I saw your byline, it was like being told again that you were better, and I'd never catch up."

I could reach out, touch his arm, say something soft. I don't. This is a wound that doesn't need a bandage; it needs to bleed dry.

He laughs, a sharp, empty sound. "You should've just told me. I'd have hated you for a week, but at least it would've been real."

"I tried, but you didn't want to hear it," I say, which is cowardly, but true. "You never did, when it mattered."

He nods, but it's more of a flinch than an agreement. "So what now?"

I don't have an answer. The lamp hums, the fridge cycles on in the kitchen, a lorry barrels down the road and rattles the pane. I wish I could freeze the room, pin this moment down like an insect, and keep it from dissolving into the next fight, the next byline, the next round of who hurt whom more.

Instead, I take a breath, let it out slowly. "Now we write the column. And we try not to fuck each other over. Just this once."

He looks at me, and for the first time all night, his face is completely open, stripped of the usual snark and self-defence. There's pain there, yes, but also something softer, like the bit of sky right before sunrise.

He says, "I think I hated you because I couldn't bear to hate myself."

There's nothing to say to that. I just nod, and the air between us shifts, imperceptible but real. A détente. Maybe even a truce.

He reaches for the laptop on the table, powers it up with a click. The screen glows blue, casting both our faces in the same artificial halo. He types a few words, stops, then glances at me.

"You want the first line, or should I?"

"Surprise me."

It's not forgiveness, or anything like it. But for a while, we write together again, shoulder to shoulder, the city outside shrinking to a manageable hum. We argue, but not like before. We disagree, but don't draw blood. We work.

And in the end, the story's better than either of us could have made it alone.

It's not love, but it's something. And for now, that's enough.

TWENTY-FOUR

PAUL

We hone and preen and edit the article for the whole day, in between stand-ups, department meetings, and a talk from HR about new standardised employment contracts that will be rolled out over the coming weeks.

It's gone half ten at night and the *Chronicle* newsroom looks like the set of a post-apocalypse sitcom: half the monitors are still on, casting blue phantoms over unclaimed chairs; a semi-circle of dead takeaway containers forming a defensive perimeter around the Features pod; the last, heroic cup of coffee clinging to its own relevance in the centre of the table. The rest of the staff are long gone, scattered to pubs, or home, or the hell of late trains. Only Grace and I remain, custodians of the blue-light graveyard, screens open, fingers ticking away at the keys in that ancient, adversarial duet.

No music. No gossip, no overhead banter. Just the gentle echo of typing and the intermittent rattle of rain against the glass, London's most enduring refrain. There's something almost religious about it. I'm not sure what denomination, but definitely one with a heavy focus on self-flagellation and the long, slow death of optimism.

Grace is sitting two desks over, half-turned so her chair's at an angle that says, "I could leave at any moment, but I'm not going to." She's in work mode: hair tied back with a Biro sticking out, jumper sleeves shoved up past the elbows, lips pressed together in that tight line she uses when she's reading. Every time she finds a phrase worth underlining, her eyebrow arches like it's being winched up by a tiny, angry crane. There are four highlighters within reach, each with a different tactical purpose. The pink one is for personal attacks. The blue is for praise, or what passes for it in her taxonomy.

I try not to stare, but the alternative is looking at my own screen, which is less fun and considerably more demoralising. The column's latest draft sits open, cursor blinking at the end of a paragraph that neither of us can quite bring ourselves to delete or improve. If you believe the project management chart, the next steps are "harmonise tone" and "finalise structure." What that really means is "argue about the angle for another hour," followed by an hour of not talking to each other while we process what was said.

Tonight, though, something's shifted. The last round of edits was clinical but not cruel; the usual bloodletting has been replaced by a sort of resigned professionalism, as if we've both agreed—silently—that the time for mutual destruction is over. Or maybe we're just too tired to keep it up.

I lean back in my chair, stretching until my spine cracks. The ceiling tiles above are speckled with old water stains, one of them shaped exactly like the county of Kent, if Kent had suffered a series of targeted airstrikes. The overhead light is down to one functioning tube, and it flickers at intervals that almost sync with my pulse.

Grace lets out a long, audible sigh. Not annoyed, just... exhausted. She taps her pen against her bottom lip, a habit so ingrained I'm not sure she knows she does it. The green high-lighter is in her other hand, poised and twitchy. I watch as she makes a note in the margin, pauses, then erases it, only to write something else in smaller, more aggressive print.

It's a perfect study in how we work: me, building up a wall of defensive sentences; her, picking through the mortar for weaknesses. I used to think the only thing holding us together was our capacity to irritate each other. Now, I'm not so sure.

"You ever wonder if we're just making the same argument, over and over?" I ask, not looking directly at her.

She blinks, surprised by the break in protocol, then shrugs. "Every relationship is a feedback loop. Ours just has better editing."

I snort, low and involuntary. "I don't know. I think we're recycling material at this point."

"It's called a motif, Callaghan. Read a book."

We lapse back into silence. She's right, of course. She always is. That's half the problem.

After a minute, she gets up and crosses to the kitchen alcove—a three-metre strip of Formica counter and a kettle so ancient it might qualify as heritage. She pours herself a glass of tap water, swirls it, and takes a long drink. The way she stands—one hip cocked, head tilted, sleeve already wet from leaning on the counter—reminds me, against my better judgement, of nights back at uni, when we'd stay up insane hours just to beat the next deadline, or just to outlast the other.

She comes back, drops into her chair, and swivels to face me.

"You're doing it again," she says.

I blink. "What?"

"The thing where you stare at the screen like it's going to finish the column for you. It's not AI. You have to actually type something."

"Thought I'd let the universe intervene," I say, but my heart's not in the joke.

She softens, just a fraction. "I read your last section. It's actually good."

"Don't oversell it," I mumble, embarrassed.

She leans forward, elbows on knees. "You know you can just say it, right?"

I pretend not to know what she means, but the flush in my face gives me away.

"That you miss it," she says, eyes fixed on the pile of edits between us. "The arguing. The writing. All of it."

I look at her, properly now, and for a second the wall of bullshit I keep between us crumbles. "I do," I say, barely above a whisper.

Grace is not built for vulnerability. She deflects, always, with sarcasm or facts or both. But this time she just sits with it, lets the air fill with everything we're not saying.

"I miss it, too," she says, and the sound of it hits me somewhere between my lungs and my sternum. "Not the drama. Just... the rhythm."

I want to say something clever, something that will make it less dangerous. Instead, I blurt, "You're brilliant, you know."

It's a car crash of a compliment. The kind that gets airbagged and replayed in slow motion at the inquest.

She blinks, startled, then smiles—small and crooked, the way she used to when I'd caught her off guard in the old days. "Careful, or I'll start to think you like me."

I do. I always have. Even when I was supposed to hate her, even when it was easier to make her the villain in my own story.

She looks away, but not before I catch the flicker of something real in her eyes. She tucks a strand of hair behind her ear, takes a steadying breath, and picks up the green highlighter again.

There's a long, comfortable silence—the kind you only get with people who have known every angle of you and decided to stick around anyway.

"We should probably finish this," she says.

"Yeah," I reply. "Probably."

We work. Not like before. Like now: two people who know how to hurt each other, but have chosen, tonight, not to. Two people who are better together, even if it's just for this moment.

TWENTY-FIVE

GRACE

The flat is freezing when I walk in, and it'll be at least an hour before the single heater in the living room kicks out enough warmth to make removing my coat feel like a safe choice.

The place looks exactly how I left it—two mugs on the table, last night's *Evening Standard* slouched against the skirting board. My phone is on seven percent. I plug it in, letting the blue-white glow flood the room.

Three new emails—two from Viv and one from the Comms team—all about tomorrow's follow-up piece. I skim, reply where necessary, then—because I'm weak—open Twitter. Grace Hampton: still trending. A shoutout from an MP gets a screenshot. Proof, maybe. Or just something to gloat over later.

For a few minutes, there's something like peace. Not the gentle, golden kind—more the after-a-fistfight variety, where your bones still hum and the adrenaline hasn't quite burned off. I breathe it in, letting the city's noise settle into the background.

At 00:11, the phone pings.

Unknown number. UK code. No name, no icon, no prior messages. Just a single line:

> Is this Grace Hampton from the Chronicle?

I blink. Could be spam. Could be a wrong number. Could be one of those 'urgent' messages that turns out to be a phishing link.

> Who's asking?

Silence. I pour a glass of water, watch condensation bead and run down the glass. Another ping:

> You wrote that piece about Kidz Trust.

I hesitate, then give in to curiosity.

> Yes. Did you have a problem with it?

> The article barely scratched the surface. You need to look deeper.

That gets my attention. No abuse, no obvious scam—just an accusation hanging in the air.

> If you know something, you should say it.

> You and your colleague didn't look hard enough.

The urge to defend Paul sparks instantly, but I tamp it down. He's perfectly capable of defending himself—and besides, I'd rather hear where this is going.

I'm listening.

Nothing. Ten minutes go by. I drink the water, check my emails again. Still nothing.

Halfway through brushing my teeth, the phone lights up.

Not safe to text about it. Too dangerous to get involved.

I spit, wipe my mouth.

Then why contact me?

The typing ellipsis bounces, slow and deliberate. Whoever this is, they want to be chased.

We can meet in person.

A long pause. I almost think I've pushed too hard—until:

14 Saxon Ave. Felixstowe. Noon tomorrow.

I read it twice. I've been to Felixstowe maybe twice in my life, both in the summer. February's a hell of a time to request a seafront meeting.

Do I know you?

Martin Cheng.

I try coaxing more, but the phone stays dark.

I lie on the sofa, staring at the ceiling, replaying every training session I've ever had—don't meet sources alone, always tell someone where you're going, keep comms traceable. I ignore every single one. Then I remember how I know Martin Cheng, and it all makes sense.

Just before sunrise, I text Paul: Road trip. You're driving. Felixstowe. Civil servant wants to talk. Bring coffee.

He sends back a thumbs-up and a GIF of a penguin shivering.

The sun comes up, the city stirs, and I sit by the window, watching the light creep across the buildings.

I don't know if it's dread or excitement. Either way, I'm ready.

You can't understand the North Sea unless it's tried to kill you at least once. This is what I'm thinking as Paul takes a corner too fast, the wind battering us so hard the entire car shimmies sideways, and a curtain of drizzle atomises against the windscreen. We're in a village so small the only pub is called The Pub, and every window is advertising "Seaview" even though the only thing visible is a wall of wet, horizontal grey. He refuses to use Google Maps, so we're running on Paul's innate sense of direction, which is not so much a compass as a very specific flavour of male stubbornness.

I try to help, straining to spot a landmark or street name through the windscreen wipers. "If you'd just slow down," I say, "we could read the street names before they blur past."

Paul smirks, never taking his eyes off the smear of cottages ahead. "If I slow down, we'll lose momentum and have to get out and push."

He's not wrong. The wind is howling hard enough to make the entire car rattle. He parks—half on the kerb, half on what looks like the remains of a paving slab—and looks at me with the kind of pride that's usually reserved for successfully parallel parking a bus.

"Why are we here again?" he asks.

"Because Martin Cheng won't talk to us any other way. If

we want to get the rest of this story over the line, we have to shake the tree ourselves." I recite this with the calm of someone who has rehearsed it in the mirror, to an audience of exactly one takeaway curry and a row of unpaid utility bills.

He shrugs into his jacket, an ancient leather thing with the arms starting to split. "Right. Lead the way, then, chief."

I do, because if there's one thing I'm good at, it's leading others into disaster. The house is three doors down, the paint a colour that used to be blue but is now mostly surrender. The garden is wild, all stinging nettle and foxglove, with a single path mowed through like the wake of a drunk lawnmower. I pull my coat tight, check the house number twice, and tap on the door.

Paul sidesteps next to me, hands in his pockets, eyes scanning the windows. "Place looks like a murder scene from a Scandi crime thriller. Type 999 on your keypad now, so all you need to do is hit 'call.'"

I ignore him. The door opens a cautious inch, revealing a sliver of face, sallow and bespectacled.

"Martin?" I say, projecting warmth and trustworthiness like a children's TV presenter.

He's aged badly—hair thinning, skin with the parboiled look of a man who eats all his meals from the reduced section. The last time I saw him, he was sweating through a suit in a government committee room, answering questions about green technology and promising the future was biodegradable. Now, he's wearing a rugby top and a face that screams: *Go away, or I'll call my solicitor.*

Paul takes over, stepping into the gap before Martin can shut the door. "We've actually crossed paths before, Martin," he says, like he's dropping a winning hand at a poker tournament. "We met at that 'Tech4Good' panel. You bought me a pint, then tried to sell me on bio-ethanol heating units. I still get spam from you."

Martin's eyes widen, as if seeing a ghost or possibly the bailiffs. He glances behind him, then opens the door a fraction more. "I remember. Sorry, I'm— Actually, can we do this another time?"

Paul ignores the cue. "We're not here to stitch you up. We just want to talk about the Bluebell Environmental contract, and why you resigned right after the payout."

Martin sags, defeated. "I shouldn't have contacted you."

"The truth is important," I say, wincing a little at my own pomposity, but shifting my weight in the doorway so he can't close it again without making a scene. "We can talk inside, if you like."

For a minute, I think he'll slam the door and call the police, but then his shoulders go slack and he waves us in. The hallway is narrow, lined with brown carpet that hasn't been vacuumed this century, and the air smells like fried onions and incense sticks.

We follow him to the cramped living room, decorated exclusively in the theme of "Coastal Retirement on a Budget." There are little wooden boats on the mantel, a faded print of a lighthouse, and an ornamental lifebuoy on the wall that says "Home Is Where the Harbour Is." The windows are covered with newspaper, the kind that doesn't get delivered to actual houses anymore.

Martin gestures to the sofa, then sits in the lone armchair, knees up, arms crossed. "You want tea?" he asks, but his tone suggests this is not a real offer.

"We're fine," I say, taking out my notebook and flipping to a fresh page. Paul sits beside me, sinking into the sofa so deeply he almost disappears.

Martin watches us, wary.

Paul is uncharacteristically gentle. "We know you were the technical director on Bluebell's bid. We know the project got fast-tracked, and we know the money vanished from the accounts within a month. We just want to know if you can tell us why."

Martin picks at the hem of his tracksuit, avoiding our eyes. "I can't talk about that," he says, voice barely above the hum of the ancient fridge in the kitchen.

"NDAs?" I say.

He shakes his head. "Worse."

Paul leans forward, elbows on knees. "Look, Martin. The thing about secrets is they have an expiry date. Our legal team is already investigating Hackney Council and has issued about forty Freedom of Information requests. When those responses come back, the council's going to scapegoat someone, probably the lowest man on the chain. You need to pre-empt that. Actually, we thought you had, and that's why you reached out. At least this way you get to tell it how it really happened."

Martin's eyes are glassy, desperate. "You don't understand. They threatened my family."

Paul's voice is soft. "Who's they?"

Martin opens and closes his mouth twice. "You know the guy who signed off on the accounts? He's not in the country anymore. And the contractors— They were all paid off through shell companies. I just did the paperwork."

I flip to the Kidz Trust published audit, slide it across the table. "This bit here," I say, "the reference numbers are identical to the ones on the 'offshore remediation' contracts and the council's purchase order. You think that's a coincidence?"

He looks at the page, then up at me. "No," he says, the word as soft as tissue.

Paul nods, slow and encouraging. "You're not the villain, Martin. But if you don't want to be the fall guy, you have to help us out."

There's a long silence, broken only by the tick of the ancient wall clock and the distant cackle of seagulls. Martin glances at the door, as if hoping for a fire drill, then says, "You can't print this."

"We can and will print anything," I say. "But we want your side, not just what we *think* happened."

He rubs his face, leaving a stripe of sweat across his forehead. "All right. The project was a front. It was always a front. The company existed to move money out of the council, via the charity, and into the hands of the people who—" He breaks off, shaking. "I didn't even know who was behind it until last week. They threatened to ruin me if I didn't play along."

I write, my pen a blur. Paul watches Martin with a look I've never seen before: a mix of empathy and pure, predatory focus.

"Who's 'they'?" Paul presses, voice low.

Martin is almost crying now. "It's all in the files. They told me to put everything in a storage unit in London. But I can't get to it. They said if I ever went back, I'd end up in a canal."

Paul looks at me, and the gears in his mind are visible behind his eyes. "Can you get us the key?" he asks.

Martin nods. "It's in the garden, taped to the leg of the trampoline."

He breathes a shuddery, miserable gasp. "If you can get the files, it's all there."

I watch as Paul takes this in, not as a story, but as a problem to be solved. He stands, stretches the stiffness from his arms. "We'll get them," he says.

Martin looks at him, disbelief and relief tangled up. "You can't go alone. They're watching. They always watch."

Paul shrugs, the same way he does when told the odds of a story panning out are next to zero. "That's our job."

I stand too, collecting my notes and tucking them away. "Thank you, Martin. We'll be careful."

He stands, but doesn't follow us to the door. His whole

body seems to fold in on itself, like a man who's already begun rehearsing his own obituary.

Outside, the wind's picked up again, slapping rain into our faces as Paul rips the tape off and pockets the small key.

The street is empty except for a single gull, picking at something unidentifiable in the gutter.

Paul starts the engine and looks at me, hair still a mess, eyes brighter than I've seen them in weeks. "You believe him?"

I nod. "Yeah. I do."

He smiles, but it's a small, tired thing. "Then let's go get the story."

I look at the house, at the dying garden, and the light still on in the window. "We might actually pull this off."

He grins, a proper one this time. "Don't get sentimental, Hampton."

I drive us away, and for the first time in months, I think we're pointed in the right direction.

If there's a hell for English agnostics, it's probably a Victorian B&B at low tide. Ours is a stone monster perched above the car park, all bay windows and faded grandeur, the kind of place that promises a "full cooked breakfast" and delivers a single banana and a teabag with a string. The inside smells like overcooked onions and the existential dread of anyone who ever failed to leave their hometown.

The woman at the front desk—sixty if she's a day, tight perm, glasses chained to her neck—gives us a look as we drag our bags up the carpeted stairs, not so much judgmental as deeply, deeply invested in the possibility of a scandal. She checks the register twice before frowning. "It's Miss Hampton and Mr Callaghan, is it? Only I see there's just the one room booked—oh, dear. There must have been some confusion." She smiles, the kind that could run a boot camp for sociopaths. "But it's the last one left. Festival week, you see."

I force a smile, the one I reserve for customer service and family weddings. "It'll be fine. We'll manage."

She brightens, leading us up the stairs, chattering about the Daffodil Festival at the local park and the unique charm of the local chippy. The room is on the top floor, tucked under the eaves. She opens the door and stands aside as if unveiling a prize on a daytime game show. "All mod cons!" she chirps, "and a lovely view of the Estuary—on a clear day."

The room is... optimistic. Two single beds with floral duvets, a dressing table that looks like it's survived a couple of World Wars, and wallpaper so loud it feels like a migraine coming on. There's a single window, steamed up and rattling in its frame, overlooking the main road and, yes, a slice of the estuary if you crane your neck and squint.

"Breakfast is seven-thirty to eight sharp," the landlady says. "If you'd like it brought up, just ring down on the phone—there." She gestures at a phone so old it could summon the dead. She lingers in the doorway, eyes darting from bed to bed, as if to make sure we don't immediately reenact some ITV drama. Then she leaves, shutting the door with the soft finality of someone who'll be listening at the keyhole.

Paul laughs as soon as she's gone, throws his bag on the nearest bed, and sprawls across it, arms out. "You sly fox, the just-one-bed conundrum."

"There are two beds. It's a twin room. That's the point. Or was Sir expecting *The Chronicle* to fork out for a suite each?"

Paul laughs, "Maybe it's just my seedy mind exposing itself."

"Maybe it is."

"Do you think she's got a hidden camera in the kettle?"

"Don't flatter yourself," I say, dropping my own bag on the

floor and opening my laptop. "She just wants a good TripAdvisor review."

He sits up, kicks off his shoes, and surveys the room. "You know, it's almost romantic. If you ignore the fact that it's haunted by the ghosts of a thousand failed honeymoons."

I pretend to type, but I'm really just staring at the screensaver. "I'll be sure to put that in the headline: 'Paul Callaghan Endorses Romance, Film at Eleven.'"

He grins, unbothered. "I've grown as a person. Also, I'm pretty sure there's an entire bottle of Lidl gin in the minibar."

The truth is, I'm wired—adrenaline and caffeine fighting a deadlock in my bloodstream. The Martin Cheng interview is replaying on loop, every detail a new rabbit hole: the papered-over windows, the trembling hands, the phrase "they'll ruin my family" that hasn't stopped echoing since we left. I open a fresh doc and start listing next steps, bullet points lining up like a firing squad.

Paul, meanwhile, is scrolling on his phone, hunting down every possible hit on the storage unit, the PO box, and the names Martin half-coughed into the air. Every so often, he mutters something about "idiots with shell companies" or "this is just like the Deutsche Bank thing," then lapses into silence.

For half an hour, we work in companionable parallel, the only sound the rattle of the window and the gulls outside, occasionally punctuated by the soft click of Paul's jaw as he worries at a chipped molar. It's so domestic it hurts.

Eventually, I can't take it. I close the laptop with a snap. "You never sleep, do you?"

He shrugs, still scanning his phone. "I'll sleep when we have the story, or when I'm dead. Whichever comes first."

"Grizzled freelancer," I say, but it comes out fonder than I intend.

He glances up, something bright at the edges of his eyes. "And you're still the only person who can out-stubborn me."

I get up, cross the tiny room, and stack my notes on the dressing table. The space between the beds is barely wide enough for a suitcase, so when I sit back down on the edge of mine, our knees almost touch.

"We're a terrible team," I say, "but we're the only one we've got."

He laughs, and the sound vibrates through the wooden floor. "You know, for what it's worth, I always liked being the underdog to your spreadsheet obsession."

"Spreadsheet obsession is a compliment," I say, and for a second, the air between us is less sharp.

Outside, the wind picks up, making the window creak and the wallpaper bulge. For a moment, we're just two people in a room, the rest of the world a thousand miles away.

"You were always good at this," I say.

He meets my eyes, serious for once. "You were always better."

For a minute, it's like the years drop away, and we're back in the student newsroom at midnight, arguing over commas and drinking crap corner-shop wine, both convinced we were going to save the world or at least break the internet. The distance between us isn't much—a handspan, maybe. He reaches out, fingers hovering over my knee, not quite touching.

There's a charge, or maybe it's just the static from the polyester bedspread, but it's enough to make my heart kick. I look at his hand, then at him.

"I missed this," I tell him.

TWENTY-SIX

PAUL

There's a point during every bad idea where you can still walk away. You can see it coming, the fork in the road, the part of the night where you laugh, say something biting, go home, and stew in the comfort of your own mediocrity. The smart money always walks. But I am not smart money, and this, right here, is the part where I fall off the edge.

She looks at me—really looks, no sarcasm, no filter. There's a silence, perfectly tuned, and then she says, "I missed this."

It lands like a brick through a bay window. For a second, I don't know where to file the information.

"The work?" I ask, because that's safer.

She doesn't blink. "You."

There's a shift in the air, some molecular realignment that turns gravity up a notch. My mouth goes dry. I want to crack a joke, call her a sap, reroute the emotional train to a siding where it can't hit anything valuable. But I don't. Instead, I sit, and wait, and let the moment hang like it deserves.

Grace stands again, walks to the window, stares out at the

night beyond. She crosses her arms tighter, shoulders hiked like she's cold, though it's warm enough in here to fog the glass. "We shouldn't," she says, voice low and raw.

I say, "We won't."

Neither of us believes it.

She turns, and the look on her face is all contradiction: tired, determined, a little bit scared. "You know you're a dickhead, right?"

"Occupational hazard," I say. "You should see the pension plan."

She laughs, a real one this time, and the tension breaks just enough that the next thing I know, she's three steps closer. Her hands are fists, not in anger, but to keep them from shaking.

I don't move. I don't dare.

She says, "If you ruin this, I will staple-gun your ears to the next *Mail on Sunday* leader column."

I say, "That's not a threat, that's foreplay."

The next movement is slow—deliberate, like she's giving me a chance to bail, like every microsecond is a referendum on the last ten years. She stops a foot away, looks up at me with that look, the one that got me through uni and three breakdowns and the day she left for London and didn't look back.

It's her move. It always was.

She reaches down, grabs the collar of my shirt, and pulls me in.

The kiss is clumsy at first, the kind of ill-advised workplace snog that never gets past the second page of an HR manual. Our teeth clash, lips miss, noses bump. We both laugh into it, which only makes the second try hotter, more dangerous, like we're daring each other to keep going.

She tastes like coffee, and anger, and something sharp I can't name. Her mouth is soft, but her grip is iron—one hand anchored in my shirt, the other sliding around the back of my neck, holding me in place like she's worried I'll disappear if she lets go.

I don't have a plan for what to do with my hands, so I put them at her waist, half afraid she'll flinch. She doesn't. If anything, she presses closer, our bodies fitting together with the inevitability of magnets in a junk drawer. I feel every inch of her: the tremor in her stomach, the heat radiating off her skin, the ragged intake of breath when my thumbs press into the small of her back.

The world does not end, but it shifts.

I want to catalogue every detail: the way her hair smells like cheap shampoo and my car, the way her lips part just before I kiss her again, the way her pulse hammers against my chest like a warning. I want to remember this, because there's no guarantee it'll ever happen again.

She pulls away first, breathless, eyes wild. "Don't get cocky," she says, but her voice wobbles at the edges.

"Too late," I say, and kiss her again, this time slow, a question mark at the end of a very long sentence.

She answers by biting my bottom lip, enough to make me gasp.

It's a war now, and I'm losing beautifully.

We break apart, hands still locked in a silent dare. I look at her—really look—and for once, she doesn't look away.

It's dangerous. It's inevitable. It's us.

The line is crossed, burned, buried. There's no going back.

I let go of her waist. She grins, a wolfish thing. "Now what?"

I shrug. "Suppose we do what we always do. Pretend it doesn't matter."

She leans in, forehead pressed to mine, her hair a curtain hiding us from the world. "Liar."

"Every time," I whisper, and kiss her again, because it's the only truth I can trust.

Grace pulls at my shirt like she's trying to rip a phone book in half. I try to help, but my hands are full of her—hair, face, the column of her neck—and by the time I get a grip, she's already yanked the first three buttons clean off. They bounce across the floor, lost to history. There's a moment of shared surprise, then we both laugh, teeth clacking together in the scramble.

It should be awkward, this undressing-by-consensus, but it's just... right. We're both in a hurry, but also not: every second is a dare, every inch of exposed skin a new front line. She tugs my shirt down my arms, fingers tracing the pale lines of old scars and newer, desk-job doughiness. I let it fall, then reach for her blouse, intent on returning the favour.

The buttons are tiny, mean little bastards, and my hands shake with adrenaline or maybe just the disbelief that this is actually happening. I get the first two, then fumble the third, then just give up and go for broke, pulling the fabric loose and pressing my mouth to her collarbone like it's a prayer. She gasps, arching into me, her hands in my hair now, grasping it tight enough to hurt.

For a second we pause, both of us taking inventory: I can hear her heart, quick and erratic, feel the heat of her skin, the rise and fall of her chest against mine. It's a feedback loop of want, and there's nothing measured about it anymore.

She sits, pulls me over to her bed, and the world compresses to this point—ridiculous, beautiful, reckless. I kneel between her legs, run my hands up her thighs, and she shudders, the old gooseflesh response I remember from a million years ago. I kiss her—softer, this time—and she bites back a moan, nails digging crescents into my shoulder.

The jeans are a problem. I tug at the waistband, and it doesn't budge.

She grins, breathless. "Tight fit."

"You're telling me," I say, but my voice is all rough edges.

She lies back, hands behind her head, watching as I try to wrangle the denim off her hips. It's ridiculous, really—there's nothing sexy about fighting stretch material—but she makes it look like a performance, each wriggle and shimmy calculated to drive me mad. She lifts her pelvis, and I get the fly down, but the jeans cling stubbornly to her thighs, a last stand against inevitability.

"Need help?" she says, mocking and merciful.

"Never," I reply, and give them one more heroic tug.

They come off in a rush, and I nearly fall over. I lift them overhead like a trophy, triumphant. In the process, my elbow connects with the bedside lamp, which wobbles, lists, and finally tips over the edge.

The crash is loud, a hollow, plastic thud, followed by a clatter. The lamp settles at a cockeyed angle, casting a wonky ellipse of light across the wall.

We freeze, staring at the carnage.

Then she laughs, a full-body giggle that turns into a howl, and I join in, the two of us half-naked and hysterical in the shambles of our own making.

"Perfect," she says, still laughing. "Fucking perfect."

I lean over her, hands braced on either side of her head. "You're a menace," I say, but it's the kind of accusation you level at a co-conspirator.

She hooks her legs around my hips, pulls me down, and kisses me again. There's no finesse left—just hunger, raw and immediate. Her hands slide under my waistband, fingers cold against my skin, and I shiver, every nerve ending on red alert.

She rolls us over, so she's on top, her hair falling around us in a curtain. She straddles me, knees digging into the mattress, eyes sharp and wild and entirely in control.

"Not so cocky now, are you?" she says, and grinds down, slow enough to be torture.

I can't speak, can barely think. I reach up, trace the line of her spine, marvel at the reality of her, the heat and the weight and the way she moves against me. It's an old rhythm, but it feels brand new—like we're writing our own manual, one page at a time.

She unclips her bra one-handed, the skill of long practice, and lets it fall to the bed. I stare, mesmerised, and she raises an eyebrow as if to say: Keep up.

I do, or at least try to. I sit up, mouths crashing together, hands everywhere—her back, her ribs, the delicate slope of her waist. She tastes like triumph. I want to map every inch of her, record it for when this is inevitably taken away again.

She slips her hand between us, and for a second, time stops. I close my eyes, lean into the feeling, let it take me. There's no fear anymore, no hesitation. Just us, the bed, the damaged lamp, and the impossible luck of being here, now.

She whispers something—my name, I think, or maybe just a fragment of it—and the sound is enough to undo me.

I lift her off me and push her gently back, her hair a halo on the cheap bedding. I take my time, trace her jaw with my thumb, kiss the hollow of her throat, let my hands roam until she's panting, eyes closed, body arching up to meet mine.

We fit. I don't know how, but we do.

I slide my hand down her thigh, take in the texture of her skin—warm and impossibly soft, goosebumps forming in my wake. She shivers, but doesn't pull away. I trail my fingers across her, and she lets out a small, involuntary sound that makes my pulse race all over again.

She lies back and opens her legs, hands gripping the bedsheet. "You're staring," she says.

I nod. "It's for research."

She laughs, a low hum vibrating against my chest. "Always so methodical."

I work down. I kiss her tummy, then her thighs, then her lips, taking my time with each. I want to memorise this, build a memory I can call up when the world inevitably turns to shit again.

She adjusts her position, and this time there's no rush, no sense that we're trying to win. She slides her leg over the back of my neck, using the pivot of her knee to guide—no, command—where I kiss and lick next.

I welcome the guidance. The permission. The insistence. I want her to know what it's like to be wanted—not as a rival, not as a sparring partner, but as herself, unadorned and unafraid.

Grace responds in kind, her body arching as I suck and kiss and lick, her breath hitching and then releasing in waves. She tangles her fingers in my hair, drags me deeper. I taste salt and sweat and the sharp sweetness that's uniquely her.

She moans—soft at first, then louder, the sound ringing in my ears, urging me on. I slow down, then speed up, chasing the rhythm we find together. She pulls at my hair, digs in her nails, no doubt leaving marks. I watch her face over the rise of her breasts, the way her mouth opens, the way her eyes squeeze shut, the flush that spreads from her chest to her hairline. She is incandescent, utterly beautiful, and for a second I almost lose myself.

TWENTY-SEVEN

GRACE

My skin is still buzzing when the room finally settles. My body is heavy, boneless, but my brain—never one to clock off at a reasonable hour—is running sprints.

Paul, for his part, looks somewhere between dazed and destroyed. His hair is a mess—my fault, entirely—and his chest is slick with sweat and something less noble. The duvet is a knot at our feet, the air thick with proof that, yes, two people can generate enough heat to power a small nation if they're sufficiently horny and insufficiently clothed.

He joins me on the pillow, and I shift onto my side, propping myself up on one elbow so I can observe him more closely. He always said I was a control freak, and he was never wrong. His mouth is open just a sliver, and there's a muscle twitching in his jaw, the ghost of some argument he didn't finish. I trace the line of his ribs with a finger, more forensic than tender, and watch his stomach jump in reflex.

He doesn't move. He doesn't even flinch, but I can feel the tension coiling in his thigh, his need to get the last word—

verbally, physically, emotionally. Too bad for him: tonight, the last word is mine.

"You alive, Callaghan?" I say, keeping my tone light.

His hand slides down from his face, revealing an eye so blue it makes my teeth hurt. "I'll need to take tomorrow off for medical observation."

I smirk. "You'd have to show up for work to do that."

He grins, but it's more grimace than challenge. "You're relentless, Hampton."

"And you love it."

He laughs, low and wrecked. "Never said I didn't."

There's a silence that could go either way, but I'm not in the mood to let him coast on the laurels of mutual destruction. I roll, slow and deliberate, until I'm straddling his hips. He looks up, startled but not resisting, and for once, I have the element of surprise. He's always been the one to tip the balance, to set the pace, to make me come undone and then act like it was an accident of chemistry.

Not tonight.

I lean forward, pinning his wrists to the mattress, and let my hair fall like a curtain around our faces. He tries to look smug, but the effect is spoiled by the flush on his cheeks and the way his pulse jumps under my hands.

"Don't get comfortable," I whisper, mouth close to his ear. "You're not the only one who knows how to take charge."

He shivers, and it's not from the cold.

For a second, we just breathe, each of us waiting to see who will move first. I slide my hands down his arms, mapping the old burn near his elbow. He's always shaking, even when he pretends otherwise. I press down, not hard, but enough to remind him who's in control.

He swallows. "Thought you were spent."

"Shows what you know," I say, and lower my hips, grinding down just enough to make him gasp. His composure cracks. It's a beautiful sound, and I file it away for future use.

He tries to sit up, but I pin him again, and this time there's real struggle in it, a friction that's equal parts frustration and surrender. He bares his teeth, a challenge.

"You gonna take a victory lap, then?"

"Don't tempt me," I say, but the truth is, I already am.

I let him go, just to see what he'll do. For a moment, he's motionless—calculating, or maybe just savouring the moment. Then he brings his hands up, slow and careful, to my waist, thumbs pressing into the skin just above my hipbones. It's a practiced move, but the look on his face is pure awe.

"You're dangerous," he says.

"So are you," I reply, and kiss him, lips just brushing his jaw, and then work my way down, slow and deliberate, mapping the territory with tongue and teeth. I kiss the old scar on his shoulder, then the hollow beneath his clavicle. His hand comes up, half-hearted, to catch mine, but I redirect it to the mattress, fingers entwined so he can't use it as a lever.

He gets the hint, but that doesn't mean he likes it.

I keep going, lower and lower, until I'm halfway down his stomach and he's breathing so hard it's almost a laugh. I pause, glance up, and catch him watching me with a look I can only describe as: "If you stop now, I'll never forgive you."

I don't stop.

I take my time, alternating between feather-light touches and the occasional deliberate scrape of teeth. Every time I pull back, he makes a sound—sometimes a hiss, sometimes a low groan, sometimes a whispered, "Fuck, Grace."

When I finally reach the part of him that's been quietly clamouring for attention since round one, I pause, just to savour the anticipation. He bites his lip, staring at the ceiling as if trying to remember how to pray.

I draw it out, slow as possible, switching up rhythm

and pressure, keeping him right at the edge but never letting him tip over. He starts to squirm, hips lifting off the bed, and I pin him with one hand, palm flat against his pelvis.

"Easy," I say, mouth barely leaving his skin.

He laughs, but it's a desperate sound. "You're enjoying this."

"More than I probably should."

He tries to reach for my hair, to guide me or maybe just ground himself, but I catch his wrist and pin it back to the mattress. He goes still, eyes dark and dilated, and I realise: I've never seen him surrender, not once, not in a decade of rivalry and regret.

It's fucking beautiful.

I ramp up the pace, adding strokes of my hand, watching every micro-expression: the way his eyebrows knot, the way his mouth falls open, the way his entire body goes taut as a bowstring just before—well.

He makes a sound I've never heard before—half gasp, half curse—and then it's over, his body shuddering under my grip, breath coming in ragged bursts. I let him ride it out, then crawl back up, lying beside him and running a hand through his hair, because I can.

For a minute, neither of us says anything.

Finally, he turns his head, eyes glazed, and mutters, "I fucking hate you."

I grin. "Liar."

He closes his eyes, smiling despite himself. "You're going to gloat about this forever, aren't you?"

"Obviously."

He shakes his head, still breathless. "I should've seen it coming."

"You never do."

He's quiet, then: "You're amazing."

It's not a word he uses lightly. I let it hang there, unchallenged.

He rolls to face me, pulls me close, and kisses me, slow and sweet, the opposite of everything we've ever been. For once, we're not competing, not even pretending. Just sharing the same bed, the same aftermath, the same unspoken promise that maybe—just maybe—this isn't a disaster in the making.

He tugs me in, wraps both arms around me, and mumbles into my neck, "If you ever tell anyone about this—"

I laugh, burying my face in his chest. "Not a chance."

We stay like that for a long time, bodies tangled, the fight gone out of both of us.

Tomorrow, the war resumes. But tonight, the field is quiet, and I'm the one who gets the last word.

He falls asleep first.

I lie awake, fingers tracing idle patterns over his skin, and think: let the world come for us.

We'll be ready.

I wake up in the middle of the night. The air in the room is electric—still charged, like it's waiting for the next lightning strike. Paul's body is a furnace against my back, his arm heavy over my waist, pinning me to the mattress. At some point in the night I must have rolled away, but he's reeled me back in, a reflex neither of us will admit to. His hand rests, fingers splayed, just under my boob, and each slow breath fans over the sweat-stuck hair at my neck.

For a few perfect minutes, I don't move. I let myself enjoy it. The warmth, the weight, the rhythm. The way his thumb occasionally twitches, as if testing the boundaries of where skin ends and ownership begins.

But the world waits for no one, and the ache building between my thighs is both a demand and a promise.

I shift, careful at first, then more boldly as he stirs. His hand tightens, not in protest, but in the sleepy, selfish way of someone determined not to lose what they've stolen. He mutters my name, the syllables fractured and low, and for a moment I wonder if he's still dreaming.

He isn't. His mouth lands on the curve of my shoulder, rough stubble scraping my skin. He nips, then soothes, then nips again, each small act of violence immediately made right. He draws me back, pressing his chest to my spine, letting me feel the full, hard truth of what he wants.

I arch into him, and he groans, voice gone wrecked. "You're insatiable," he says, words muffled by my hair.

"Occupational hazard," I shoot back. My whole body is awake, buzzing with anticipation and the certainty that we're nowhere near finished.

He rolls me onto my back, hovering over me. I watch his eyes—hungry, adoring, still a little disbelieving—and I feel the urge to ruin him all over again.

I hook my leg around his, pulling him closer, lining us up in a way that's deliberate and filthy and utterly without shame. I want to see him lose himself. I want to see him break.

I guide him inside me, slow at first, just the tip, a taunt more than a gift. He holds back, biting his lip, every muscle in his body set to "suffer." I make him wait, shifting my hips, taking him in increments, relishing the hitch in his breath every time I steal a little more.

When he finally pushes all the way in, he shudders so hard I think he might actually fall apart, and my body echoes the sentiment. He buries his face in my neck, and for a moment I feel his chest hitch—like he's trying not to cry, or maybe just trying to keep from saying something he can't take back.

"Jesus, Grace," he manages, the words half-strangled.

I wrap my arms around his back, nails digging in just enough to leave marks. "You wanted this," I whisper, and he nods, ragged, thrusting harder, deeper, until the only things left in the world are the creak of the mattress and the sound of our bodies meeting.

It's chaos. It's messy and desperate and glorious. Years of wanting, years of holding back and pretending not to care, years of fighting for the upper hand—all of it explodes in the space between us, a detonation of everything we've never said.

He pulls back, locking eyes with me, his mouth softening into something dangerously close to tender. "You're fucking incredible," he says, and this time there's no sarcasm, no mask.

I want to answer, but the words get lost in the flood of sensation as he angles just right, and I can't help the whimper that escapes me. He grins, triumphant, then bends to kiss me, the movement rough and perfect. I bite his lip in retaliation, and he growls, speeding up, the rhythm turning frantic.

We're both close, and we know it. There's no need for games anymore. I want him to see me come, want him to know what he's done to me. I dig my fingers into his shoulders, legs wrapping tighter, and let go.

He follows a second later, a low, guttural sound ripped from somewhere deep inside. For a long time, neither of us moves.

The sweat cools. The air is thick with the smell of sex and old dust and something new—a sense that this, whatever it is, isn't temporary. Not just the physical. The rest of it, too.

He props himself up on one elbow, face inches from mine. His hair is a disaster, his eyes red and soft and utterly unguarded.

"You okay?" he asks, voice barely above a whisper.

I nod. "Never better."

He searches my face, looking for the catch, the punchline, the first sign of retreat. He doesn't find it.

"Good," he says, and kisses me again, softer this time. A punctuation mark, not a prelude.

We lie like that, tangled together. I trace circles on his forearm, counting the scars. He plays with the ends of my hair, winding them around his finger like he's trying to anchor himself to the moment.

There's so much I want to say, but none of it fits. So instead, I close my eyes and breathe him in, memorise the feeling of being wanted, of being held. Of not having to fight, even for a little while.

He's about to say something—maybe even something important—when my phone goes off, loud and shrill, shattering the moment.

I answer it, bracing for the landlady's voice. Instead, it's Tess from the newsroom, her accent twice as Northern when she's stressed. "Grace, sorry to call so late. It's urgent."

"What's happened?"

"Sarah says the leak's going public. Someone's tipped off the *Standard*, and they're trying to put together an article about the council's connection to Kidz Trust. If you want your scoop, you need to file pronto. Otherwise, it's gone."

The room is suddenly smaller, the urgency telescoping everything down to a single, breathless point.

"We're on it," I say, grabbing for my laptop. "Thanks, Tess."

I hang up, turn to Paul. "We have maybe six hours before the story dies. If we want to use the key, we have to move."

He's already on his feet, bag half-zipped, adrenaline burning off all the softness from a minute ago. "We can be in London in two hours."

I stuff my notes into my bag, shoving chargers and pens in after. "Let's do it."

He nods, and for a moment, we're perfectly in sync: showering, packing, prepping, back in the trench together. We don't talk about what just happened. There isn't time. But when our eyes meet across the chaos of recovering underwear from tangled bedsheets, I know we'll have to. Later.

As we rush out, I pause in the hallway, hand on the banister. "You know, if this works—"

He stops just behind me, eyes wide. "If this works?"

"We'll have to celebrate," I say, almost daring him.

He grins, the old edge back in his smile. "I'll buy you breakfast. Or a proper gin."

I nod, and we race the wind down the stairs, into the street, past the sleeping landlady and her sad, singular banana.

The night is alive with possibility and impending doom. We get in the car, slam the doors against the cold, and drive.

And for the first time in a long time, it feels like maybe—just maybe—this is what it means to win.

TWENTY-EIGHT

<hr>

PAUL

The storage unit estate off the Old Kent Road is a masterpiece of urban anxiety: floodlights, security fencing, razor wire, and the wet glimmer of concrete corrugated by a thousand pointless bollards. It's gone three in the morning, and the air's so cold the windscreen fogs before we've even killed the engine. I have to lean into the heater's useless breath to make out the lot numbers.

Grace has the key and the sense of urgency, both of which make her the natural point person. She's already out of the car, coat zipped and collar up, every line of her body directed at the far end of the lot. The place is a warren—three tiers of units, every door the same shade of chemical blue. I keep close, the torch from the glove box rattling against the loose change in my pocket, hands raw and slow with cold.

We find the storage locker in the back row. The lock is new, black as oil, and the hasp gleams like it's been licked clean by a meticulous robot. And it's lying on the ground. The shutter has been rolled down, but not all the way.

Grace hesitates, just for a second, then yanks the roller door up. It's heavier than it looks, and shudders halfway before she muscles it the rest of the way. The interior is the size of a large bedroom, with the aroma of damp chipboard and the earthy tang of cardboard in slow decay.

But the smell isn't the only thing waiting for us.

Movement. Fast, peripheral, behind a haphazard stack of crates.

I freeze, because my body knows better than to announce itself in a dark room with unknown company. Grace is already a step ahead, phone out, thumb poised on the torch. I nudge her arm—*don't*.

Whoever's in there is good. They've stopped moving, even their breathing tamped down, but I know the sound of someone trying not to be heard. It's the kind of silence that has intent.

Grace whispers, not looking away from the stacked boxes: "Do we—?"

I mouth: *Wait.*

A minute passes, maybe two. Time slows and rearranges. My hearing calibrates: every drip, every scuff of gravel from outside, the nervous tap of Grace's nail against the back of her phone. My own pulse, amplified in my ears, makes it hard to count the seconds. Then: a scrape, softer than a whisper, but enough.

I step through the threshold and flick the torch on, aiming low. The beam rakes over a jumble of banker's boxes, a ratty suitcase, the uneven shadow of a person hunched behind an archive box with "BBELL ENV. 2025" scrawled on the side in marker.

"Not a great hiding spot," I say, trying for bored, but my throat is dry. "You want to stand up and explain, or should we call the police and let them do the honours?"

The shape straightens, not much taller than me, but much

slimmer. Black hoodie, black gloves, something balled in one fist—a torch, not a weapon. There's a moment where I think maybe they'll try to bluff, but they don't. They just look at me, eyes sharp and unblinking under the hood.

Then they speak, voice distorted by a mask or maybe just the effort of not being recognised: "Back off. This isn't your business."

Grace edges forward, chin up, no fear in her at all. "It is now. You're the one trespassing. You want to tell us what's in those boxes?"

The figure shifts, gaze darting between us. I can see now: the face is blurred by a neoprene mask, the sort cyclists use to keep the wind out. Their right hand twitches. Not getting ready to punch, but ready to run.

"No one needs to get hurt," the voice says, and now it's obvious: female, or a good impression of one. "Just walk away."

I step forward, keeping the light just out of her eyes. "If you're here for Bluebell's records, we already have copies. There's nothing left to steal."

A beat. "Then why are you here?"

I think about lying, but Grace cuts in before I can. "Because we're journalists. You're not the first to try and torch evidence, but you might be the first to do it in front of witnesses."

That lands. The body language flickers—fear, then calculation. The gloved hand tenses, releases. Then, as if a decision's been made, the intruder lunges for the boxes, grabs one by the handles, and makes a break for the open corridor.

I move to block, but she's faster than she looks, and the edge of the torch only catches the sleeve of her jacket as she shoulders past. Grace yelps as a box careens into her shin, but she doesn't let go of her phone. I give chase—there's no time to think, only to react.

She's quick, feet light even under the weight of the box.

Down the corridor, past two turns, skidding on the wet concrete. I sprint after her, breath burning in my chest, shoes slapping echoes off the sheet-metal walls. She reaches the gate at the end of the row and, with a surge of desperation, hurls the box over the top of the security fence. Papers scatter, shrapnel of invoices and printouts exploding in the orange glare of the streetlamp.

I catch up just as she starts up the chain link. She's halfway up before I even get a hand on the mesh. I try to grab a foot, but she twists, lands a boot to my shoulder, and I lose grip, falling back hard. She's over and gone, sprinting into the dim playground of back alleys and scaffolding.

I want to follow, but my lungs are full of needles, and my arm is already going numb where she kicked it. By the time I get to my feet, there's nothing but the wind and the angry chorus of my own gasping.

I stand for a minute, hands on knees, swearing quietly into the night. Then I look up. Grace is already gathering papers from the pavement, her face tight with focus and something else—something like vindication.

I limp back, trying not to look as winded as I feel. Grace doesn't say anything, just shoves a fistful of documents at me. I take them, scanning for names, numbers, anything useful, but my hands are shaking too hard to read.

Inside the unit, nothing's on fire. The remaining boxes are intact, but someone's been through them with a fine-tooth comb. The suitcase is unzipped, contents ransacked: a tangle of old cables, a half-dozen USB drives taped together, a printout labelled "Tender Award: Confidential." Grace is already in the suitcase, peeling off strips of gaffer tape to get at the drives.

I drop to my knees next to her, and together we work in silence, scooping every document, every scrap of hard evidence, into a bin bag from the back of the car. The whole time, I'm replaying the break-in, trying to decide if the intruder looked familiar, or if it was just the shape of desperation that's common to everyone who ends up in stories like these.

When we've got everything, I lower the shutter, spin the lock back through, and we stand for a moment in the hard glare of the floodlights. I look at Grace, really look at her, and she's shivering—but not with cold.

"We need to get these somewhere safe," she says, hugging the USBs to her chest like a litter of kittens. "They'll come back. They always do."

I nod, even though my whole body is screaming for a stiff drink and a hot bath.

Back in the car, the adrenaline dies down, and what's left is a blank, vibrating edge. Grace is already sorting papers into piles, the overhead lamp illuminating the hard lines of her profile. I drive us out of the industrial estate, taking three left turns in case we're being tailed, and only relax when we're back on the main road.

She doesn't speak, not until we hit the roundabout at Elephant and Castle. "You think it's the same person who threatened Martin?"

I think about the voice, the mask, the calculated violence of the break-in. "Wouldn't bet against it."

Grace swears, low and eloquent. "This is big, isn't it?"

"Someone's willing to break and enter, maybe even start a fire, just to stop us." My own words sound thin and performative, but for the first time in a long time, I feel like the story is real—real enough to get us both killed, or at least properly sued.

She turns to look at me, and there's a wildness to her that's equal parts fear and delight. "We should get these to Legal. Like, now. Before they come after us."

"*Chronicle's* closed until seven."

"We've got lanyards, security will let us in," she says, and it's not a question.

I grip the wheel and floor it through the next amber.

As we drive, Grace dials up the intensity, sifting through the printouts, reading aloud the bits that matter. "Here—look. Council wiring instructions. Two million into a Seychelles account. The dates line up with the Bluebell project, but the account holder is different. Shell company, probably."

I steal glances at the pages, trusting her to know what matters. My hands have stopped shaking, but I can feel the buzz in every muscle. The night is thin and vicious, and every headlight behind us is a suspect.

We make it to the *Chronicle* without incident, and Grace is out of the car before it's even in park. We take the side entrance, her hands so full of evidence she can't even dig out the security fob. I do it for her, because that's what I'm good for: keys, doors, and the idiotic optimism that we can outrun whoever's behind this.

Inside, the building's dead quiet. The newsroom is a sleeping beast, monitors blinking at idle, the only sound the distant, hydraulic sighs of the building's ancient plumbing.

We spread the loot on Grace's desk, her monitor the only glow in the universe. She's in her element, scanning and copying, every motion efficient and practised. I hover, because there's nothing else to do, and watch her work.

After an hour, she straightens, eyes red but alive. "Got it all. Multiple backups. Even if they trash the office, it's safe."

I flop into the chair opposite her, brain on the edge of collapse. "You think this is worth it?"

She laughs, the sound brittle but real. "If we live to see the byline, yes."

I want to say something clever, something to bring it back to earth, but the only thing that comes out is: "You're brilliant."

She looks up, surprise flickering, then softens. "So are you, sometimes."

We're both listening for footsteps that never come, the ghost of danger humming between us.

I'm supposed to be helping, but mostly I pace. The corridor outside the Features pod is a runway of half-dead plants and awards for "Best Content Strategy," none of which have anything to do with what we're doing now. I keep watch for the security guard, for assassins, for any sign that the outside world gives a toss about what happens within these four walls. Nothing. Just the city beyond, orange and feral.

When I drift back to the desk, Grace is deep in the process: USB after USB, each one feeding a new tree of folders, each folder crammed with the kind of evidence that would make a compliance officer weep. She's methodical, even at this hour, naming everything with the date and initials. Every few minutes, she leans in and squints, as if she's trying to find a hidden message in the grain of the pixels.

I hover in the liminal zone between useful and unnecessary. She doesn't notice, or pretends not to. The glow from her monitor makes her look impossibly focused, like she's the only person in the world who isn't held together with chewing gum and self-loathing.

She mumbles, "You want to look through these or just pace all night?"

I force a smile, slouch into the chair next to hers. "I'm great at moral support."

She side-eyes me, but there's a quirk at the edge of her mouth. "You're not even moral."

"Support, then." I scroll through a folder, click into a spreadsheet. Rows and rows of numbers, most of them lies. My eyes glaze in record time.

But I take the hint and for the next hour, we work in parallel, as if the argument of the last few weeks, years really, never happened, as if we're just two kids in a library, trying to outsmart a test that's already been written.

"Found something. You want to see?"

I nod, because that's what you do.

She pulls up a PDF. The first page is a cover sheet from an offshore accountancy firm. "This is where it gets fun," she says, tapping the screen. "Transfers from the council to the charity, and then they went here, and here, and then straight to two private equity funds—one in the Caymans, one in Luxembourg. Shells, but if you look at the directors..."

She clicks on a LinkedIn profile, and I look at the female face on screen.

"What am I supposed to see?"

Grace scoffs. "You really do need spoon-feeding, don't you?" she says as she makes a letterbox gap with her thumbs and forefingers, and holds them over the image. "Our friend from the storage unit?"

I look at the eyes and the bridge of the nose and the small indentation below the eyebrow—it's the same woman. "That was her."

"I know. And guess what? She's on the board of the holding company."

I squint at the name: Eleanor Chambers. I don't recognise it, but I know the type—one of those serial lobbyists who move sideways through government, always a step ahead of the fire.

Grace reads my face, grins. "Bingo."

She's so alive right now, more herself than I've seen in months. I can see it winding her up, the thrill of being smarter than everyone else in the game. It's magnetic, in a way that makes my teeth hurt.

I try to focus. "So what's the play?"

"We take it to Sarah, and we run it first, before the *Evening Standard* joins the dots. It's going to make people furious."

"That's the idea," I say, but my voice is thin.

Grace looks at me, head cocked, as if she's trying to calibrate the tone. "You okay?"

"Yeah. Tired." I rub at my face, the stubble catching on my palm. "Just... tired."

She goes back to the screen, but the mood's shifted. The air is sharper. She knows something's off, but doesn't want to say it. That's always been our weakness.

A half hour later, she calls over. "There's something wrong with this one."

She turns her monitor, shows me an image: a blurry scan of a handwritten ledger, the kind that doesn't belong in any digital archive.

"See these entries?" she says, finger tracing the line. "Payments to 'Consultant – JC.' That's not standard. If you're laundering, you don't use initials."

I read the line, the penmanship weirdly familiar, but I can't place it. My brain is running on fumes and shame.

She's waiting for me to say it. To connect the dots.

I can't. Instead, I say, "You've got what you need now."

She blinks, confused. "What does that mean?"

I stand too fast, nearly tip the chair. "It means you can finish this without me."

She's hurt, but hides it with anger. "Are you for real right now? After everything that's happened? It's *our* story. We're on the verge—"

"Of what?" I snap, and the echo is louder than I expect. "Of making the same mistake we always make? You break the story, you get promoted, I get left behind, and the whole cycle starts over."

Her mouth tightens, but she doesn't look away. "That's not fair. It will be both of us on the byline."

"It's true, though."

She doesn't answer, just stares at me, jaw clenched. Behind her, the city flickers, dawn bleeding in from the Thames.

I grab my jacket, my battered bag, and head for the door.

Grace calls after me, "Paul—"

I pause in the corridor, but don't turn around. "Just finish the story, Grace. You don't need me. You never did."

I walk out. The lift is slow, the kind that lets you feel every floor between you and the exit. I stare at my reflection in the mirrored walls, at the face I've spent years pretending belonged to someone else.

When the doors open, I step out into the cold, and for the first time all night, I know exactly what I'm running from.

TWENTY-NINE

GRACE

I have the whole newsroom to myself until I look up at half-past six to find the Features desk is in full metabolic surge: subeditors mainlining sausage, egg, and bacon baps, Liv orchestrating the daily scrum with a sequence of "urgent" hand waves, and every desk phone bellowing at intervals designed to induce panic. The heating is on the blink, as usual, but the cold is almost a mercy. I want to feel numb. I want to be untouchable.

The last twenty-four hours have ground my brain to a fine, gritty paste. I don't think I got more than two hours of sleep in Felixstowe. I can't remember the last time I ate. There's a taste of metal in my mouth, and the inside of my wrists are tattooed with red pressure marks from resting on the edge of my desk.

I type. And type. And type. The words come out harder than I intend, the sentences sharpened to points that could draw blood if you handled them carelessly. I pull up the evidence from last night—scans of the USB drives, shaky photos of the ledgers, a ropey audio file of Martin's panicked confession—and drop it all into the doc. Each paragraph is a small, contained explosion. Each transition is a grenade.

The newsroom does its thing around me: Liv's voice rising above the melee, tech support swearing at the printer, a parade of desperate freelancers orbiting the coffee machine. They know I'm working on something huge. There's a sense of accelerated entropy, like the whole place could combust at any minute. I don't care. I can't. The screen is my only horizon, the column inches the only measurement of time that means anything.

The coffee next to my keyboard goes cold in fifteen minutes. I don't notice until my hand is halfway to my mouth, and the taste is so bitter it nearly makes me retch. I sip anyway, just to prove I'm still alive.

I hit Save. I read the whole thing from start to finish, out loud, just to hear how the anger sounds in daylight. My voice is flat, but the text is on fire. It's the best thing I've ever written. It's the worst thing I've ever felt.

There's a shuffle of footsteps, then Liv appears, holding a fresh cup in one hand and a fistful of paper in the other. "You look like death's admin assistant," she says, offering the coffee as a bribe.

I accept it, wrapping my hands around the cup as if it might warm more than just the skin. "Been worse," I say, voice shredded.

She glances at the monitor, scanning the headline and the byline underneath it. "No Paul?"

I hesitate, just for a second. "He made it clear we're not a team."

Liv sets her papers down, the gesture gentle. "He's a good writer. You're a better one." She doesn't say the rest. She doesn't have to.

I look at her, really look, and for a moment I want to tell her everything—the fight, the history, the endless recursive proof that some things never heal, no matter how many times you rewrite the ending. Instead, I say, "Thanks," and mean it.

Liv walks away, her presence leaving a wake of calm in the aisle. I watch her go, then pull up the document again. The mouse hovers over the Send button. I hold it there, a moment longer than I need to, just to see if the universe will intervene.

It doesn't.

I click send.

The article launches into the world with a single, silent movement. The system logs the submission, stamps it with my name, and that's it—twenty-four hours of real investigative journalism, months of rage, a decade of grudges, and a night of raw, unbridled sex, compressed into three thousand words and an exclusive label.

I stare at the byline for a long time.

GRACE HAMPTON.

Just that. No partner. No footnote.

The rest of the office swells and shifts, a living organism of deadlines and deliverables. I know there will be fallout: Board meetings, lawyers, a parade of damage-control emails and frantic phone calls. There will be applause, and anger, and someone will probably cry in the kitchen. For a few hours, maybe a day, it will feel like we've done something that matters.

But for now, it's just me and the cold screen, and the sound of my own heart, as loud and empty as a broken drum.

I finish my coffee. I close the laptop. I stand and stretch, the joints in my back popping like bubble wrap.

I don't know where Paul is. I don't know if he'll ever come back, or if he even wants to.

But I know what I did.

I shoulder my bag and walk to the lifts, but instead of pressing down, I press up.

There's a view from the roof of the *Chronicle* building that makes you feel like you could fall forever and still end up landing in the same city. I sit with my feet dangling over the edge, half-watching everyone going about their business. The sky is that blue-grey nowhere colour, the kind that doesn't have a name but does have a temperature: too cold to be comforting, too familiar to be bracing.

I look at the Chronicle homepage on the phone, the headline, the opening paragraph I can now recite verbatim. It's proof I was here, that I did something real.

It should feel like triumph. It should taste like winning.

Instead, I just feel tired. Not the kind you sleep off, but the sort that accumulates, layer after layer, until it's the only thing holding you upright. My head hurts, my wrists ache, and my heart is a tight, over-tuned string that might snap if anyone so much as looked at it sideways.

There's a thump as the fire door is shouldered open behind me, then the slow, deliberate steps of someone who knows I'd rather be left alone, but isn't going to allow it. Liv appears, hair in a perfect bun, trainers immaculate, two paper cups clutched in one hand. She sits beside me without a word, not close enough to touch but close enough to count as a gesture. The wind is louder higher up, and it snatches the steam from the coffee and sends it somewhere south of the river.

She holds out a cup. I take it, even though I don't want it. This is the kind of peace offering you don't refuse, not if you want to keep your dignity.

We sit parallel, twin statues, watching as the city gets paler and meaner. Liv isn't like the others; she doesn't fill the silence with motivational quotes or ask if you're "processing your feelings." She just sits, waiting, as if patience is its own kind of pressure.

I crack first. Of course I do.

"I thought it would feel better than this," I say, not even bothering to keep the bitterness out of my voice.

She shrugs, eyes fixed on the Gherkin's glass and steel teeth. "It usually doesn't. Not at first."

I set the coffee on the ledge, hands curling around the paper like a lifeline. "Everyone's already forgotten about it. Half the comments are about my lipstick, or whether I'll sleep with the next Deputy Mayor for a quote."

"They won't forget," she says. "You pissed off the right people."

I almost laugh, but it catches in my throat. "What if all I did was make things worse? The old guard gets fired, the new guard just learns how to be sneakier. Nothing changes. I'm not even sure I changed."

Liv pulls her knees up, balancing the coffee between her trainers. "You did. You're just the last one to notice."

I look at her sideways, searching for the catch. She's not being ironic. That's the trouble with Liv; you can't out-cynic her, because she's already accounted for it in the maths.

"I'm tired," I say. The words come out small. "Not just from the work. From—" I can't finish the sentence, so I gesture at the skyline, a sweep that's meant to take in the entire miserable enterprise. "All of it. The rivalry. Pretending not to care. The knowing that no matter how hard you push, someone's always waiting to take your spot, or to see you fuck it up."

Liv leans back, palms braced on the roof's edge. "You don't have to pretend. You care. It's why you're good."

My eyes sting, but I refuse to blame it on anything except the wind.

"I just thought," I say, voice wobbling on the last word, "that it would mean more. That it would fill in whatever's missing."

Liv's quiet for a long time, long enough that I start to think maybe she's fallen asleep with her eyes open. She sips her coffee, sets it down, and says, "You didn't just break the story, Grace. You broke yourself a little, too."

That lands. It lands so hard I have to grip the ledge with both hands to keep from sliding right off.

She doesn't reach for me, or say it'll be okay. She just lets it hang there, the truth of it, shimmering in the new sunlight.

I watch the trains crawl along the bridges, the planes cut contrails across the sky, and people entering and exiting buildings. London doesn't care about the things you lose to keep it moving, but for a moment, up here, it feels like someone does.

I wipe my nose with the back of my sleeve. Liv pretends not to notice.

I let myself stay for a while longer, alone but not unaccompanied, suspended somewhere above the place where things get broken and the place where they get fixed.

THIRTY

PAUL

The newsroom is on life support. It's long past the hour when news happens, but the security lights are on, so the place glows with the sickly blue of a fish tank and the faint, ever-present aroma of disinfectant.

The laptop screen is the only other light in the room. My eyes are already fried from twelve hours of scrolling, but I keep reading. I have the *Chronicle* homepage open, and at the very top, above the fold, above the latest sponsored content and the "most read" sidebar, is Grace's article.

Her byline sits alone. All caps. No ampersand, no "with reporting by," no italicised footnote about additional research. Just GRACE HAMPTON, as sharp and final as a scalpel. The headline is taut and unsentimental: "COUNCIL FRAUD EXPOSED: INSIDE THE SHELL GAME COSTING LONDON MILLIONS."

It's good. Maybe the best headline I've seen on this site in months. The subheading is even better. The opening paragraph? Vicious and precise, the way only she can do it.

I read it once, then again, looking for cracks, but there aren't any. She doesn't quote me. She doesn't even mention me. She doesn't have to. I see myself in the negative space between her sentences: the sources I chased, the files I flagged, the voice notes she never acknowledged but always, somehow, used to reconstruct the scene better than I ever could. Her prose is cleaner than it used to be, but the edge is the same. The bit that turns every hard fact into a tiny, shining blade.

There's a photo too, halfway down the column. Grace in the background, pen in her mouth, glare on her glasses as she stares at a stack of evidence. I remember the day Tess took it, before we actually had much in the way of real evidence; I'd been making fun of the jacket she was wearing, a mustard thing with leather elbows, and she nearly stabbed me with her Biro. Now the photo is embedded for all of London to see: the face of integrity, the sole author of the best story *The Chronicle* has published all year.

My coffee is cold, the mug welded to the desk by a ring of sugar residue and neglect. I drink it anyway, the bitterness a small price to pay for the illusion of staying awake. The only other sound is the cleaning crew dragging a Henry Hoover through the advertising pod. The whine is oddly soothing. I let it fill the silence that's otherwise packed tight with regret.

I finish the article, then scroll through the comments. Most are unhinged, as always, but the top one is a single line: "Hampton for Editor-in-Chief." My stomach turns. Not because I disagree, but because I think that would be a good move. She's earned it. All of it.

I click away from the browser, try to focus on my own unfinished column. But the words just clot, refusing to move. I type the same sentence three times, then delete it, then start again, then close the document altogether. There's no point. Not now.

I sit back in the chair, listen to the hum of the building,

and try to piece together where it all went wrong. Not just the story. Not just the move over from the *Express* to the *Chronicle*. The whole fucking timeline, from Sheffield to now. Every time I thought I was doing the right thing, I ended up standing in someone else's shadow, hands empty. Every time I ran, it was away from a future I didn't think I deserved.

I'm staring at the ceiling, tracing the cracks in the acoustic tile, when I hear someone at the door.

It's Jamie, the only person left in the building who knows how to use the espresso machine. He's wearing a puffer coat and headphones and looks like he's walked in from a different climate. He sees me, pauses, then leans against the glass wall with his arms folded.

"You look like someone drowned your dog," he says, not unkindly.

"Didn't have a dog," I reply. "Maybe I was the dog."

He smiles, just a little. "Whatever's going on between you and Hampton, it's fucking with your head. And your copy. You know Sarah's noticed, right?"

I give a noncommittal shrug, but he's right. The decline started weeks ago, and I can see it even in my own drafts. The columns are lazier, the arguments thinner, the punchlines all recycled. I'm on autopilot, coasting, waiting to be fired.

Jamie walks over. "You talk to her yet?"

"She's got nothing to say," I lie.

He sits on the edge of the neighbouring desk, the one with all the ancient "Save Local News" badges.

"Don't be a wanker, Paul. You're not fooling anyone. Least of all, her."

I laugh, but it comes out flat. "I don't think she cares. She's got the byline. She's got everything she wanted."

He looks at me for a long time, then shakes his head. "You ever think that maybe you're the one who wanted it more?"

I want to argue, but the words won't come. I'm tired. So fucking tired.

Jamie stands, stretches, and heads for the door. "Talk to her. Or don't. But if you're going to let her break you, at least make it entertaining for the rest of us."

He leaves, the glass door whispering shut behind him.

Eventually, I pull up my email, then my personal archive, then the Dropbox I haven't touched since before the world went to shit. I start scrolling—it's everything I've ever written. Old essays, half-finished stories, screenshots of social posts from when Grace and I first started at Sheffield together. I find a photo: us at the student paper, beer bottles in hand, a printout of our first joint feature spread across the table. She's laughing, mouth wide and unguarded. I'm not looking at the camera, my eyes are on her.

There are dozens of these, each a small, perfect wound. The night we snuck into the student union vice-president's office to dig up evidence for the housing scam story. The morning after, when we both turned up to the interview in the same clothes, her eyeliner still smudged from tears or from laughter, I never figured out which. The week she let me sleep on her sofa after my flatmate torched our kitchen. The night we accidentally kissed and never mentioned it again.

I keep clicking. It's compulsive, this archaeology of failure. Each file is a thread back to a version of myself that still thought any of this would make a difference. That believed journalism mattered, that the stories could fix something broken, even if it was just the small things. That believed, in some feral, idiotic way, that Grace would always be there, and that together we could take on the world or at least the editorial board.

I click into an old doc, the very first feature we ever published as a pair. The byline is there, in bold, our names side by side:

By Grace Hampton & Paul Callaghan

It's ugly, this version of us. Full of typos and grandstanding and the kind of earnestness you can only get away with before you turn twenty-one. But it's alive. It's fucking alive. I read the first paragraph, then the second, then the whole damn thing, and for a moment I can hear her voice beside mine again, trading jokes, building sentences, shaping the story together.

I stare at the byline for a long time.

The truth is, all my best work has her fingerprints on it. The scoops, the columns, even the edits that drove me mad at the time. Every story that mattered had a trace of Grace in the margins. Every story that mattered, mattered because of her.

I close the laptop, the fan whirring to a stop. The room is quiet again, the city beyond the windows a distant shimmer.

It was never about the byline.

It was always about her.

After the eulogy comes the resurrection.

The city is sleeping now, or at least pretending. Out of the newsroom window, the Thames glows with the reflected glow of streetlamps and the occasional headlight. For once, I don't feel the urge to disappear into it.

I sit for a minute, hands loose in my lap, and try to remember the last time I fought for something that wasn't already lost. There's no answer. But there's a phone, and I reach for it.

Liv picks up on the second ring, her voice half static, half cigarette haze. "You're lucky I'm up. If this is about extending your deadline, you're dead to me."

"It's not the deadline," I say. "I need to return the favour."

She's silent for a beat, then, "You're serious. Proper serious."

"Yeah. Proper."

"What do you need?"

I run through the list fast. Liv doesn't scoff or judge, just starts planning out loud, then she tells me she'll be here in thirty minutes.

"Thank you," I say, but it doesn't feel like enough.

"You owe me a kidney. Or at least a bottle of Bombay Sapphire."

"Both," I say. "Promise."

She hangs up, leaving me alone with the weight of my own optimism.

Liv hefts a backpack onto my desk and grins. "Hope that's everything."

"You're a star, thank you."

She gives me a look—half smirk, half something like pride —then disappears, her footsteps already fading.

I open the backpack and take out the Post-it Notes inside, and start writing. The words come out hot, not like blood this time but like adrenaline. I build the story from the inside out, not as a takedown or a confession, but as a kind of love letter. Not just to Grace, but to the whole fucking mess we made together.

I work straight through the night. By dawn, the building is awake again, the first shifts trickling in, the newsroom slowly repopulating. I don't stop.

It's not a victory, but it's something.

Maybe it's even enough.

THIRTY-ONE

GRACE

The morning after a big scoop is the closest thing journalists get to a resurrection. You walk into the office and the whole world looks different, like you've changed your own blood type overnight and everyone else is running on the wrong version. The doors of the *Chronicle* hiss shut behind me, and there's a second where I think the city's actually gone quiet for once.

I'm wrong, obviously. The building is humming. Phones ringing, printers vomiting paper, interns power-walking towards their next character-building humiliation. But something's... off. There's a tension in the air, like the charge before a thunderstorm. I make it as far as the first bank of lifts before I see it.

Every surface—every wall, every pillar, even the glass of the fire doors—is covered in Post-its.

Hundreds. Maybe thousands, all stuck in uneven rows, some curling at the corners, all in a spectrum of neon colours that makes my eyes ache. At first, I think it's some kind of prank, or a mass breakdown of the stationery budget, but then I start to read.

The first one, on the left by the vending machine, just says: "Congrats, Chief. You made the rest of us look slow." A blue square, someone's aggressive capital letters.

The next one: "EXPOSED: Editor-in-Chief's Secret Stash of Tesco Gin," and I know instantly it's from Liv, the handwriting a dead giveaway. There are others: "Girlboss energy, but not in a bad way," "You spelled 'malfeasance' right on the first try," "Hot takes hot messes." There's one that just says, "Never change. Or do. Up to you."

Then, as I move closer, I spot the ones in a different hand. A messier, slanting scrawl, each letter fighting its neighbour for space. Paul's handwriting.

Some are headlines: "Hampton & Callaghan Torch Vice-Chancellor (Metaphorically)." "Student Paper Stays Up All Night, Drinks City Dry." "Breaking: Sheffield's Two Most Annoying People Join Forces." Some are fragments of in-jokes: "Next time, let's just burn the admin building." "I still owe you a sandwich. Or five." "Thought you'd go easy on me after the second pint, you maniac." Some are clipped from old student issues, yellowed at the edges, or laser printed with stories we wrote side by side. One is a scan of the first time our names ran together on a front page, circled three times in biro.

I follow the wall of notes down the corridor, reading as I go, the ache in my chest growing with every step. I start to notice a pattern, a phrase that repeats every few feet: "You're the story worth chasing."

By the third time I see it, I have to stop and put a hand to the wall. The surface is rough under the paper, and I realise, stupidly, that I'm shaking. I keep moving, colleagues watching from the corners of their eyes, trying not to smile. There are more notes now, written in handwriting I don't recognise. I run my fingers over them as I pass, half-expecting them to be hot, like fresh ink.

The trail leads me to the breakroom. Of course it does. I push the door open, and there he is.

Paul stands in the centre, looking like he slept in his clothes and then lost a fight with a hedge. His hair is a disaster. There's a smear of ink on his chin and two different socks visible above his battered trainers. In his hand is a single yellow Post-it.

He doesn't say anything at first, just stands there, eyes wide, like he's not sure if this was a good idea or the worst one ever.

I close the door behind me and lean back against it, crossing my arms. "You've redecorated."

He tries for a grin, but it lands somewhere between sheepish and terrified. "Figured it was your turn for a wall of shame."

There's a silence. The kind that only exists when everything that needs to be said has already been printed in the morning edition, and now all that's left is the errata.

"I was wrong," he says, voice steady but not strong. "About the internship. About you. About all of it."

He glances at the note in his hand, then holds it up like a peace offering. "I thought—if you hated me, it would hurt less than losing you." He laughs, short and ugly. "Turns out, I just got the pain in early and stretched it out for seven years."

I let the words settle, the way you let whisky burn its way down before you start to feel anything.

He takes a step closer. "I'm not sorry for the fights. I'm not even sorry for being a prick sometimes. But I am sorry I kept running when I should've just... stayed. With you."

I look at him for a long time, taking in the lines at the corners of his eyes, the way his hands shake just a little. The Post-it trembles between his fingers.

"You're a terrible journalist," I say.

He blinks once. Twice.

"Your sources suck," I continue. "You miss deadlines. Your handwriting's shit. But your timing?" I step forward, close enough to take the Post-it from his hand and press it to his chest. "Your timing is finally not awful."

He laughs, and this time it sounds like him. "That's the nicest thing you've ever said to me."

I reach up, tangle my fingers in the back of his hair, and pull his face down to mine.

The first kiss is a mess—teeth, nose, and the taste of over-sweet vending machine coffee. He freezes for a second, and I think he might actually pass out from the effort of not fucking it up, but then he kisses back, hard enough that I have to catch the counter to keep my balance.

Somewhere in the corridor, someone whoops. The door swings open, and Liv leans in, mug in hand, eyebrow arched so high it's practically in her hairline.

"Finally," she says, and lets the door shut with a bang.

We break apart, breathing heavily, and for a second, it's just us in the room, the silence full of everything we never said.

Paul grins, wide and unfiltered. "Is this going to be an HR problem?"

I shrug. "Only if we get caught."

He pulls me in again, softer this time, and we stand like that, holding on for dear life, until the day and the deadlines catch up with us.

Later, when we come up for air, the corridor is still a riot of Post-its, and the newsroom is humming, and the world outside is still the same cold, ugly, beautiful mess.

But we're here. And that, for once, feels like enough.

THIRTY-TWO

—— ♥ ——————

ONE YEAR LATER

GRACE

You can tell a lot about a relationship by the state of its shared bookshelf. Before Paul moved in, my shelves were a colour-coded battalion: history, current affairs, and the odd, guilty thriller lined up with military precision. Paul's collection, by contrast, was like the aftermath of a small but determined earthquake—paperbacks bent double, old *Private Eyes* with the spines half eaten by mildew, and about forty-seven pamphlets on publishing ethics I'm convinced he's never actually read. The morning he arrived, he "just temporarily" dumped his entire library on top of mine, and I'm still finding stray copies of Zadie Smith and "classic journalism" anthologies wedged behind the radiator.

Today, though, the shelves look—if not neat, then at least less haunted. This is because my mum is coming over for tea, and the first thing she does in any flat is judge you by your storage solutions. There's a running joke in my family that she can diagnose a person's moral fibre by the way they file their old receipts and payslips. If she ever finds out that Paul sorts his post, unopened, into "to be ignored" and "to be actively destroyed," she'll report us both to the local vicar.

I lean against the doorframe, arms crossed, surveying the carnage we've just managed to conceal. The laundry basket is at last back in the cupboard where God intended; the living room floor, which for the past week has looked like a donation bin for failed gym memberships, is more or less visible. Even the mugs—previously in a state of semi-permanent migration from sofa to desk to windowsill—are, for now, all inside the actual kitchen. It feels unnatural, as if we're about to be burgled by a *hygge* coach.

A clatter from the bedroom signals that Paul has finally finished his morning "wardrobe process." He emerges in a pair of black jeans and a shirt that might once have belonged to an actual adult. He is holding aloft a single, ratty sock like it's forensic evidence from a particularly squalid crime scene.

"Explain this," he says, in the accusatory tone of a man who has spent a decade writing for tabloids.

I take the sock and examine it. Navy blue, hole at the heel, weird bleach stain near the toe. "It's definitely yours. I haven't worn socks with sheep on them since Year Eleven."

He snatches it back and frowns. "You said they were cute."

"For a fifteen-year-old, they are."

He looks wounded, which is absurd, but that's Paul: always the martyr, even in a sock dispute.

"Grown-ups," I say, hanging the word in the air like a threat, "don't throw their laundry into wardrobes."

He sniffs, offended. "Creative storage solutions, actually. It's called horizontal filing."

Before I can reply, the doorbell buzzes. For a split second, Paul looks genuinely terrified, as if the Ghost of Girlfriend's

Mum has materialised and is about to quiz him on the taxonomical history of oven gloves.

He straightens his shirt and smooths his hair with both hands, then stands very still, like a schoolboy about to be graded on his handwriting. I resist the urge to laugh, mostly because my own stomach is doing slow somersaults. My mum's met Paul already, but that was when we were students; this time it's as my significant other. It's been years since I introduced anyone to my mother, and the last time didn't exactly end in a standing ovation.

I open the door. There she is: five foot four, floral scarf, and a look of bemused scepticism that she's honed over four decades of teaching secondary French. She leans in for a kiss, then wipes lipstick from my cheek with a tissue she produces from the sleeve of her cardigan.

"Grace, darling. You look tired. Are you eating properly?"

Paul is standing behind me, hands in pockets, and she sweeps him into the force field of her presence without missing a beat.

"Hello, Paul." She says it like it's a confession rather than an introduction.

He offers a hand, then immediately aborts and goes for a slightly awkward hug. "Hi, Mrs Hampton, it's been a while."

She appraises him up and down, then beams. "Call me Marianne. Glad you kept the long hair, it suits you."

I snort. Paul actually blushes. He's six-two and skinny as a scarecrow, but something about his demeanour—possibly the sheep socks—makes him look about twelve. He's never more attractive to me than when he's being slowly flayed by my mother's cheerful scrutiny.

She shrugs off her coat and glances around the flat, eyes darting from bookshelf to kitchen and back, no doubt compiling a full psychological profile.

"You've been tidying," she says, not a question. "Good for you."

Paul looks at me, panic flickering. "We try."

"Mmm," she says. "I'll put the kettle on, shall I?"

He nods, then immediately regrets ceding control of the kitchen. Mum makes a beeline for the cupboards, her laser gaze noting the arrangement (alphabetical, with a sub-row for herbal) and the state of the mugs (all handle-facing, no visible cracks—my work). I watch Paul try and fail to intervene as she selects the least embarrassing teapot and sets about brewing enough English Breakfast to resuscitate a small regiment.

I stand back and watch the scene unfold, equal parts mortified and delighted. We've survived worse than this, I remind myself. There was the time I accidentally CC'd my mum on an email about the "obscenely robust" taste of university canteen lasagne. She sent me a recipe, annotated with notes about the protein content of actual mince.

Paul sidles over and mutters, "She's a force of nature. Should we be scared?"

"Nah," I say. "She's here for you, not me."

He stares. "That's much, much worse."

Mum reappears, tea tray in hand, and gestures at the kitchen table. Paul sits, legs crossed at the ankle, radiating nervous energy. Mum pours, then turns her attention to the actual interview.

"So. How are you finding London?" she asks, stirring her own tea with clinical precision.

Paul hesitates, as if suspecting a trick. "Big. Loud. Never boring."

She nods. "You from the North, originally?"

"Leeds," he says, and I can hear the extra grit in his voice, his accent sharpening out of self-defence.

She smiles, almost approving. "Good. Grace needs someone who can stand up to her."

He grins, "I try. I've got the bruises to prove it."

She laughs, then launches into a barrage of questions about work, living arrangements, and the philosophical merits of "artisan" sourdough. Paul answers them all with the sardonic charm he usually reserves for hostile sources, and before long, even the air between them feels lighter. There's something almost... familial about the way they spar, a weird echo of the debates I grew up listening to at every dinner table for eighteen years.

I refill the mugs and retreat to the window, half-listening as Paul tells a story about an undercover reporting gig at a cat show gone wrong. Mum interrupts with, "I never understood why anyone would want a hairless cat, but then again, I've never tried vegan cheese either," and Paul loses it, shoulders shaking with silent laughter.

It's a kind of miracle, this peace. I watch the two of them, feeling a prickly warmth in my chest that I'd normally ascribe either to indigestion or poorly contained feelings. I wonder if this is how normal people do it—just invite their baggage round for tea and see what sticks.

When the biscuits are nearly gone and Mum is scribbling down the address of "a real butcher, not that Tesco nonsense," Paul catches my eye over the table and gives me a small, conspiratorial wink.

The thing about my mother is, she doesn't really "visit" so much as colonise. Less than an hour after her arrival, she's already moved from sipping tea to "just a quick tidy," and is currently rearranging the shoe rack with the ruthlessness of a junior officer on drill inspection. She tuts at the muddy trainers ("Outdoor footwear belongs by the door, darling, or else you'll have to mop twice"), then shifts her gaze to Paul, who's hovering in the background like a man waiting for the firing squad.

"Stand still," she instructs, and before he can protest, she's at his collar, fingers quick and decisive. "There. You're presentable now. We can't have the neighbours thinking I raised my daughter to live with a scarecrow."

Paul blinks, caught between mortification and delight. "Thank you, Mrs— Marianne."

She fixes him with a look that would make a lesser man combust. "You're welcome, love."

I snort. Paul blushes so hard the tips of his ears go pink.

We settle in the living room. The table is a relic that came with the flat, the surface marked with ancient mug rings and a single, defiant burn that's the result of a failed stir-fry and a moment of extreme hubris. Mum wipes at it anyway, then folds herself into the armchair like a cat seeking out the one patch of sunlight. She accepts her mug of tea with the air of a queen being presented with the royal sceptre.

"So," she says, wrapping both hands around her cup. "How's the domestic experiment progressing? Have you driven each other mad yet?"

Paul laughs, and to his credit, manages a fairly solid dead-pan. "Only on Mondays. She hoards the good coffee and makes me listen to Radio 4 during breakfast."

Mum beams. "It's called a civilising influence, Paul. You could use a bit of it."

"See?" I say. "It's not just me."

Mum sips her tea, then surveys the walls with the cool detachment of a property valuer. "Have you considered painting? Something brighter, perhaps. This beige is rather... funereal."

I roll my eyes. "We're tenants. If we so much as look at a paint chart, the landlord doubles the rent."

She sniffs. "You should still try. A home should have colour."

Paul, sensing an opening, says, "We could always go for a radical accent wall. Like neon green."

Mum raises an eyebrow. "Maybe not quite that extreme."

She turns to me, softening. "Are you happy, darling?"

It's a simple question, but it lands like a bomb. I nod, swallowing the urge to say more. Mum's always been able to spot a lie at fifty paces, and right now, I can't even muster a good one.

Paul, perhaps sensing the mood shift, puts a hand on my knee, just for a second, then pulls it back like he's worried Mum will think he's trying to influence my answer. I can't help but smile, because it's such a Paul thing to do: supportive, earnest, but a little bit self-conscious.

Mum catches the moment, her expression flickering between approval and smugness. "Took you long enough to get round to it, didn't it?"

Paul grins, a lopsided thing. "Some things are worth waiting for."

"Oh, listen to you, Mr Romantic." She shakes her head, but she's pleased.

The conversation turns to work. Mum wants all the details, down to what kind of computers we use and whether the new editor-in-chief "has any backbone." Paul fields her questions with the skill of a man who's been grilled by police and pensioners in equal measure. When she tries to quiz him about our cleaning schedule, he defers to me with a "Grace is the true organiser." She's delighted by this answer, and makes a note to "put that in the Christmas letter."

By the time the biscuits are gone, and the tea's gone cold, I'm feeling oddly content. Mum isn't here to judge, not really. She just wants to see me settled, and maybe—just maybe—see Paul sweat a little.

After she leaves (with a promise to bring over a "proper"

casserole next week), Paul and I collapse onto the sofa. He lets out a long breath, like a diver surfacing after a deep plunge.

"Your mum is terrifying," he says.

"She likes you," I reply. "Trust me, that's the worst it'll get."

He snorts. "Wasn't so bad, I suppose. She didn't even mention the Brexit mug."

"That's next time."

We sit in companionable silence, listening to the faint creak of the building as it adjusts to the day. Outside, the city hums, oblivious. Inside, it's just us, the warmth of Mum's visit lingering in the air.

"Some things are worth waiting for, huh?" I say, nudging his leg.

He grins, pulling me closer. "Not all things. Some things are worth fighting for, too."

I rest my head on his shoulder. For once, I let myself believe it.

We spend the rest of Sunday the way I imagine normal people do: alternating between chores, snacks, and the deep, unspoken relief that comes with surviving a parental inspection. At some point, Paul attempts to build an IKEA bookshelf that's been waiting to be introduced to a screwdriver for months, while I pretend not to notice his increasingly creative swearing. I make it to three o'clock before giving in and helping him decipher the instructions, which are remarkably simple.

By four, the flat is as close to perfect as it's ever going to be. Mum's lasagne is in the oven (she left it with a note: "DO NOT MICROWAVE"), the new bookshelf stands upright, and the city outside has quieted to the gentle drone of buses and kids on skateboards. We're on the sofa again, feet tangled, Paul reading the weekend supplement while I scroll Twitter. I'm halfway through a thread on why jam should be refrigerated when he nudges me.

"Look at this," he says, holding up a page. It's the *Observer*, with an image of my article front and centre, my byline in the headline font. "You went viral."

I groan. "That was days ago."

He grins. "Doesn't matter. You're famous. The trade minister is resigning, you know."

"Allegedly."

He laughs. "You're not even going to enjoy it, are you?"

I hide my face in the cushion. "It's not— It's just a job. The next thing will be twice as grim."

He tugs the cushion away, fixes me with a look that says: *Stop being so bloody humble.* "You're a pain in the arse, Hampton, but you're the best pain in the arse in the business."

I stick my tongue out, which is probably the most mature response available.

He leans back, arm around my shoulder. For a minute, we just watch the light change on the ceiling, the slow creep of afternoon fading into evening. It's not dramatic. It's not even particularly memorable. But it feels... permanent, somehow.

Mum texts at half five: "Did you eat the lasagne? It has layers." I reply with a photo of the empty dish and Paul making a thumbs-up face. She responds with three heart emojis and a GIF of a hamster eating a grape.

It's ridiculous, but it makes me smile. Maybe this is what people mean when they say "settling down"—not giving up, but finding a place where all the madness can just... rest, for a bit.

Paul nudges me. "Bet you a tenner the PM's gone by Christmas."

I grin. "You're on. Loser cooks."

He raises an eyebrow. "You mean, loser orders takeaway?"

"Obviously."

He laughs, then pulls me closer. "You know, if you'd told me two years ago that I'd be living with my arch-nemesis, I'd have said you were clinically insane."

I snort. "If you'd told me I'd like it, I'd have checked myself in."

He kisses me, quick and soft. "So. What's next for London's premier muckraker?"

I shrug, suddenly uncharacteristically shy. "I dunno. We'll see."

He squeezes my hand, and for once, there's no punchline.

The future is unwritten, but right now, it's enough. The sofa, the Sunday, the city spinning outside. There's warmth here. There's hope.

There's us.

And that's more than I ever thought I'd want.

THE END

Want to keep reading? Check out Mind the App, a slow-burn, enemies-to-lovers romcom full of heart, humour, and tech-fuelled tension.

She's small-town America. He's London.
It's complicated.

Mind
The
App
alia smith

CHAPTER ONE

DANNY

The gear shifter is mocking me.

"Why," I mutter through gritted teeth, "is it *here*?" My hand flails against the sleek steering column, grappling with the absurdly located lever that refuses to cooperate. It's like trying to solve a Rubik's Cube while blindfolded and mildly concussed. Who decided this was better than a proper gearstick? Americans, apparently.

"Alright, Danny. Breathe. This isn't rocket science. Just twist it into—" A surge of power jolts me forward as the car lurches violently toward the curb. *Brilliant.*

From behind me, a horn blares—a deep, aggressive honk that can only belong to an oversized pickup compensating for something. I glance in the rearview mirror and see the driver gesturing wildly, his face contorted in what I can only assume is either rage or constipation.

"Yes, mate, I hear you. Loud and clear," I murmur under my breath, throwing him a tight-lipped smile through the mirror. Another honk. Brilliant. Now it's a duet of shame because someone else has joined the symphony from further back. Perfect. Nothing like a public audience to really highlight your incompetence.

"Alright. Focus." I square my shoulders and grip the wheel, which feels suspiciously sticky. The rental agency did promise 'thorough cleaning,' but I'm starting to suspect their definition of clean is... flexible.

"Okay, approach slowly. Tiny adjustments. You've got this." My tank-like SUV inches forward, the nose barely nudging into the tight space between a minivan that looks like it's been parked there since 1987 and a shiny red convertible. Of course, the only available spot in this entire town is so narrow it might as well come with a sign that says, "*Good luck, sucker!*"

Another honk erupts, longer this time, accompanied by what sounds like muffled shouting. My anxiety spikes, but outwardly, I plaster on the kind of calm expression one might wear while delivering a quarterly earnings report. Cool. Collected. Not at all about to combust internally.

"One more try," I say aloud, as if the SUV needs reassurance. Glaring at the dashboard, I twist the futuristic gearshift again, gentle this time, hoping it miraculously shifts itself into reverse. Instead, I end up in neutral, the engine completely giving up, mirroring precisely how I feel inside.

"Sure, just take your time, buddy!" comes a sarcastic shout from the pickup driver. His window's down now, and I catch sight of his cowboy hat bobbing as he shakes his head. Cowboy hat. Of course. Why not?

"Thank you for your patience," I mutter under my breath, though every syllable drips with venom. My pulse thrums in my ears as I finally manage to align the vehicle properly. Or as close to properly as one can get when the steering wheel seems to have its own parking-assist agenda and the pavement markings are faded relics of a bygone era.

"Last time I rent a car in a country where they think super-sizing is a personality trait," I grumble as I throw the vehicle into park—or at least I hope it's in park. The flashy lights don't exactly inspire confidence.

With a final, triumphant lurch that feels more like the SUV giving up on me than the other way around, I manage to wedge the tank—sorry, rental—into what might generously be called a parking space. It's crooked. Not just "slightly off" crooked, but "did-a-drunken-raccoon-park-this?" crooked. One tire kisses the curb like it's trying to apologize for my existence, while the rear end juts out into the street with all the subtlety of a toddler's tantrum.

Taking a deep breath, I smooth down the front of my suit jacket and push open the door with as much poise as a man can muster while exiting what is essentially a vehicular crime scene. My shoes hit the pavement, polished leather against small-town asphalt, and I step away from the SUV with an air of calculated indifference. Chin high, shoulders back, as if I haven't just spent ten minutes wrestling with a steering column like it insulted my mother.

And then I hear it—a slow, deliberate clap.

"Well done, sir!" A grizzled voice floats over, tinged with amusement, followed by another clap. And another. I glance up to find an elderly couple perched on a nearby bench, their weathered faces lit with matching grins. The man is clapping slowly, theatrically, while his wife sips from a thermos adorned with stickers that read things like "Live, Laugh, Lobster" and "Willow Cove Forever."

"Bravo!" she adds, raising her thermos in mock salute.

"Thank you, thank you," I say with a dazzling smile, sketching a sarcastic little bow in their direction. "Always happy to provide top-tier entertainment."

"Parking's an art form around here," the old man says,

tipping his flat cap at me. "You'll get the hang of it—eventually."

"Can't wait," I reply dryly, resisting the urge to adjust my tie. Instead, I turn on my heel and stride away, leaving behind the awkwardly parked SUV and my shredded dignity like yesterday's emails.

The air shifts as I move further into Willow Cove, trading the chaos of the main street for something quieter, softer. The faint scent of salt lingers, mingling unexpectedly with cinnamon, and I can't tell whether it's coming from a bakery or some kind of candle shop.

Overhead, strings of bunting crisscross between buildings, their pastel triangles fluttering lazily in the breeze. It's aggressively quaint, like someone took a postcard and made it three-dimensional. The post office sits on the corner, its red-brick façade adorned with cheerful flower boxes. A bell above the door jingles every time someone enters or exits. It's absurdly charming, the kind of detail that would make city planners roll their eyes. But I guess that's the point, isn't it? To scream *small-town America* loud enough that even people in orbit could hear it.

I pass a shop with a hand-painted sign that reads *Scones & Stones: Crystals and Pastries.* Of course. Because why wouldn't you combine baked goods with New Age mysticism? Inside, I catch a glimpse of shelves lined with glittering geodes and a counter piled high with what look like blueberry scones. A woman in a flowing cardigan gestures animatedly at a customer, holding what appears to be a chunk of quartz the size of a small cat.

Despite myself, I take in the details—the tidy cobblestone sidewalks, the clusters of locals chatting outside the hardware store, the way laughter spills out from an ice cream parlor. It's... nice. Annoyingly so. Like someone designed it specifically to make big-city outsiders feel both charmed and out of place. Well, congratulations, Willow Cove. Mission accomplished.

Walking past the ice cream parlor, I catch sight of a sun-bleached newspaper stand tucked between a bench and one of those oversized planters overflowing with petunias. The *Willow Cove Gazette* sits front and center, the bold headline practically shouting to be noticed: *"The App No One Asked For: How Tech is Turning Small-Town Charm into Corporate Blah."*

Charming. Subtle. Definitely not aimed at me.

I stop, tilting my head as if I've misread it. Nope, still there. Still passive-aggressive in font size seventy-two. Beneath the headline, there's a grainy photo of what I assume is the town council office, though the angle makes it look more like a rustic barn. A caption reads, *"Progress or Plunder? Locals Weigh In."*

"Well, this should be riveting," I mutter, paying for a copy. The paper crinkles against my fingers as I flip it open. A faint whiff of ink and newsprint hits me—nostalgic, in a way that feels almost antiquated. Like vinyl records or rotary phones, it's something you wouldn't bother with unless you were determined to make a point about authenticity. I scan the byline: *Riley Hayes, Feature Writer.*

"Right then, Riley," I say under my breath. "Let's see what you've got."

The editorial takes up half the page, framed by an aggressively earnest stock photo of a laptop next to a coffee cup. I skim the opening paragraph, my smirk fading as I read. It's sharp. Too sharp. Words like *"soulless,"* *"exploitation,"* and *"algorithmic mediocrity"* jump out like arrows aimed straight at my ego. There's even a not-so-veiled jab about "tech executives who wouldn't know community values if they tripped over them in their bespoke loafers."

"Ah, good," I mutter dryly. "She's subtle too."

Still, I can't stop reading. Her writing has a rhythm. She

skewers the whole tech-for-the-sake-of-tech mentality, disman-tling every talking point my company has ever used to promote our platform. And damn it, she's... kind of brilliant at it. Artic-ulate, passionate, unrelenting. The kind of voice that doesn't just poke holes in your argument but rips the whole thing apart and serves it back to you on a platter, garnished with sass and righteous indignation.

For a moment, I forget to breathe. My chest tightens—not in a *you-may-be-having-a-heart-attack* way, but in a *your-confi-dence-is-being-flattened-like-roadkill* kind of way.

"Who *is* this woman?" I murmur, scanning for a photo or bio. Nothing. Just her name in neat little italics. *Riley Hayes.* Sounds like someone who's probably wearing practical shoes and glaring at me from some corner of the universe right now.

I fold the paper with more force than necessary, shoving it under my arm. There's a flicker of something unsettling in the back of my mind—half irritation, half admiration. It's maddening. On one hand, how dare she take aim at my project like that? On the other hand... damn, if she doesn't make some valid points. Infuriatingly valid.

"Great," I mutter as I start walking again. "Just what I need. A small-town crusader with a flair for theatrics and a thesaurus."

I stride down Willow Cove's postcard-perfect main street, dodging a gaggle of teenagers on skateboards and a woman walking what appears to be a mop with legs. The folded copy of the *Willow Cove Gazette* burns under my arm like a branding iron, its headline—"*The App No One Asked For*"—seared into my frontal lobe.

"Fix the app rollout," I mutter to myself, as if saying it out loud will somehow summon competence. Get the US launch back on track, earn a hearty pat on the back from the London office, and maybe—just maybe—the product director promotion will be mine. Easy, right? Except, now there's this... *Riley Hayes*. This faceless, word-slinging assassin who's decided my app is the devil incarnate and Willow Cove is her hill to die on.

"Practical shoes," I say under my breath, picturing her as some humorless crusader in orthopedic loafers. Probably wears cardigans with elbow patches. Drinks herbal tea. Owns a cat named Socrates. And yet, even as these snide thoughts churn in my head, I can't shake the sharp-edged brilliance of her writing. It's unsettling. Like discovering a rival chess player who's ten moves ahead before you've even figured out where the horsey piece goes.

Lost in my spiraling thoughts, I almost walk straight past the town hall—a squat, brick structure with peeling paint and a flagpole leaning at an alarming angle. As I veer toward the entrance, something—or rather someone—catches my eye.

She's standing just outside, pinning a brightly colored flyer to the community noticeboard. Her auburn hair is swept up in a messy bun, strands escaping to frame her face in a way that looks effortless, but probably isn't. A battered leather messenger bag hangs off one shoulder, and she's biting her lip in concentration as she smooths out the paper against the board.

For a split second, I forget how to move. She's... striking, in an unpolished sort of way. The kind of person who doesn't try to catch your attention but somehow commands it anyway. But then she glances up—and our eyes lock.

Hazel. Her eyes are hazel. Sharp and discerning, like she's already cataloging every flaw in my existence. My crooked parking job flashes through my mind, along with the slow clap from that elderly couple. Brilliant.

"Hi," I blurt, because apparently, my brain has decided to throw dignity out the window.

"Hi," she replies, her tone flat and vaguely suspicious. There's a flicker of *something* in her gaze—probably my English accent, throwing her slightly. Or maybe I'm imagining things. Either way, her eyes narrow slightly, and my palms start to sweat.

"Nice day, isn't it?" I hear myself say, the words tumbling out before I can stop them. Smooth, Danny. Truly the pinnacle of eloquence and wit.

Her lips twitch, not quite a smile. "If you like salt air and tourists blocking traffic."

"Ah. Yes, well," I stammer, feeling the weight of her judgment—or what I assume is judgment—pinning me to the spot. "Tourists. What a nuisance."

"Mm-hmm." She adjusts her bag, looking me up and down. Not in a flirty way, mind you. More like a mechanic inspecting a car for faults. "You new in town?"

"Just visiting," I say, attempting my most charming smile. It feels painfully forced, like I'm auditioning for a toothpaste commercial.

"Figured," she says, and there's something almost playful in her voice now, though her expression remains unreadable. "Well, welcome to Willow Cove. Try not to run anyone over while you're here. We drive on the left side on this side of the pond."

She turns and pins another flyer to the board—something about a town potluck—and steps back to inspect her work. I can feel her judgment radiating off her in waves, even as she pretends not to be bothered by my existence. It's almost impressive, really. A masterclass in passive-aggressive small-town hostility.

"Right, well," I mutter, adjusting the strap of my laptop bag and trying to summon what's left of my dignity. "I'll just...

get out of your hair, then. Wouldn't want to block any more traffic."

"Good idea," she replies, not even bothering to look at me this time.

Ouch. Okay then. Message received, loud and clear.

I turn on my heel and walk briskly down the street, ignoring the heat creeping up the back of my neck. Honestly, it's fine. Totally fine. If she wants to think I'm some hapless tourist who shouldn't be trusted behind the wheel, so be it. Let her think that. I'm not here to make friends. I'm here to fix an app, prove myself to my bosses, and then get the hell out of Dodge—or Willow Cove, rather.

CHAPTER TWO

RILEY

My boots are propped up on the desk, a lukewarm coffee cup balanced on my knee, and my morning is already circling the drain. The door to the office creaks open, and Elaine strides in like she owns the place, which, technically, she does. She's waving a piece of paper like it's the golden ticket to journalistic doom. Her heels click against the hardwood floor, each step radiating purpose and a subtle warning: brace yourself.

"Good morning, Riley," she says in that clipped tone that tries to sound warm but mostly just sounds like she's about to assign me something awful. My eyes flick to the press release in her hand, and my stomach sinks.

"Let me guess," I say, not bothering to move my feet off the desk. "Another groundbreaking initiative to revolutionize our lives by selling us things we don't need?"

"Close," Elaine replies, dropping the paper onto my desk with a flourish. The words "Artisan App" and "local engagement" leap out at me like an unwelcome pop-up ad. "You know that piece you did last week on the *Makers' Mart* app? Well, you got their attention. There's a senior product manager flying in from their UK office. He'll be here for two weeks, leading some community outreach project. They want us to cover it."

I let out a groan loud enough to make Elaine raise an eyebrow. "I think I bumped into him this morning. I can't believe they actively want to engage with me after I tore them a new one. Wow. It's brave, I'll give them that."

"Look, just meet the guy, see what's going on."

"A tech firm thinks they can waltz into Willow Cove with their sleek apps and overpriced lattes and call it 'engagement'? This town doesn't even have decent cell reception half the time."

"Well, apparently, they think we're worth the effort," Elaine counters, crossing her arms. "And since you're our resident cynic with a penchant for colorful commentary, I thought you'd be perfect for the follow-up story."

"Perfect?" I repeat, sitting up straight and giving her my best incredulous look. "Elaine, I'm allergic to PR fluff. You know this. It's in my medical records."

"Riley," she says, leaning over the desk, voice dropping into her no-nonsense editor mode. "You're doing it. Like it or not. The Chronicle needs this coverage, and you need a byline this week."

"Fine," I say, grabbing the press release and scanning it with a mix of irritation and dread. "But if this ends with me having to write about how some British guy redefines the meaning of artisanal bread, I'm quitting."

"Noted," Elaine says with a smirk. She turns on her heel and heads toward her office, leaving me to stew in my misery.

I stare at the press release again, the name "Daniel Winter" glaring back at me like a neon sign. Senior Product

Manager. UK Office. Local Engagement Initiative. I shake my head, tossing the paper onto the desk.

"Welcome to Willow Cove, Daniel Winter," I mutter under my breath. "Prepare to be unimpressed."

I stop just inside the door of the town hall, boots scuffing against the freshly buffed wood, and take in the spectacle before me. There it is—the pop-up tech booth in all its misplaced glory, smack dab in the middle of the room where we usually hold bake sales and PTA meetings. A sleek black banner hangs above a glossy table, its minimalist white font declaring: "*Create. Connect. Share.*" The words practically beg for an eye roll, so I oblige them. Twice.

There are iPads. Of course, there are iPads. They're propped up on little stands, their screens glowing with what I assume is some kind of app demo, complete with pastel graphics and soft-focus stock images of suspiciously happy people holding pottery. My gaze drifts to the far corner, where a stack of branded tote bags sits. Each one is stamped with the company's logo—a stylized swirl that looks vaguely like a cinnamon roll trying too hard to be modern art.

"Because nothing says 'support local artisans' like mass-produced corporate swag," I mutter under my breath.

The setup couldn't be more out of step with Willow Cove if it tried. This is a town where the farmers' market still uses handwritten signs, where Mrs. Callahan's honey jars come with crooked labels she prints on her ancient inkjet. The last time someone tried to introduce anything "cutting-edge" here, it was Mayor Thompson's ill-fated attempt at a digital suggestion box. The thing crashed within a week, mostly because half the town still refuses to use anything newer than AOL.

I scan the room again, noting the perfectly symmetrical arrangement of chairs around the booth, the carefully placed flyers fanned out across the table like some kind of corporate peacock display. Everything about it screams calculated precision, and I hate it. It's too slick, too polished, too... fake. Like they think they can slap a shiny veneer over their intentions and no one will notice what's underneath.

"Not on my watch," I mutter, digging into my bag for my notebook. The leather cover is battered from years of abuse, but it feels solid in my hands as I flip it open and click my pen.

"Pop-up booth at town hall," I scrawl at the top of the page, then underline it twice for good measure. My handwriting slants unevenly, the way it always does when I'm annoyed. Below it, I start jotting down notes: "iPads everywhere—overkill" ... "banner looks like something from a dystopian startup" ... "tote bags = insult to actual artisans."

My pen hovers midair as another phrase bubbles up in the back of my mind, sharp-edged and insistent. I hesitate for a moment, then write it down in bold capital letters: *"DIGITAL COLONIALISM."*

It's a loaded term, sure, but it fits. This isn't just about an app; it's about outsiders coming in and pretending to understand our community, acting like they're saving us while they quietly dismantle everything that makes this place unique. The thought fuels a fresh wave of irritation, and I press my pen harder against the page, underlining the words until the paper tears slightly.

"Perfect," I mutter, flipping the notebook closed. My gaze shifts back to the booth, where a couple of stand builders are fussing over the placement of yet another flatscreen display. One of them steps back, tilts his head, and gestures toward the banner like he's Michelangelo critiquing the Sistine Chapel.

"Yeah, that'll really win over the guy who whittles spoons

for a living," I say under my breath, shoving the notebook back into my bag.

The fork in my hand hovers over the half-eaten pile of sweet potato fries on my plate as Ava raises an eyebrow at me, her grin downright wicked.

"Okay, so tell me again," she says, leaning forward with her elbows on the table, "why you're not *at all* interested in the cute British guy who's apparently taken over town hall with his floppy hair and boyish good looks?"

"First of all, 'cute' is subjective. Second, if by 'taken over town hall,' you mean he's set up a soulless tech shrine to late-stage capitalism, then fine. And third"—I stab a fry into the ketchup for emphasis—"I'm just doing my job, Ava. This isn't about him."

"Uh-huh." She drags out the word, her tone dripping with disbelief. Her coffee cup hovers near her lips as she takes a slow sip, watching me over the rim like she's waiting for me to crack. "So it has nothing to do with how you've said the word 'tech bro' approximately seventy-three times since we sat down?"

"Tech bro is a *genre*," I shoot back, waving the fry dramatically. "He's not special. He's... he's just another corporate pawn here to sell us snake oil and call it innovation."

"Right," Ava drawls, smirking. "And that's why you were glaring at his pop-up booth like it personally insulted your mom."

"Because it did," I snap, pointing the fry at her now. "Metaphorically speaking. My mother is this town, Ava. And he"—I gesture vaguely toward the direction of the square, even though we can't see it from here—"is here to exploit her."

"Wow." Ava sets her coffee down and clasps her hands

together like she's praying. "You're officially projecting onto Willow Cove. I'm impressed, really."

"That's not—" I start, but she cuts me off with a raised hand.

"Don't get me wrong, I love this for you," she says, grinning wider now. "The passion, the outrage. It's all very... Jane Austen's heroine meets Erin Brockovich. But you know what they say about the lines between hate and other feelings being razor-thin, right?"

"Stop it."

"Riley Hayes," she crows, clapping her hands together. "You're flustered! Oh my God, you have a crush on the tech bro!"

"Absolutely not," I say, stabbing another fry. "What I have is a healthy disdain for everything he represents. The accent and cheekbones don't change the fact that he's bad news wrapped in a well-tailored suit."

"Again, *very* specific observations for someone who's not been paying attention," Ava teases, popping a fry into her mouth.

"Ugh." I drop my fork and press the heels of my hands against my forehead. "This is why I hate having lunch with you. Everything turns into some kind of rom-com subplot."

"Hey, I'm just saying—" Ava starts, but I cut her off with a pointed look.

"Enough. I don't care about him. What I care about"—I sit up straighter, jabbing a finger at the table for emphasis—"is making sure this town doesn't get steamrolled by some slick app that thinks it can replace actual human creativity with algorithms and buzzwords. That's it. End of story."

"Uh-huh," Ava says again, clearly unconvinced but mercifully letting it go. For now. She sips her coffee like she knows something I don't, and it takes every ounce of self-control I have not to throw a fry at her face.

"Anyway," I say, grabbing my notebook from where it's wedged under my elbow. "I've got work to do."

"Of course you do," Ava says. "Just try not to swoon too hard while you're, you know, dismantling the patriarchy or whatever."

"Goodbye, Ava," I mutter, standing up and slinging my bag over my shoulder.

"Good luck, Riley!" she calls after me.

Outside, I take a deep breath and square my shoulders. Whatever Ava thinks, this isn't personal. It's about Willow Cove—about preserving what makes this place special. I'll dig deeper, ask the tough questions, and expose this whole initiative for what it is. No distractions. No nonsense.

"Game on," I mutter under my breath, heading back toward the square.

The sound of a heavy-duty stapler misfiring is what first catches my attention.

"Come on, you bloody—" The voice, clipped and British, slices through the late afternoon air like it doesn't belong here. Like it's wandered in from a BBC period drama and gotten lost in small-town Willow Cove.

I glance up from my notebook—just a quick look, I tell myself—and there he is. Mr. Big Tech himself, the guy I bumped into this morning, standing next to that pretentious pop-up booth, wrestling with a piece of poster board that's come loose.

He's tall, annoyingly so, his dark hair styled so perfectly it probably has its own HR department. His shirt looks like it costs more than my monthly rent, and he's wearing some kind of tailored navy blazer that screams *Look at me, I'm important!* It's all very polished. Very corporate. Very... not Willow Cove.

And yet, despite his whole *Bond, Jame Bond* vibe, he's currently losing a very public battle with a staple gun.

"Really?" I mutter under my breath, leaning against the wall to watch the show. "This is the guy they sent to save us?"

Danny—or whatever his name is—yanks the stapler back and examines it like it holds the secrets of the universe. He frowns. Adjusts his grip. Tries again. The sound of another misfire ricochets around the room, followed by an exasperated sigh loud enough to rattle the bunting hanging above the stand.

"Brilliant," he mutters to himself, his accent thickening with frustration. "Just brilliant."

I can't help it. A laugh slips out before I can stop it, quiet but sharp. He freezes, his head snapping up in my direction like he's just realized he's being watched. For a second, his eyes meet mine—blue and piercing, the kind that probably makes boardrooms go silent when he walks in.

"Problem?" he calls out, his tone all crisp politeness layered over obvious irritation.

"Not for me," I say, raising my eyebrows. "But you might want to switch to tape before you staple your fingers together. Just a suggestion."

His jaw tightens, and I feel an almost smug sense of satisfaction at the way his carefully curated mask cracks, just a little. He glances down at the stapler, then back at me, like he's debating whether to engage further.

"Thank you for the... advice," he says finally. "But I think I'll manage."

"Sure you will." I push off the wall, slipping my notebook into my bag. "If you survive the stapler, that is."

"Very funny," he mutters, turning back to his poster board.

"Welcome to Willow Cove," I call over my shoulder as I walk away, my voice laced with sarcasm. "Try not to break anything while you're here."

As I cross the square, I can't resist one last glance over my shoulder. He's still there, still struggling, but now there's something... almost endearing about the way he's muttering to himself, trying to wrestle the board into submission. Almost.

"Digital colonialism," I mutter to myself, pulling out my pen and underlining the phrase in my notebook. "Yeah, this is going to be fun."

SUBSCRIBE TO ALIA'S MAILING LIST
&
RECEIVE YOUR FREE NOVELLA

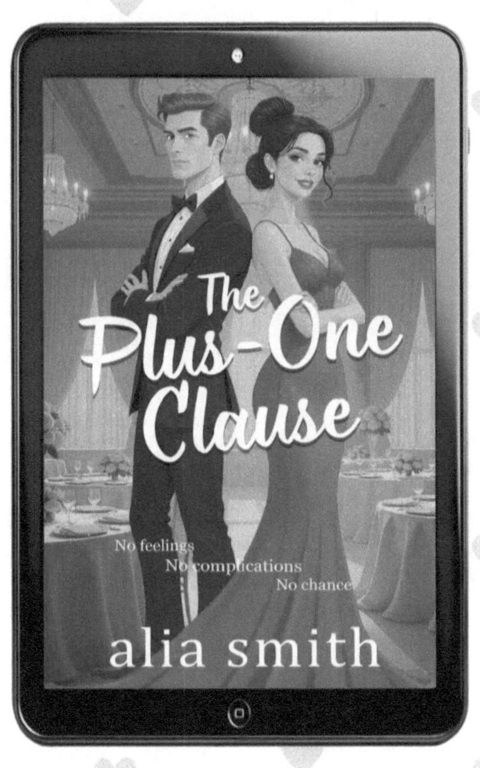

www.aliasmithbooks.com

AUTHOR'S NOTE

Hi,

Thanks so much for reading *Hot Off the Press*!

It was a lot of fun to write. I truly hope it was an entertaining read.

If you enjoyed it I would be incredibly grateful if you'd be so kind as to leave a review.

Reviews really help authors for a number of reasons, not least, providing feedback on what readers like and improving visibility of the book on online retail sites.

Thanks in advance and I look forward to reading your thoughts.

Alia xx

ABOUT THE AUTHOR

Alia Smith writes heart-warming romantic comedies filled with wit, charm, and just the right amount of chaos.

When she's not crafting love stories, she can usually be found curled up with a book, getting emotionally invested in reality TV, or attempting to keep Galaxy—her cat and chief muse—from sitting on her keyboard.

She lives in a cosy Oxfordshire home, where she firmly believes that every great romance starts with a good cup of tea.

www.aliasmithbooks.com

 instagram.com/aliasmithbooks
amazon.com/author/aliasmith

BINGE THE SERIES